A LIFE CHOSEN

Sydney Rutherford

Published by Black Hat Publications

ISBN: 978-1-0670159-0-9

To D, for the Saturday mornings.

1

The smoked-meat sandwich was the only thing worth ordering at Gino's Deli. The mountain of tender brisket piled on top of a slice of rye smeared with yellow mustard was simple, unpretentious, and a bit stringy—much like the owner, Gino Castelli. He was an old friend of the family, his grandfather having arrived on the same boat from Sicily as Montreal mob boss Giorgio Russo. Or so the story went.

Rayan assumed the decision to swing by Gino's that afternoon had less to do with the sandwich and more to do with family loyalty, something his capo, Mathias Beauvais, did not take lightly. It was rare for the two of them to stop to eat. Most days, they took lunch as they drove, any breaks between jobs kept brief. But today was different. Mathias had been invited to the boss's residence to meet privately with Giorgio Russo. Even Rayan, who occupied the lowest rank in the group's hierarchy, knew what an honor that was.

They sat in a small booth at the back of the deli, flanked on one side by the frosted display of meat and fish and on the other by a large window overlooking the street. Through the glass, Rayan could see the sheen of a recent shower coating the sidewalk outside.

"You're wrong," Mathias said from his seat across the table, taking a bite of his sandwich and chewing slowly. He'd been interested to discover that Rayan had finished reading Dante's *Divine Comedy*. "Each circle is a digression."

"I didn't say they were equal," Rayan countered.

"But you don't agree with Alighieri's order."

"No."

Mathias picked up his cup of coffee, gray eyes betraying his amusement. "Then what, in your esteemed opinion, is worthy of unseating treachery?"

The door chimed, and a large man strode into the shop, his eyebrows thick, almost touching. He stepped over to the counter and spoke loudly in English. Mathias glanced up, a flicker of annoyance crossing his face.

"Violence," Rayan replied absently, his attention shifting to the disagreement the customer appeared to be having with Gino's son behind the register. Nick Castelli was waving a hand in the man's face, telling him to leave. The man reacted by knocking over a rack of newspapers by the door. It fell to the floor with a clatter.

Mathias put down his coffee. "Pick them up," he ordered from across the store.

The man turned to look at them, his face darkening. "The fuck did you say?" He strode toward their table.

Rayan stood, instinctively placing himself between the mammoth of a man and his boss. "He said, pick them up," he echoed in a low voice, tilting his chin toward the pile of fallen newspapers.

"You gonna make me?"

Rayan slipped a hand into the pocket of his slacks, and his jacket fell open to reveal the Beretta resting against his ribs. The man straightened up, glancing at Mathias then back to Nick at the register, who was shaking his head. Without a word, the man returned to the front of the store, stooped awkwardly to gather the newspapers, and dumped them onto the counter. With a last look in their direction, the man stumbled out of the shop and onto the street. Rayan took his seat as Nick gave him a brief salute.

Mathias pulled a pack of Du Maurier Signatures from his jacket pocket and lit one. He smoked in silence, their earlier conversation abandoned. Rayan wondered if his thoughts were on the impending meeting with the boss. If Mathias had any reservations, he gave no indication. He was as impenetrable as ever, his sharp features set in the usual half frown so that he appeared perpetually irritated.

When Rayan had first started working for Mathias, getting through a job without a single rebuke counted as success. His capo's approval lay in his silence. From there, Rayan had trained himself to intuit, to the point where Mathias could instruct him with a look alone. It was an unexpected intimacy, allowing him to understand the man from the subtlest of glances and read the underlying message in his tone. Mathias was different from anyone he'd ever encountered, something about him encircling Rayan and drawing him in.

A foolish endeavor from its very inception—his want to be close to Mathias. Rayan knew now what it had spawned and its potential for frightening repercussions. He'd made peace with the futility of these feelings, knowing that the only way he could demonstrate them was in service to his boss. And so he had done just that, honing himself into the best possible tool he could be.

"On the house, gentlemen," Nick said as they stood to leave and ushered them out like visiting dignitaries.

"Regards to your father," Mathias said, looking down at his watch. They were running early.

"Did Tony say what it's about?" Rayan asked as they walked to the Mercedes, which was parked outside on the street.

Antonio Giraldi was head of the family's collections department and oversaw the formal lending side of the group's activities. Mathias had worked directly under Tony for years. Collections covered everything from bailing out failing local businesses to topping up a politician's kitty during a tough election year. The catch, of course, was the ludicrously high interest—and what would happen if they didn't pay. This was where Rayan's capo had proven efficient: clients rarely delayed payments when Mathias appeared at their door.

"We'll find out soon enough," Mathias replied, pulling open the passenger door and getting into the car.

Mathias had been to the boss's private residence only once before. The stately brick townhouse was situated on what the cops called Mafia Row, a manicured stretch of the Ahuntsic suburb that housed not only Russo and his wife but several close members of the family as well.

Giorgio Russo, head of the Fifth Family in Canada, had always considered Montreal the true gem of the north. It was home to the largest faction of the Sicilian Mafia outside of Italy. Even the American-based Cosa Nostra, having been decimated across the border by the FBI, had come to accept the concentrated heft of the family in Quebec. The province's radical cultural history and restrictive access to the RCMP—the country's national police service—made it prime breeding ground for the group's activities.

Since he'd made *caporegime* with a territory under his jurisdiction, Mathias had found himself one step closer to Russo's inner circle. The man who had always appeared a remote figurehead was now extending an invitation to Mathias to meet in his home and converse with him on a first-name basis.

Rayan pulled the car into the driveway in front of the boss's house. He cut the engine as Mathias reached beneath his jacket to unfasten the gun strapped to his shoulder holster. The absence of its weight against his chest left him feeling exposed, but the rules were clear—bringing a weapon to a meeting with Giorgio Russo meant one thing and one thing only.

"Wait here," he said, handing Rayan his gun.

Mathias stepped out of the car and straightened his jacket. Climbing the steps to the front door, he marveled at how quaint the operation appeared from the outside. Here lived a man with his finger in every major deal in the city. Hundreds of thousands of dollars passed through the family each week, and this was where Russo had chosen to enjoy his prominence—a modest two-story brick house in suburban Montreal.

Stefano, the boss's personal handler, answered the door and let Mathias into the foyer, where he was unceremoniously frisked. After determining that he was clean, Stefano led him into the salon, where Mathias took a seat in one of the overstuffed leather chairs. Stefano stood by the door with his back to him as they waited.

When Russo arrived, Mathias was surprised to see him on the arm of a dour-looking nurse. There was a pained slowness to the boss's approach, each step an uncharacteristic display of weakness. Mathias moved to greet him, clasping both hands in his.

"You've caught me on a bad day, Beauvais," Russo grumbled as the nurse helped lower him into a chair. "High as a kite from these new pills they've got me on." He let out a phlegm-filled cough.

While Mathias had nothing but respect for the man, there was no way around it—the boss looked terrible. Pale as paper, his skin sagged over cheeks speckled with angry red veins. His eyes were sunken and watery, framed by dark circles.

"Coffee," Russo said, snapping his fingers at the nurse standing with Stefano by the door. As she disappeared into the hallway, the old man turned to Mathias. "Tony says you brought in over a hundred last month."

It wasn't the first time. Month after month, Mathias's share of collections revenue vastly outstripped that of anyone else in the division. As a result, Tony had increased Mathias's lending capacity and extended their reach into the greater province.

"Business is booming," he said with a shrug, deflecting the praise.

Russo smirked. "Isn't it?" Mathias pulled out his cigarettes and held them up, but the boss waved his hand. "Go ahead. One of us might as well enjoy himself. I can't have a fucking smoke for the next two weeks. Doctor's orders."

Mathias placed one between his lips, ducked his head to light it, and took a long drag, aware of Russo following his movements enviously.

"We've been watching you. Who knew the son of Freddie Mancini's *goomah* would make it this far?" He chuckled.

Mathias smiled indulgently, swallowing the familiar spike that rose in his throat.

"The world's changing, I say," Russo continued. "As much as we try to uphold the traditions of the old country, I don't like to ignore talent. That's how you stagnate, and then someone else moves in."

The boss stared at him, and Mathias held his gaze. He was well aware of his own deviation from family tradition. His mother was French, set up for years on his father's dime. Even if his old man could be traced back to Sicilian soil, Mathias would still remain the son of a whore.

"You're ambitious," Russo said. "I like that. Frankly, we need more captains like you. There'll always be the question of your parentage, but you can climb higher yet."

Mathias tapped the end of his cigarette against the ivory ashtray on the table beside him, keeping his hand steady as his thoughts whirled.

"Tony's put you forward for *santista*," the boss announced. "He's setting up a commercial branch within the division. Wants you to lead it."

Mathias fought a grin. After all these years, Tony was finally giving him his due. The nurse walked in with two small cups of black coffee. She handed Russo his and placed the other on the table next to Mathias.

"Tony and I go way back. His recommendation means a great deal."

Mathias nodded. "It's an honor, boss."

There was a long silence as Russo slowly sipped his espresso. "I've had some health concerns as of late," he said finally.

Mathias stilled at the admission.

"Nothing serious," the boss continued—a lie that would remain unchallenged. "But the whole situation has given me a chance to, shall we say, observe my own mortality."

Mathias now understood why the man's public appearances had been few of late. If rival groups were to find out about a possible power vacuum on Montreal turf, it would mean an end to the shaky peace the family currently presided over with a heavy hand. Here in the safety of his home, Russo was being candid, which could only mean things were already shifting behind the scenes.

"When these sorts of things happen, it can put ideas in people's heads," Russo said pointedly. "Succession is a seductive subject. I want to be sure I can count on you to follow the right people if the need arises."

Stefano shifted at his post, eliciting a creak from the floorboards beneath his feet.

The right people? "Of course," Mathias said.

Russo put down his coffee. "Good. There are those on the council that consider you an asset. Keep them close."

This news had Giovanni written all over it. The man had taken an increasing interest in Mathias over the last few years. Giovanni Bianchi was head of the Quintino, a council of four that consulted directly with the boss. Besides Russo, the Quintino were the most senior members of the family, both in age and in rank.

"Of course we're talking theory here, Beauvais. This old man has bounced back from worse."

The sentence lacked conviction, and Mathias noticed how taxing even talking seemed for him. He nodded, stubbing out his cigarette.

"Ah, give us a fucking smoke, will you?" Russo said, motioning to the nurse to take away his empty cup.

Mathias pulled out his pack and handed the boss a cigarette. He leaned forward to light it for him. Russo exhaled with the pleasure of a dying man discovering water in the desert.

"Who listens to doctors anyway," he muttered between puffs.

Mathias took a sip of his coffee, which had already cooled, and placed the cup back on the table. A thin trail of smoke curled above Russo's head as he watched him steadily.

"You're a good soldier, Mathias. A bit too smart for this business, but you make up for it in loyalty. I didn't have much to do with your father, but I heard he was a pretty solid bookie. Retired now?"

"So I've heard."

"How is he? Missing the action?"

"I wouldn't know," Mathias said. From the little he knew of his father, a life lacking in action was the kind he enjoyed.

Russo finished his cigarette, and Mathias passed him the ashtray. The older man's hand shook as he crushed the smoking butt. He signaled to the nurse, and she appeared at his side and helped the boss slowly rise from his chair. With that, the meeting was over. Mathias stood, and the two once again clasped hands.

"Don't get too comfortable. I may call on you," Russo said.

"I'll be ready."

The boss gave Mathias a knowing smile, clapping a hand on his shoulder. Then he allowed the nurse to lead him out of the salon. Mathias waited until he was gone before returning to the entrance with Stefano. He retrieved his jacket and was shrugging it on when the front door opened and the boss's son stepped into the foyer.

Piero Russo was a good ten years older than Mathias, somewhere in his midforties at least, yet carried himself like a plucky twenty-year-old. The dye in his graying hair gave it an unnatural black sheen but did little to detract from the deep lines that crisscrossed his face, which was pulled into a permanent sneer.

"Look who it is," Piero said with a chuckle, clasping Mathias's hand and slapping him on the back. "Come to pay your respects?"

"When I can," Mathias replied. He'd hoped to avoid Piero during his visit, yet here he was, cornered in the lion's den.

"*Patri* has been under the weather lately, but he's a bull, I'm telling you. He'll be back up and running in no time," Piero said.

"He seemed well."

"Of course," Piero said, pulling off his coat and handing it to Stefano. "You talk some business?"

"Tony's requested help with the department."

"Boss has taken quite an interest in you."

His tone was easy, but Mathias saw the hard glint in his eye. Piero liked to think himself a master of subterfuge, but his true intent was glaring. He did not like Mathias. The fact that his father had summoned him only served to remind Piero of his success.

"So it seems." Mathias pulled open the door, the rush of fresh air a welcome relief. Russo's praise was more of a half-truth—Mathias's loyalty only stretched so far. "Good to see you, Piero," he said, not waiting for a reply as he closed the door behind him.

He made his way down the steps, attempting to curb his irritation. Officially, Piero had been given authority over the group's betting syndicate, but the man was a gambler and a notorious pussy hound. He frittered away division profit and poked his nose into Narcotics, trying to get a cut for himself behind the scenes. The only reason the syndicate continued to function was due to the efforts of division head Domenico Lombardi. And everyone turned a blind eye to Piero's activities because he was Giorgio Russo's son. Mathias did not doubt that Piero thought himself worthy of succession and would claim it as his birthright. He could not think of a worse leader with whom to entrust the future of the family.

Mathias looked up to see Rayan standing by the car, watching him approach. Even here, outside the boss's own home, Rayan waited as though expecting to be called on at any moment. The man's appearance had a fluidity that defied classification—ochre-flecked eyes the color of coffee, honeyed skin that lightened over the long winter months, hair an inky black. The ambiguity of his features allowed him to slip between identifying groups. The Algerians might claim him, as could the Cubans. To the family, he was simply an other, lumped in with all non-Italians and considered equally inferior.

Russo talked about talent surpassing lineage. Mathias had learned this lesson himself. Rayan, an *estraneo*, with his background muddied beyond recognition, had proven more competent than any soldier he'd worked with.

2

Not yet sixty, Mathias's mother, dressed in her finest on a weekday morning, peered out the window in the kitchen. She lived on the top floor of an extravagantly decorated triplex in the Plateau and had been there since before he was born.

"I was thinking of updating the balcony furniture," she announced.

Mathias placed the brown paper bag of deli meats and cheeses down on the dining table, already planning his exit. "Were you expecting me to care?" he asked evenly.

His mother straightened up and gave him a dirty look as she turned away from the window. "Your French has gotten terrible. Too much of that Quebecois filth and far too much English." Marguerite sighed. "And to think of all the money we spent sending you to the best schools."

We. He knew exactly who she'd persuaded to make that happen. Mathias set his jaw, saying nothing.

His mother was Parisian and hadn't let the move to Canada erode her staunch national superiority. Quebec culture never ceased to repulse her, and she couldn't understand why the local government was so eager to preserve what she believed to be a flawed bootleg of the original.

"But you're looking good," she said, walking over and giving him a charming smile. "You know, you remind me of your father in those early years."

Mathias felt his temple twitch. "Before he married someone else?"

His mother's face darkened, her keen temper flaring—a trait Mathias had inherited. As a child, he'd learned to avoid the worst of her moods. As an adult, he deliberately stoked them.

Calming herself, Marguerite moved toward the table, absently poking through the bag from the boulangerie. She retrieved the thick white envelope Mathias had placed at the bottom and slipped it into her purse, which sat on the counter. Her life had long been financed by dirty money, first his father's, now his. Yet she still had the gall to act like it was beneath her. Mathias took pains to avoid visiting his mother. When he did, it only served as a reminder of how much he disliked her. Still, it was an enduring obligation he couldn't seem to shake.

"Your father's not well," Marguerite said after a long pause. She continued unpacking the contents of the bag, not looking at him. "Lung cancer. It's terminal."

Mathias frowned. This was the first he'd heard of it. Then again, he'd made a conscious effort to avoid anything to do with his father for the past decade.

"They say he doesn't have long," she continued.

Mathias felt a dull ache behind his forehead, tightening like a vise. So the old man was dying.

Marguerite glanced up and gave him her most pitiful look. "I want you to visit him."

He let out a snort of laughter. Over the years, his father had made it very clear how little he needed Mathias and his mother. "He's got his real family for that. Wasn't that the plan all along—play the odds to make sure he had someone by his side when he keeled over?"

His mother's expression turned stony, her light-blue eyes darkening into tiny pins. "How you dare to act so ungrateful is beyond me," she said, her voice wavering. "After all he's done for us—"

"Ungrateful?" Mathias's fists clenched instinctively. "We both know who benefited the most from this little arrangement. Should've listened to him and got rid of me when you had the chance."

His mother's hand came flying toward his face. He caught it easily and squeezed her wrist in warning before letting it drop. They'd established the futility of these outbursts a long time ago. Standing in silence, they stared each other down.

"The old man deserves everything he gets," Mathias muttered finally. He left his mother standing in the kitchen, slamming the apartment door behind him. As he scaled the stairs to the street, the ache in his head grew to an insistent throb.

They'd completed the last job of the day—an impromptu visit with a surprisingly accommodating city councilor—and Rayan was driving them back to the office when Mathias's phone began to ring. It was Tony.

"Sonny has a runner. Owes shy of fifteen grand. Not a good look if we don't catch him quick."

While Mathias had assisted in expanding the division's share of white-collar lending, Collections still relied heavily on protection fees—overseen by Franco Ricci—and rounding up betting arrears. That particular task fell to Salvatore "Sonny" Alvisi, who was always letting clients one-up him. He doled out money like the family was some kind of charity.

"Let him clean up his mess," Mathias said.

"His mess becomes our mess when punters start thinking they can borrow and run."

Mathias lowered the phone. "Pull over," he instructed Rayan. The man slowed the car, turning onto a side street. "It's past five, Tony. I'm not chasing Sonny's fuckups all evening."

"Then you better start looking." The line went dead.

Mathias swore under his breath. He punched in Salvatore's number, and he picked up on the first ring. "Who's the runner?" Mathias asked.

"Mathias!" He sounded out of breath. "Fucking *medigan*, Connor Armstrong. He's deep in the hole."

"And you gave him more money?"

He began to stutter. "Did right by us before. I reckon he's been borrowing to pay someone else."

In the background, Mathias could hear the roar of a hockey game and the murmur of voices. "Where are you?"

"I'm hitting up a couple of the regular spots, see what I can find."

Mathias clicked his tongue. "He's done a runner, Sonny. He's not going to be at the regular spots." He hung up and shoved his phone into his pocket. "You're a gambling addict who owes money to the mob. Where do you go?" he muttered.

"Somewhere I can bet it all to earn it back," Rayan replied.

Mathias looked at his second, surprised by the insight. "No one's going to carry him. He's on our blacklist."

"No one that kicks back to the family."

"That leaves Franklin, Javier..."

"Belkov," Rayan added.

Fuck. Of course. The Russians coexisted fairly peacefully with the family in Montreal, though they were champing at the bit to fill any power vacuums family politics opened up. They had to be kept on a short leash to prevent them from overstepping. And Viktor Belkov, the city head, was a loose cannon at best. The Bratva operated, among other things, a gambling syndicate that sucked in the trash the family threw out. The stakes were higher, of course. And the Russians did not play games.

"Head to Laval. We'll start with Belkov." Mathias figured he had enough leverage to convince the man to cooperate.

His second pulled the car back onto the road, and they drove toward the highway, speeding through the darkening city.

There was a restaurant in Laval that Belkov owned, the Château Suzdal. It looked nice enough from the outside—families with kids at big tables—but naturally, out back, he ran any number of rackets, from drugs to prostitution. Mathias and Rayan found him in his back office, feet up on the desk, half-empty glass of vodka in hand, sipping it like it was water.

"Beauvais, to what do I owe the pleasure? We're not due until next month."

Belkov always seemed a little drunk, as though he required a minimum amount of booze to function. The Russians paid monthly fees for use of the port, which the mob had controlled for decades. While the family dealt in the local narcotics circuit, the Russians had their hands on the harder stuff, which they shifted south across the border to their contacts in the States. As long as their imports didn't compete and they paid their dues on time, Russo didn't have a problem with them.

"I'm looking for Connor Armstrong. Wanted to see if he was on your books."

Belkov held up his bottle of Green Mark, and Mathias waved him away. He'd had the misfortune of sharing one too many drinks with the man before.

"I'll help you if you tell me whether the rumors are true."

"Rumors?" Mathias asked.

The Russian waggled his eyebrows. "About Russo. How long does he have?"

Mathias looked hard at the man. "That desperate you're listening to rumors now?"

Belkov laughed and swilled his drink. "You're hedging."

"Sorry to disappoint. Russo isn't going anywhere."

"Let me ask you one thing, Mathias," he drawled in his thick Russian accent. "If he keeled over tomorrow, would you be ready?"

The Bratva boss reached beneath the desk and pulled out an antique revolver. In an instant, Rayan appeared in front of him, the gleam of his gun catching the light as it lined up with Belkov's head. From behind, Mathias could see his second's body tense in expectation of the shot.

"Bang!" the Russian crowed, dropping the revolver onto the desk and holding his hands up in mock surrender. "You got me!" He cackled with laughter then downed the rest of his drink.

Rayan stood between them, still poised to shoot. Mathias glanced at the door, where Belkov's own lackey stood, fingers resting on the handle of a pistol tucked into his waistband. He put a hand on Rayan's shoulder, and he lowered his gun, his eyes flicking to Mathias for the briefest of moments before he stepped back.

Feeling red-hot anger sweep through him, Mathias strode up to the desk and placed both palms on the glossy wooden surface. He leaned in close, his mouth curling upward in mock civility. "Just for that, I'm adding twenty to next month's dues, you crazy Russian bastard," he said in a low voice. "Pull your gun on me again, and you're finished. We'll flush you out of this city like a filthy fucking rat."

"My apologies." Belkov leered, leaning back in his chair. This was what he'd wanted—to put on a show and make sure the family knew the Bratva weren't completely pistol-whipped. "Here I was thinking you could take a joke."

Mathias straightened, leveling his gaze at him. "Connor Armstrong."

"Try Le Singe Doré," Belkov said. "There's some action there tonight. If he's on our books, that's where he'll be."

Mathias turned and pulled open the door. The noise from the restaurant filtered through as he strode down the hallway, Rayan at his heels.

"*Brasseux de marde,*" Rayan muttered as they walked across the parking lot. He was still keyed up, jaw tight, mouth pulled into a scowl.

They got in the car and headed back toward the city. Mathias stared out the window, recalling Belkov's thinly veiled threat. *Who is giving him information about Russo? What exactly is he planning?*

Rayan and Mathias made their way through the crowds at Place d'Armes. It was well into the evening, and people were spilling from the various bars and clubs along the strip. Rayan couldn't help but feel strange as they passed through the melee. How different their Friday night activities were in comparison.

Rayan noticed two women with their eyes fixed on Mathias, whispering excitedly as he strode past. He gave his boss a sidelong glance. Mathias was dressed as he always was—impeccably, his muscular frame filling out his designer suit, dark-brown hair combed back, his strong jaw betraying no hint of stubble. No wonder they were staring. He was imposing, exuding a kind of authority that was hard to ignore. Rayan blinked, quickly looking away.

They turned into Chinatown, where red lanterns framed the streets. Music blared from a karaoke bar on the corner. Le Singe Doré was located along a side alley, a nondescript brick building with a hairdressing salon fronting the street and a small speakeasy round back. Behind the bar and through a maze of narrow corridors was a series of rooms where the Russians ran various betting rings.

Mathias strode down the alley and pulled open the door to the club. It was dark, with a low ebb of music in the background. Black leather booths dotted the room. It must have been early, because the place was practically empty. Mathias walked to the staff entrance and pushed through the doors into a brightly lit corridor.

They approached the first room, and Mathias turned. "The fuck does he look like?"

Rayan shrugged. He'd never heard of the man before that night.

"Goddamn wild-goose chase," his boss muttered and stalked into the room.

Three large screens lined the walls. There were several tables packed with men glued to the games on television. In the corner, someone was mixing drinks.

A short bald man stepped in front of them. "What do you want?" he asked in a thick Russian accent.

"We're looking for Connor Armstrong," Mathias replied, his eyes sweeping the room.

The man looked them up and down. "Who're you with?"

"Who do you think?" Mathias shot back.

Rayan could tell he was losing his patience. Bad things happened when his capo lost his patience.

The Russian glowered. "What makes you think I can help you?"

Mathias retrieved a wad of bills from inside his jacket, peeled off a few, and held them out. Baldy grinned, taking the money and pocketing it.

"He's over there. Table on the right, red jersey."

They walked over to the table. Armstrong's eyes were fixed on a screen where a hockey game was playing. He gripped the table hard, muttering something, maybe a prayer. He was going to need it. Mathias stepped in front of him, blocking the screen.

"Hey, man—" Armstrong started.

Rayan stood behind him, placing a hand on his shoulder, and pushed him into the chair. Armstrong went rigid.

"Fuck," Armstrong whispered.

"My associate and I would like to talk to you outside," Mathias said.

"Are you with Sonny?" he asked quickly, his words tripping over one another. "Y-You can tell him I've got the money."

Mathias's eyes narrowed. "Do I look like Sonny's messenger?" His voice was measured, but Rayan could hear the malice beneath. "If you've got the money, we don't have a problem." He placed a hand on the table between them. "But we both know you don't."

Mathias met Rayan's eyes, inclining his head toward the door. Rayan yanked Armstrong up by his arm and led him out of the room. They emerged into the alley, the sound of the karaoke bar filtering through from down the street. He pushed Armstrong up against the brick wall, Mathias stalking behind him like a tiger.

Armstrong gave them a winning smile, but it wasn't enough to hide the slight tremor of his lips. "This is all a misunderstanding."

He looked like the kind of man used to talking his way out of trouble. It was a shame Rayan's boss didn't like to talk.

Mathias glanced down at the Rolex on his wrist, his frown deepening. "I don't take kindly to my time being wasted."

Rayan moved forward, but Mathias held up his hand, his eyes darkening like a gathering storm. A pile of wooden pallets sat stacked to one side of the alley. On top were several severed panels, the nails still embedded. Mathias stepped over, picked one up, and tested its weight in his hand. He advanced toward Armstrong, taking his time, making him sweat.

Armstrong visibly paled. "I'll get you the money, I swear. I'll have it by the end of the week."

Backed against the wall, he had changed his tune. Mathias rolled his neck. Then he raised the plank and slammed it against Armstrong's knee with a crack, violence flashing like lightning across his face. Armstrong screamed, pitching over and falling to the ground. He clutched his leg, looking up in disbelief. Mathias raised the board once again.

"Please, wait, please, don't!" Armstrong babbled.

There was a thwack as the wooden slat made impact with his other knee. Armstrong curled up on the ground, whimpering like a child.

Mathias cast the plank aside, and it clattered across the alleyway. "Now let's see you run."

3

Mathias pulled out a chair and took a seat at the table in the VIP room at the back of Le Rouge, an unremarkable suburban strip club in Maisonneuve. The place was a local institution. Owned and operated by the boss himself, it functioned as the de facto meeting place for most high-level discussions of family politics. Not that the punters throwing notes at the girls on stage would know. The club offered certain private services as well, and typically, that was how any given meeting would conclude, with high-ranking attendees dispersing to the curtained enclaves with their strung out stripper of choice.

Made members came here regularly to discuss business with the various division heads. Sometimes Giorgio Russo was present. This was never announced, and as far as Mathias knew, only Giovanni had advance warning of his attendance.

Tony arrived shortly after Mathias and took a seat beside him at the far end of the table. A squat man in his early sixties, the Collections boss saw no need to dress up for the occasion. His wrinkled white button-down strained against an ample gut, and his graying hair was slicked to one side in an attempt to hide the ever-expanding bald patch on top of his head.

Russo wasn't here tonight, and there was the noticeable absence of his son. At the head of the table, the Quintino were assembled: Enzo Carbone, Armando Bernardi, and Gabriele Giordano, with Giovanni in the end chair—an almost interchangeable set of salt-and-pepper combovers and designer suits.

Several of the men had their seconds stationed by the door—the ones they trusted, at least. Talk that went on behind these doors did not leave the room. If you couldn't trust a grunt to keep their mouth shut, they were relegated to the corridor, though most of them eventually snuck out front for a glimpse of the real action. Rayan stood with the others in the room but off to one side, avoiding the regular banter, his face betraying nothing.

Giovanni kicked off the meeting with a round of liquor then settled into his seat as the various heads of each division provided their monthly status reports. Betting was down for a third month, interest in the flagging hometown hockey team at an all-time low. Tightened security had tied up several cross-provincial routes for Narcotics. The take by Collections was up, as usual, proving it again to be one of the strongest divisions.

It was what Tony lived for. He'd long ago abandoned the idea of upward mobility—despite personal ties to the boss and an impeccable family history—and was instead intent on the cultivation of his department. Tony had seen too many comrades run to their deaths on the promise of a higher position in the family's ranks.

In many ways, Mathias was fortunate to have started out under a boss like Tony Giraldi. He'd been given clout and greater jurisdiction, whereas other division heads would have balked at the prospect. All Tony cared about was the bottom line, and because Mathias knew how Tony worked, he knew how to deliver.

The overview was coming to a close when the door opened and Piero walked in. He held up his hands in mock apology, smirking as he took a seat in one of the few chairs left empty. There was a mutter of disapproval from some of the older stalwarts. Giovanni gave a signal, and the hostess came in with refills. Once the room was placated, the councilman once again took the floor.

"Before we wrap up, Tony's making some changes."

Mathias steeled himself. He'd suspected they would use the meeting to announce the new promotion. He glanced at Piero. The man sat, seemingly unaware, fiddling with a pack of cigarettes.

Tony cleared his throat. "As you've heard, I'm making too much damn money while the rest of you sit around jerking off."

The room rippled with laughter.

"Commercial lending is through the roof—we're setting up a branch within the division to capitalize on the uptick. Mathias Beauvais, who's had a hand in this particular development, will head it. All commercial contracts from Sherbrooke to the Mount now go through him. Any questions?"

There were several nods from the men at the table, indicating their assent. Mathias recalled the boss's praise. His achievements hadn't gone unnoticed.

"That's settled, then," Giovanni said, raising his glass. The table followed suit, and Mathias downed the remainder of his scotch in acknowledgement.

"That's quite the promotion," Piero said from his seat, his drink untouched. "Heading his own branch? Wasn't so long ago Beauvais was shaking dealers down for protection money. You thought this through, Tony?"

Beside him, Tony huffed, a ruddiness appearing along his fleshy neck. Mathias placed his glass down with a thunk. The room had gone quiet.

"Ask your father. He approved it," Tony retorted.

Piero's face darkened. "Maybe as a favor to you." He inclined his head toward Mathias. "But he's not one of our own."

"Need I remind you the man's father has ties to the founding family," Giovanni reprimanded sharply.

"Then why doesn't he carry his name?"

Mathias stood, his chair scraping noisily across the floor. He would not lose face—not here in front of these men. "If my loyalty's in question, let's settle this now," he said smoothly, refusing to let the anger register in his voice. If they had heard about his success, they'd also heard about his reputation. There was a reason people paid Mathias quickly.

"Your loyalty is not in question, Mathias," Giovanni said, holding up a hand in conciliation. "Neither is your ability. The man brought in a hundred alone last month." He turned to address Piero. "Almost enough to bail out your division. Think carefully about what you say next."

The boss's son said nothing, instead taking a long swig from his glass. Piero's ever-growing incompetence was well known among members of the family's inner circle. Mathias felt Rayan's eyes on him but did not meet his gaze.

Next to him, Tony thumped a fist down on the table. "Beauvais has worked under me for the past ten years. Ain't gonna find anyone as dedicated. He's got the stomach for this job and the smarts to keep things profitable." Under his breath, he said, "Not one of our own, my ass."

There was a rumble of agreement from the collection of men, who began to stand and clasp hands with Mathias, offering their congratulations. Piero remained seated, an insult he knew would be taken seriously, as did everyone else at the table.

Giovanni came over when the group had thinned and slapped him on the arm. "You're a *santista* now. Try not to disappoint."

"I won't," Mathias replied, masking his fury.

The old man's face turned serious. He leaned in. "Come to the club next Thursday. I have something to discuss."

"Finally!" exclaimed Narcotics head Filippo De Luca, opening the door to the room and beckoning over the hostess. "Let's get the girls in already."

21

Mathias watched the woman's mouth move down his cock as he sat in one of the club's private booths, spurring a mixture of pleasure and revulsion. He hated these jack-off sessions the elites were so insistent on having, a meeting to discuss business devolving into an excuse to take some girl behind a curtain. Just another display of the posturing required to maintain support in the family's upper echelons.

Mathias tried not to look too closely at her kneeling form clad only in a lace thong and black heels. He tried not to think about the numerous other pricks that had filled her mouth. It didn't help that he was still seething from the events of the meeting. Piero's words were fixed in his mind: "Not one of our own."

A muffled moan came through the wall beside him, and his stomach turned. What he regarded as a selfish pursuit, performed without show or ceremony, took on a garish quality when transplanted to the seedy titty bar. The old man coming next door was almost enough to make his dick soft. He cast about, as he had so many times before, searching for something—anything—to trick his body into submission.

Behind the curtain, he heard Rayan shift his weight. He was stationed outside to ensure Mathias's privacy and protection. It was almost midnight, and his second had been on his feet all day. The sound was a reminder of his presence, a sudden intrusion. The thought of him standing so close, knowing what went on mere steps away, filled Mathias with a strange surge of desire. He swallowed his surprise, swiftly pushing the thought aside, but his mind kept returning to it as if caught on something.

Rayan appeared clearly in his head—the contours of muscle visible through the man's shirt, the faded scar that ran down his neck, partially hidden by his collar. The way his mouth was set in a hard line on his angular face, bottom lip fuller than the top. The flick of the girl's tongue along his shaft made his breath quicken, and Mathias bit back a groan. When had these images implanted themselves so vividly in his brain? It was as though all this time, he'd been unconsciously taking stock, filing them away. The jut of Rayan's knuckles as he gripped the steering wheel, the smoothness of his skin... Mathias pressed his nails into the soft flesh of his palm as the sensation built, unable to shake the thoughts loose. He saw Rayan as he'd appeared before him in Belkov's office, face unyielding, body tense. He'd looked at Mathias, his eyes for an instant betraying the softness Mathias remembered from the day they'd first met. *What would that face look like when he lost control?*

Mathias's teeth clenched, and he came abruptly, with an intensity to the release he hadn't felt in months. His hand shot out to steady himself, and he pushed the woman away. Standing, he turned and fastened his pants. The girl looked up meekly, kneeling before him on the carpet, and disgust once again cut through the haze of pleasure that had overcome him.

Mathias reached into his pocket, pulled out a roll of bills, sliding off a handful, and laid them on the table. He took several slow breaths, smoothing his hair expertly, before feeling composed enough to venture out from behind the curtain.

There Rayan waited, staring straight ahead as Mathias emerged. Not for the first time, he was grateful for the man's propensity for staying silent. Without looking at him, Mathias moved toward the exit, Rayan following dutifully. He did not want to catch a glimpse of his second's face—did not want to see what his mind had so quickly conjured in that dim room.

"He was out of line." Rayan steered the car through the parking lot outside Le Rouge, still angry at having to stand by as Piero Russo insulted his boss.

"The man's a hack," Mathias muttered, staring at the road. He appeared distracted and subdued, despite the evening's festivities.

Usually, on nights like these, once they peeled off into the dark, his capo—eyes slightly less sharp, features softened by the booze—actually talked. He didn't instruct, didn't reproach, but talked. Rayan looked forward to those fleeting moments, the only time he ever felt brave enough to address the swirl of questions in his mind.

"What Piero said..." Rayan had seen the way Mathias had stiffened at the man's barb. "It's because your mother's French?"

He knew Mathias was only half-Italian and had always assumed that was the reason behind the frosty reception he received from some of the family stalwarts. Rayan's boss remained silent.

"Thought Italians only married Italians," Rayan remarked offhandedly.

"Who said she was married?" There was a sharpness to the way he said it.

Rayan felt a prickle of danger. He'd traversed past the clear boundaries marked for him. In that moment, he remembered a conversation he'd overheard one evening at the club while waiting for Mathias to emerge from a private meeting with Giovanni.

A stout man in a foul mood had appeared in the corridor, his second trailing behind him. "How that son of a whore made it into a room with Bianchi, I'll never know."

At the time, Rayan hadn't registered the insult, dismissing it as general envy, something Mathias—smart and upwardly mobile—was often subject to. Now he understood.

Having already overstepped, he felt the need to double down. "You're a better captain than any of those men."

Mathias sucked his teeth. "Maybe. But to the family, blood is everything."

Rayan coasted the car to a stop at a red light and stifled a yawn, his body heavy with exhaustion. He ached to kick off his shoes and collapse, but the thought of the long night ahead filled him with dread. The dreams were back. So were the thoughts that circled mercilessly as he lay awake in bed.

"You look like shit," Mathias said.

Rayan glanced up to see his capo observing him. He froze. This wasn't part of the deal. In the years he'd spent working with Mathias, he'd become an expert at making sure his life did not come up for discussion.

"Having trouble sleeping," he conceded.

Mathias paused as though mulling it over. "I'll arrange something the next time we're at the club. Take your mind off things."

Rayan blinked. He couldn't think of anything less appealing. It was bad enough having to stand outside that curtain and try not to think about what was happening behind it. "Not really my thing."

"What, pussy?" Mathias baited him, razor-sharp.

Rayan's jaw tightened, a familiar turn of panic in his stomach, before he realized Mathias was teasing. "No," he said gruffly. "Working girls."

Mathias snorted. "Uppity, aren't we? Suit yourself."

The light changed, and Rayan stared straight ahead as they sped through the empty streets. Anything to escape his capo's gaze.

4

Mathias placed a carved wooden box of Dominican cigars on the desk in front of Tony Giraldi and pulled up a chair in his small corner office. Tony leaned forward with a grunt, opening the taut black seal and holding the box up to his nose. He nodded approvingly, offering the contents to Mathias.

"I can't stand the damn things," Mathias said, waving him away. It was the day after the announcement at Le Rouge, and he'd decided he owed Tony for putting him forward. Despite the transience of working for the family, he believed in giving credit where it was due.

Tony selected a cigar. He tapped the end down on his desk before raising it to his lips. He ran the division out of a second-floor commercial space on Saint Laurent Boulevard. Operating under the guise of Capital Lending & Consulting, he had everything meticulously recorded—contracts, invoices, receipts. If Revenu Québec wanted an audit, Tony would be ready and waiting. But delve a little deeper, and one might note the impressive scope of their client list and discover the true nature of the services billed, which covered the occasional friendly consultation with the likes of Mathias.

Tony held his lighter to the end of the cigar and puffed several times to get it started. A thick plume of smoke settled over the desk between them. He pulled the tube out of his mouth and turned it over in his hand, inspecting it. "They're good."

"They'd better be, for what I paid for them."

"I suppose my congratulations are in order," Tony said, raising an eyebrow.

"As are my thanks," Mathias said. "For the recommendation."

"You know me—the more work I can throw your way, the easier my life gets."

Mathias smirked.

"And who the fuck else was gonna do it? Franco? Sonny? Christ, we'd be a goddamn laughing stock. Just look at that business with Armstrong."

Mathias scowled. As if he needed the reminder.

"Surprised you managed to wrangle him in the end."

Wrangle was an interesting choice of words.

Tony fixed him with a level stare. "Speaking of promotions, with you heading Commercial, the rest of the division could do with a reshuffle. Get you some extra muscle and maybe give the kid his big break. Think he'd be up to running his own team?"

Mathias felt himself stiffen, tempering the immediate jolt of possession that passed through him. The thoughts that had arisen so intensely the previous evening had not abated. Instead, they lingered, coloring the way his second had appeared that morning as he stood waiting at the Collections office—different somehow, as though in sharper focus.

"He's quick, knows the rounds, the clients," Tony continued. "Hell, he's been shadowing you long enough. Seems a waste keeping him on as a meat shield."

"Rayan's an outsider," Mathias said, careful to sound indifferent. "Without family ties, no one will work under him."

Tony shrugged. "A captain without the title. That old-school bullshit is overrated anyway. Money talks, my friend. How do you think you've gotten so far?"

"He works with me," Mathias replied flatly, ending the exchange.

A silence fell between them. Tony took another drag on his new cigar. "Must be some kind of a record."

"What is?"

"Three years now, isn't it? With the same second. I remember when we were down to a monthly rotation."

"I blame your subpar recruitment. You should've seen some of the idiots you sent my way. Surprised I didn't end up with a hole through my skull."

"Kid must be doing something right."

Mathias narrowed his eyes. "He knows how to keep his mouth shut—that's all."

It wasn't all, but the longer explanation eluded even him. Rayan hadn't started out as a model soldier—far from it—yet somehow, he'd turned into one of the few people Mathias trusted completely. He had proven more than competent at every turn, his loyalty silencing the constant distrust Mathias felt with other men.

Almost a year after Mathias had dropped the skinny kid he'd found by the container terminal at Guillet's compound, Rayan had reappeared in the Collections office. They'd been short a driver, and Tony pulled a favor with the city's eminent nose-powder distributor. It was a last resort. Those who worked for Georges Guillet were not known for their reliability. Rayan had proven otherwise.

Mathias had never told Tony about his initial encounter with his second. He didn't know what had compelled him to pick Rayan up that day or why he hadn't simply left the man to his own fate. It had been remarkably out of character, struck by something he couldn't name. Even now, the decision unnerved him. Regardless, he'd resolved things in his own way. Besides the obvious, the next best method to ensure silence was complicity. Running for Guillet meant getting your hands dirty—driving for the family, dirtier still.

Truth be told, Mathias hadn't thought he would see the young man again. He hadn't even asked his name. Most who landed at Guillet's ended up running then using then dead. But he figured if the kid played his cards right, it was better than being out on the street. And then he'd shown up at the office, bulkier than before, hair cut short, a blankness about him. Gone were the eyes that broadcast every tumbling emotion, revealing the frightened boy for all to see. He'd managed that at least. Despite the time that had passed, Mathias couldn't shake the image of the young man's face as he'd watched his brother fall.

"This is Rayan Nadeau. He's driving for Franco."

Mathias showed no recognition. Neither did Rayan.

After a couple of months of Rayan driving, Tony was impressed enough to bring him on full-time. Mathias had dropped yet another second, and there was an opening that needed to be filled. He'd given Rayan one month—not that he'd bothered to tell him about that. If he didn't show promise, Mathias would send him back to Tony. Rayan shadowed him through his daily tasks, a silent specter hovering just within earshot. Mathias was hard on him. Part of him wanted him to quit, but he showed up each morning again and again.

Mathias had him checked out that first week and came back with a folder two inches thick: child protection, father MIA, mother dead. There'd been a series of group homes before he ended up on the street, and that was when the police record began. Petty theft, carjacking. And now, as though tempting fate, Rayan had been roped into the largest criminal organization in North America. He was resilient—Mathias would give him that. He knew how to survive.

Eager to change the subject, Mathias leaned back, folding his arms. "Last night, what the fuck crawled up his ass?" He avoided mentioning Piero by name. You never knew who was listening, and he was the boss's son after all.

Tony snorted, a look of contempt settling on his lined face. "He's as useless as they come. Gambles away division profit and still thinks he's in the running for a position on the council."

Mathias raised an eyebrow. "Does he, now?"

Tony waved his hand in dismissal. "Despite the inherited clout, he's dead jealous of anyone who gets ahead on their own merit. Probably 'cause he's got none to speak of."

Mathias was still pissed the man had shown him up at his own promotion. Even so, it was good to know he'd ruffled Piero's feathers. Mathias was starting to get the attention he deserved and, even better, was alienating the prick in the process.

Mathias hesitated on the steps of a house that was all too familiar. The orange brick facade, the black shutters, the boxwood hedge that marked the property line—he'd ventured out here many times as a child, often during his mother's days of silence when she forgot he existed. He would take money from her purse and roam about the city or take the train to Longueuil and stand across the street from his father's house, waiting for a glimpse of the man's family, careful to make sure they didn't see him. He'd return to the apartment disappointed, his mother exactly as he'd left her.

The first time Mathias had come, as a boy of eight, he'd followed his father home after one of the rare occasions when he'd stopped by their apartment. Mathias wanted to see tangible proof of his father's real family, the one he went home to every night. And sure enough, Mathias ended up here. He stood behind a tree and watched Freddie Junior and his younger brother, Tommaso, kick a soccer ball around the front yard. Distracted by his father's retreat into the house, Mathias didn't realize he'd been spotted until the older boy was standing in front of him.

"I know who you are," the boy hissed as Tommaso ran over, drawn by the commotion. "And I know what they call you, bastard!"

Mathias recalled the sharp pain of the boy's foot in his guts before blackness descended. The next thing he knew, his old man was pulling him off a bloody Freddie Junior. Mathias's fists were raw from where they'd made impact. His father yelled at him and sent him home by himself, all the way across town, as night began to fall, picking his legitimate sons over Mathias. Even at that age, he had understood.

All these years later, Mathias had still never been inside the house. He strode purposefully up the steps and rapped loudly on the dark wooden door. It was a Sunday afternoon, and he shouldn't be here. After the visit with his mother, he'd been adamant about not seeing his old man. But it had followed him doggedly—a paralyzing need to show his father what he'd become so the man would know he'd been eclipsed by the son he never wanted.

There was a shuffling sound on the other end of the door, and it cracked open, a woman peering out suspiciously. Sofia. He barely recognized his father's wife—time had not been kind. Her eyes widened, and the door began to close.

Mathias stuck out his hand, easily holding it ajar against her weight. "Nice to see you too. We can make this easy, or we can make it hard."

Sofia scowled, but she was no match for his strength. She grudgingly let the door swing open. "What do you want?" she asked sourly, lips pursed.

"I'm here to see my father."

Her frown deepened. "Federico is in no shape for visitors."

Mathias felt a familiar clench in his stomach. He moved forward so that he towered over the slight woman. "I don't think you understand," he said quietly. "I'm here to see my father."

Sofia stared him down, no doubt weighing the repercussions of refusing to let a ranked member of the family into her home.

"Fine," she said finally, stepping back to let him in. "But I don't want to see you here again."

The woman had no need to worry. There wouldn't be a next time.

"The door at the end." Sofia gestured down the hallway. "He's in there."

Not bothering to knock, Mathias pushed open the door to reveal a darkened room, the curtains still drawn. His father lay under a mountain of covers, looking smaller than he'd ever seen him. Mathias was seized with a dread that stilled his body. It wasn't simply the shock of seeing the man, who had always filled him with a mixture of hatred and fear, but of seeing him so pathetic. The cancer had robbed him of any authority he might once have held, his body pale and wasted.

Mathias felt an overwhelming need to leave, to get as far away from him as possible, but it was too late to back out. The last time they'd met, Mathias had been convinced he'd outgrown his father's grip on his life. Yet here he was, flooded with the same familiar feeling, the same longing for approval, as though he was still a boy.

Like a child turning on the light to assuage a fear of lurking horrors, Mathias walked to the window and pulled open one of the curtains, allowing a stream of afternoon sun into the room. Illuminated, this particular monster was easier to face, with his hair all but gone, cheek bones protruding, and eyes sunken. The unwelcome light hit his face, and he squinted then blinked rapidly. It seemed to take him a while to adjust, which was fine, as Mathias no longer knew what he wanted to say.

"Mathias?" His hoarse voice burst to life. "Is that you?"

"It's me."

A smile swept across his father's face. "I was wondering whether your mother—"

"I didn't come here to talk about her," Mathias cut in.

His father paused, head bobbing slightly. "How are you?"

"Finally taken an interest?"

Freddie shrugged, looking even more frail. "You're my flesh and blood. When you don't have much time left, you realize these things are important."

Mathias froze, white-hot anger locking his jaw. The man had spent a lifetime acting as though Mathias didn't exist, saving the pleasantries for when he was sick and senile, rotting away in bed.

"They've made me *santista*."

His father—who'd spent most of his adult life working for the family—nodded in acknowledgment. He'd never strayed far from the bookie house or courted danger the way Mathias had. "You've become quite the soldier," Freddie said almost wistfully. "With your education, I'd always imagined a different path for you."

The hurt was physical, like a blow to the chest. Mathias made sure his face gave nothing away, but he fell silent in an attempt to regain composure. His father began to cough, reaching for the glass of water by his bed. The old man tried to sit, his trembling arms barely able to lift him from the mattress.

Mathias watched, not moving to help. "What exactly did you imagine?" he said finally. "You know nothing about me."

His father placed the glass back down, leaning heavily against the headboard. "Your mother told me things. Heard you studied overseas, that you're pretty clever. All I'm saying is working for the family ain't all it's cracked up to be."

"For you, maybe," Mathias retorted. "Look how well you did, if this dump is any indication. Couldn't even afford to keep your sidepiece."

"Watch your mouth!" his father snapped, eyes darkening, a flash of the heavy-handed man he remembered from his childhood showing through.

Shortly before Mathias left Université PSL and returned to Montreal, his father had terminated the decades-long arrangement with his mother, cutting her off completely. Apparently, it was expensive maintaining two families, but more to the point, with his mother cresting forty, Mathias suspected she'd simply reached the end of her shelf life.

The old man appeared to lose steam, mellowing once again. "I know you take care of her."

"Only because you don't. Being a better man has proven surprisingly easy."

"Your mother—"

"Everything you've done, and she still pines over you."

His father looked at him with watery eyes. "I've made mistakes—I can admit that. As I said, you start to look at things differently when confronted by your own mortality."

"No." Mathias shook his head. "There's no absolution here. The sooner you're in the ground, the better."

The words left his lips with vitriol, almost clanking against his teeth on the way out. All his life, his father had loomed before him, someone he'd foolishly fixated on to give him purpose and justify his decisions.

"Where is he?" demanded someone from the hallway.

Mathias knew that voice—it was his father's eldest son. Sofia must have called him. The door swung open, and Freddie Junior appeared, his face red with anger.

He stuck out a thick finger at Mathias, who stood by the window. "You need to leave now. Get out."

Mathias took in the man's paunch, his receding hairline, and the ruptured blood vessels across his nose. *This was the kid I tried to measure up to?*

"Did you hear me?" Freddie Junior spluttered.

A slow smile spread across Mathias's face. "What are you going to do?" he asked menacingly.

His father's namesake shrank back as if slapped. Mathias held his gaze, suppressing the urge to lay hands on him. As a young boy, he'd fantasized about beating him senseless many times. Mathias waited for his father to intervene, but the man was silent.

So much for looking at things differently. Mathias had grown tired of the nostalgia. "He's all yours." Leaving his half brother gaping in the room, he walked past a glowering Sofia and out the front door.

In his car, as he was pulling away, Mathias took one last look at the house, and this time, he felt nothing.

Mathias wasn't sure exactly when Giovanni Bianchi had sought him out. Giovanni deliberated at length about most things, so it would have been some time before he decided to formally make his acquaintance. The meeting itself, he did remember. Mathias had accompanied Tony to one of the regular division briefings when Giovanni pulled him aside for a nightcap. He'd heard things about the young captain and wanted to see if the rumors were true.

From there, they began a discreet exchange of information, fueled by their shared ambition. For Mathias, that meant a higher rank and his own division. For Giovanni, well, those aspirations could only be hinted at while the boss was still alive. The councilman needed his eyes and ears, the contacts he'd built around the city, and the alliances he'd forged with rival group heads. Mathias needed Giovanni's clout. Son of one of the founding fathers from Sicily, the man had been born into family ranks. As an enduring member of the Quintino, he belonged to the small circle of people the boss trusted implicitly—more brother to Russo than counsel. He was a mage of the old ways and knew more about how the family worked than anyone else.

He also drank like a fish, the only man besides Belkov that Mathias had trouble keeping up with. Giovanni liked to let people know he was in control. He picked the drinks, ordered the food. The man, dressed in a tailored gray suit, looked like a young retiree, down to the slick side part and manicured mustache. Perhaps his unassuming appearance was the very reason Giovanni felt the need to remind everyone who called the shots.

The waitress brought out their fourth round of drinks, and Mathias's empty stomach growled in protest. Yet it proved a welcome distraction from thoughts of his father, which had been surfacing unprompted since the afternoon he'd stopped by the old house.

They were back at Le Rouge, in one of the small meeting rooms far from the clamor of the crowd out front. Rayan waited in the hallway. Usually privy to most of Mathias's business, he was not included in these meetings with Giovanni. To be of any use, they had to be strictly off the record.

"I know you've got a chip on your shoulder, Beauvais." Giovanni leaned forward to clink glasses. "Hell, no *goomah*'s boy has ever made it this far in the family. So you shake things up, get some attention. But now you're a *santista*. That's going to rub some people the wrong way."

"Some people," Mathias said, lifting his own glass and reluctantly taking another swig of scotch.

"We all know he was out of line at the meeting. Poor form. Only reflects badly on him."

"No," Mathias said, frowning. "It reflects badly on me to have the boss's son show such disrespect."

Giovanni spread his hands. "He shows disrespect to everyone. He disrespects the traditions, throws his weight around. Just wait. His time will come."

Mathias raised an eyebrow.

Giovanni gave him a slow smile. "Ah, now we come to it. You've seen the boss. What did you think?"

Mathias set down his glass, picked up his cigarettes, and lit one. He couldn't think of a way to answer the question without sounding disloyal.

"Exactly," Giovanni said. "We need to be prepared."

"The Quintino?" Mathias asked.

Giovanni nodded. "Ultimately, it comes down to us to agree on a succession plan."

"Boss wanted to know if I'd follow the right people."

"Russo does not want his son to head the family," Giovanni said, taking the cigar holder from his breast pocket and placing one between his teeth. Mathias leaned forward to light it for him. "But Piero will make a bid. He thinks of it as his birthright."

"And what does the council think?"

Giovanni exhaled, giving Mathias a knowing look. "Piero doesn't have many friends on the council, or in the family for that matter. But the friends he does have are very motivated. They have a lot to gain from his rise to power."

"So it'll end in mutiny. A split within the group," Mathias said, tapping the end of his cigarette in the ashtray. No longer dubious theory but a plausible reality. Those loyal to Russo would be pitted against greedy low-tier soldiers fueled by Piero's promise of a sizable payout.

Giovanni held out his hands, the corners of his mouth turning down. "Not if we can get ahead of it."

Mathias knocked back the rest of his drink. "What are you suggesting?"

"Allies. The rest of the city will sit back and let us kill each other, but whoever holds sway over our competitors will come out ahead. This is where you come in. You've made the rounds, haven't been afraid to get your hands dirty. You've ingratiated yourself to many of the groups here."

"I think you might be misinformed. I'm hated by most of the groups here."

Giovanni laughed, waving his smoking cigar between them. "Hate and respect go hand in hand. And they do respect you. You're not old Italy, and you work with an outsider. Somewhat removed from family politics. If the ship is sinking, you're the one they'll approach to start cutting deals."

Mathias took a long drag from his cigarette, thankful for the moment to temper a flash of anger. He resented his assumption of control, yet Giovanni was right—most of the men up high who pocketed the money had no idea how things on the street worked. They were unconcerned with the agreements and historic affiliations that led to a tenuous peace among their rivals.

"I don't like to negotiate," Mathias said, hiding his annoyance.

Giovanni shrugged. "Any great victory involves compromise. But it's early days—something to keep in mind for now. Be civil. Don't go burning bridges."

Mathias thought of his recent visit with Belkov. There was a fine line between burning bridges and cracking down on insolence.

The old man pressed the small black button beneath the table, signaling the waitress. "Now, how about another round?"

5

Despite the establishment's relative safety compared to the constant danger that marked their line of work, they were jumped while walking from Le Rouge to the car. Mathias, drunker than usual after his meeting with Giovanni, had passed Rayan the keys on their way out the door. They were steps away from the Mercedes when the man appeared, stooped and hooded, the glint of a hunting knife in his hand. He moved erratically, bouncing from foot to foot. His words slurred when he told them to hand over their wallets, shuffling awfully close to where Mathias stood with hands in his pockets.

Rayan's capo looked amused. "You have no idea what you've gotten yourself into."

Mathias, in part due to the liquor, did not see this tweaked-out man as a threat. But Rayan had encountered many of his kind on the streets of Montreal—unpredictable, willing to put a knife in your back for the food in your hand. He gripped the keys, the metal digging into his palm.

Mathias's unruffled demeanor made the man even more jumpy. Rayan slipped the car keys into his pocket, mentally noting the gun against his chest, how quickly he could get to it, and how much damage the man could do before then. In the dark, it was hard to see exactly who they were dealing with under the hood, but Rayan could hear the man grinding his teeth.

"The fuck you talking about? Wallet now!"

Mathias reached into his jacket and pulled out a roll of bills. He began to peel them off, one by one. The man froze. This was not what he'd expected.

Rayan tried to catch Mathias's eye. *What was he doing? Fucking with him?* His boss had been especially hard to read the past few days. Preoccupied, prone to lashing out. And now this. He was being unusually reckless.

"How much does a bump cost these days?" Mathias asked. The junkie hissed and snatched at the money, but Mathias stepped back, holding it out of reach. "Not so fast."

Then the man lunged. Mathias moved to avoid the knife, but the edge of the blade grazed his forearm as it passed. In the end, Rayan didn't reach for his gun. Even before he saw the blood, he'd tackled the dopehead to the ground, the knife clattering out of reach, and pummeled the man with his fists until he stopped moving.

"Fuck," Rayan whispered.

The hood slipped back to reveal a kid of nineteen or twenty, his cheeks mottled with acne scars—not much older than Rayan had been when he first met Mathias. But it was another face he saw, flickering like an apparition in the dim light. He put the back of his hand by the kid's mouth. *Still breathing.*

"Leave him," Mathias said. Rayan stood to see that he'd removed his jacket and was inspecting the blood blooming on the sleeve of his white shirt. "Scum."

"I'll call the doc."

Dr. Olivier Martin, who operated a private clinic in the South Shore, had a long-standing—and highly lucrative—arrangement with his capo, which included his personal number on speed dial.

Mathias shook his head. "Let's go."

Rayan reached into his pocket for the keys, and his fingers brushed his phone. He glanced back at the kid lying in the parking lot. He could just give them the address and hang up without leaving a name.

"Don't even think about it," Mathias said coldly, seeing straight through him. "Better for everyone if he drowns in his own blood."

"One less strung out piece of shit to deal with?" It came out harsher than Rayan had intended. He realized his nails were biting into the flesh of his palms.

Mathias gave him a hard look. "You don't live in that world anymore, Rayan."

They got in the car and drove the rest of the way to Mathias's apartment in silence, the blood drying on Rayan's knuckles as he clenched the steering wheel.

While they were waiting for the elevator in the garage beneath the building, Mathias turned to him. "If you feel sorry for everyone that tries to fuck you over, you will not last long in this business."

It wasn't the first time he'd imparted this lesson. Years before, shortly after Rayan had graduated from driver to second, Mathias relieved him of his weapon as it shook in his hand. He still remembered watching with a churn of shame as Mathias completed the task he'd found himself unable to do. Much had changed since then. Rayan had mastered this particular principle, save for the odd reminder.

The elevator doors opened with a ding. They stepped inside, and Mathias punched in the floor access code, grimacing. Rayan's gaze fell to the stain on the man's shirtsleeve. He felt his anger dissipate. His capo's blood was proof of his failure. Once in the apartment, Rayan stepped into the kitchen and washed his hands long and hard in the searing-hot water, exorcising the junkie's muck from his fingers.

"There's a bottle of Macallan in the cabinet. Bring it here," Mathias called from the living room.

Rayan opened one of the cupboards, half expecting it to be empty. Instead, he found shelves of neatly stacked packets, jars, and cans. It didn't take him long to find the scotch, displayed in a glass cabinet with a wide selection of liquor bottles in varying shapes and sizes. He took down the bottle and fished a small tumbler from the adjacent drawer.

In the living room, Mathias sat on the sofa, his shirt left on the floor. Rayan placed the scotch and the tumbler down on the coffee table. Then he threw off his jacket, rolled up his sleeves, and went to raid the hallway bathroom cabinet. When he returned with supplies, he found the glass abandoned, his boss opting to drink straight from the bottle.

Rayan sat next to him and started to clean his arm, gently exposing the cut beneath the blood. He felt a wave of relief. It wasn't as bad as he'd initially thought. "Make sure Martin has a look at this," he cautioned as he finished sterilizing the wound and began on the bandage.

"Count yourself lucky it's not worse," Mathias admonished him.

"Don't fuck with an armed junkie," Rayan retorted, pulling tight on the fabric. "Makes my job harder."

His capo snickered, raising the bottle to his lips.

Busying himself with taping the end of the bandage in place, Rayan spoke to his hands. "Something on your mind?"

Mathias swallowed, pausing. "Do you know your father?"

Rayan glanced up, not sure what had brought this on. They'd left one night when he was a child, and Rayan hadn't seen his father since. The man hadn't even shown up in court after his mother died. He remembered the social worker using the term *child abandonment* as he and his brother sat on a hard wooden bench in front of the judge, the starch on his borrowed button-down shirt making his neck itch. All these years, he'd never felt the urge to find him. No doubt, he was still living in the old weather-beaten house where Rayan had grown up.

"I don't have a father," he said after a moment.

"Easier that way."

Rayan saw a sliver of the man slip past the impenetrable exterior. So they were alike in that way. It made sense. One didn't get into this business on the merits of a happy childhood. He became aware of the warmth of Mathias's skin beneath his fingers and the quickening of his own pulse. But his capo was looking past him, thoughts elsewhere.

When Rayan came back from putting everything away, Mathias was stretched out on the couch, eyes closed, his bandaged arm resting on his bare chest. He paused, startled to find himself with an uninterrupted view of the man. He was usually careful, snatching glimpses here and there. He'd always found Mathias painfully beautiful. Even more so when he was like this—unguarded, sedate.

Rayan walked down the hall in search of a blanket. He'd been inside Mathias's penthouse a few times but only in passing. It resembled a showroom, as though no one really lived there. No photos, no papers strewn about, no unopened mail. Rayan stopped in front of the open bedroom door. The bed was made, nightstands clear of clutter. He stepped into the room and opened the wardrobe. Lines of perfectly pressed clothes hung from floor-to-ceiling racks. A stand displayed a small collection of Rolex watches. It smelled of Mathias. Of his cologne, his scent. Rayan closed the wardrobe and grabbed the throw blanket from the end of the bed. He made his way back to the living room.

Careful not to wake him, Rayan draped the blanket over his sleeping form. In the dim light of the room, Mathias's face tilted toward him. The hard lines had softened. Those disapproving lips were parted, his hair mussed and tumbling across his forehead. Before he could stop himself, Rayan reached out and brushed the pad of his thumb against Mathias's temple. His fingers itched to run through the man's thick dark hair. Rayan pulled his hand back as though stung, his heart pounding with a paralyzing fear. Careless. He could not afford to be this careless.

After picking up his jacket from the back of the sofa, Rayan let himself out, locking the door behind him.

Like a curse, Mathias's question conjured unwelcome thoughts of the past. They surfaced—snatches of memory Rayan had worked hard to bury. Back at his apartment he found himself unable to sleep. He lay in bed, fighting the pull of the clock on his nightstand. Recognizing the futility of willing himself to sleep, he sat up, flicking on the light. He opened the battered copy of *Terre des hommes* he kept by his bedside but found himself reading the same sentence over again. It was too late to be this distracted. The book, usually enough to coax his mind to consider the possibility of sleep, was closed to him. Since he'd first begun to decipher words on a page, books had been his comfort, his Ambien. He couldn't recall who'd taught him to read—school had been an extravagance, a joy denied at every opportunity. He figured, like most things, he'd simply taught himself.

Rayan remembered little from his childhood—he hesitated to even call it a childhood. His mother, a Lebanese refugee, and his father, an older Quebecois army veteran, were mismatched from the start. To this day, he could not understand why they'd married and why they'd had him and his older brother, Tahir. It must have stemmed from a shared decision to cling to the other as protection from life's uncertainty. They were both cut off from their families, she by circumstance, he by choice.

Rayan learned quickly that he had no love for his father. If André Nadeau had taught him one thing, it was how to hide. Whether to escape a fierce beating or conceal the parts of himself he knew were different.

As soon as he was able, he began to shape the person he was based on everything his father wasn't. He clung to his mother and would have done anything to see her happy. His brother, on the other hand, took on their father's life lessons as his own. Rayan's last memory of the man was the night they'd left, his mother glancing over her shoulder as they walked quickly from the house, a boy in each hand. Their father looked on from the doorway, illuminated in the dark. A silent, fearsome figure.

She didn't know how to drive, so they walked the two and a half miles to the bus stop. Several years later, living in a small apartment they couldn't afford, she locked herself in the bathroom and never came out. His brother went in when the custodian arrived to force the door. Fortunately, he'd spared Rayan the details.

Rayan flipped to the front of the book and traced the inscription with his fingers. Made by his mother's hesitant hand, it was all that was left of her. She'd struggled with her adopted language but had written it carefully regardless, the French words stilted, sentimental, except for the final line, her profession of love, which she inscribed boldly in *al-abjadiyah*, the Arabic script. His mother, who had given all her love but received so little in return, could only express it in her native tongue.

After her death, he and Tahir had spent a couple of years bouncing around in state care—group homes, the odd foster family. They never stayed long. In the popularity contest that was child placement, two teenage boys weren't exactly in high demand. It was his brother who convinced him they were better off on their own. That was when home became the streets of Montreal. For a while, they got by on the kindness of strangers, the unhoused community rallying around them, showing them the ropes and where to make a couple of bucks panhandling. But it soon became clear they would need more to survive. They started stealing cars, roaming through the city, careful not to hit the same neighborhoods too often. Rayan learned to drive in a stolen car, a shiny white SUV with black leather seats. They would drive around like they were other people, better people, and leave the cars with a man in Brossard who paid them a small fee for their trouble. Sometimes they stole other things as well.

It didn't take long for Tahir to get into the hard stuff. It was surprising how easily it flowed through the streets. Guys who couldn't afford a sandwich somehow had enough for a hit. The carjacking didn't cut it anymore, and Tahir began running for his dealer, a man named Jean Bastien. Rayan managed to avoid getting formally involved yet was often pulled in by association. Trailing his brother as he ping-ponged around town, going from soaring highs to crushing lows. By this time, Rayan had perfected his camouflage, hiding behind a mask that changed shape depending on who was peering in. He benefitted from his brother's affiliation, but it pained him to admit how much like his father Tahir had become. Rayan knew it was only a matter of time before something happened. There'd been the occasional run-in with police, but the wrath of street politics licked at their heels, especially when Tahir, flush with growing authority, began stealing from Bastien. Loyalty, which had tied the brothers together, started to fray. Tahir grew erratic, paranoid, no longer recognizable.

Rayan closed the book and turned off the light. He lay in the dark, flexing his fists. They were already starting to stiffen. There would be bruises in the morning. He closed his eyes and realized his heart was racing. It wasn't mention of his father that had brought the past back in high definition. It was the junkie he'd beaten into the pavement.

On a day when his brother had been tasked with delivering a cut to Bastien's mob associate, Tahir had taken off with the money. It didn't take long for the dealer to find him. Tahir had made it as far as the port's southernmost container terminal. Bastien took Rayan along as collateral. Deserted on a Sunday, the terminal was a wide expanse of concrete that ran along the Saint Lawrence River, dotted with shipping containers in stacks of twos. Parked at the end of a dirt track off the main road, Rayan could see the swell of the river through the maze of freight, swollen with spring snowmelt. While Bastien's lackeys dragged Tahir to where he and the dealer stood waiting, a black car pulled up, and two men in suits stepped out. Rayan hadn't seen many mafiosi in his time, but there was no mistaking that these men were with the family.

"It's a bad week when I have to see your face twice," the taller of the two said to Bastien. He was young and well-built with hardened features set in a scowl.

Bastien reached to pick up the scuffed sports bag one of his men had dropped at his feet. Rayan recognized the bag—it was Tahir's. He looked over at his brother, whose arms were pinned behind his back. His face was bloody. If he'd seen Rayan, he didn't show it.

"Apologies. We ran into a minor problem. You'll find something extra in there for your trouble." Bastien handed the bag over to the man's partner, who set it down on the hood of the car and began counting. There was a blur of movement as Tahir broke free and began to sprint. Without hesitation, Bastien pulled his piece from the waistband of his jeans.

Akhi... Was it thought or said? Rayan only recalled the taste of the word in his mouth, never to be spoken again. There were two shots. The second tore through his brother's chest, and he fell to the ground, unmoving.

"Problem solved," Bastien said, stowing his weapon.

Rayan stared, the only sound his heart thundering in his ears. Forced to bear witness, he could not tear his eyes away. One final familial duty.

"Get rid of it," Bastien instructed his men tersely. They picked up Tahir, his shirt already darkening, eyes open yet unseeing, and carried him to where the crane dock dropped into the river.

We belong to Allah, and to Him do we return.

The words came to his mind unbidden, like a lyric from a children's song. It had been a lifetime since he'd last believed his mother's stories of faith and repentance, read from the special book she'd carried with her from a mystical homeland. His hands began to shake, a tremor that rose from inside his body, pushing through to his fingertips. He saw his mother kneeling on the living room carpet, Tahir's arms looped around her neck as she kissed him.

"It's all here," the man who'd counted the money announced, popping the trunk and moving to stash the bag.

"Who's the kid?" The tall mafioso was looking at him, and their eyes met for an instant before Rayan dropped his gaze.

"Junkie's brother," Bastien said. "Want me to take care of him too?"

The man was quiet. Rayan felt his slate-gray eyes on him, the thread of his life casually placed in this stranger's hand.

"One dead kid, cops look the other way," he said finally. "Two's bad for business."

Bastien shrugged. "Your call, Mathias."

"If you're late again next month, a little extra won't cut it."

Bastian shrank, giving him a curt nod. Without another word, the dealer and his men got into their car and pulled out, Rayan already forgotten, left to his fate.

"Who're you with?" the man called Mathias asked, addressing him in English.

Rayan searched for words but found his mind blank. Seeing Tahir dead on the ground had rendered him mute. He stared back, saying nothing.

"Don't make me ask again." Mathias reached into his jacket, and Rayan wondered how it would feel when the bullet pierced his skin, tearing through him, shredding his insides. But instead of a gun, he pulled out his cigarettes.

The fear parted for an instant, allowing Rayan to think. "No one."

"Smart kid." Mathias lit up and took a drag. "Smarter than your brother, at least. It's not a good idea to steal from the family."

Rayan remained silent, still convinced he would kill him.

"What did you see here today?" Mathias asked, giving him a pointed stare. This time, Rayan did not look away.

"Nothing," he whispered. The thought of denying his brother's existence while his body sank to the bottom of the Saint Lawrence was too much to bear. He felt a swell of tears and swallowed hard, refusing to let them come.

"Good." Mathias exhaled a plume of smoke. He appeared to be considering something. Rayan did not know much about the family, only that if you traced any street activity far enough, it led to them.

"Roll up your sleeves."

Rayan obliged, pulling his sweater up to his elbows to expose the unmarked insides of his arms. Users were unreliable. They had nothing to lose.

"Come with me."

Rayan's feet moved on their own. There was little choice in the matter—he couldn't risk refusing a member of the family, someone with the power to make Jean Bastien flinch. He could take his chances and run, like his brother. But to where? He had nothing—and no one—to go back to.

"You Quebecois?" Mathias asked as they walked around the black Mercedes to where his partner waited, a frown on his face.

"*Oui.*"

"I'm tired of speaking English," Mathias said in French. He gestured toward the car. "Get in." Then he turned to his subordinate. "Drop him off at Guillet's."

"Boss?" the shorter man asked, eyeing Rayan suspiciously.

Mathias took another drag on his cigarette before flicking it to the ground. "He's short on runners. Might as well get some use out of the kid."

In bed, Rayan felt sleep encroaching, covering him like a heavy blanket. For most of his life, he'd been treated like he had no future, the long line of social workers, court registrars, and police officers always with that same look of pity, like he was the sad result of an unfortunate past, broken and unsalvageable. But Mathias had looked at him, standing before the river that had swallowed his brother, and seen a flicker of possibility. Alone in an unforgiving city, it was more affirming than anything anyone had given him since his mother's death. He could be useful, worth something at least. He was not nothing.

So Rayan had taken that possibility and held it tightly. That was the beginning, he knew now, when he had seen something in Mathias that others did not see, a kernel of feeling Rayan had buried deep, its tendrils growing despite his futile attempts to cut them back—gratitude manifesting loyalty and admiration breeding devotion. Because he knew on that day, had he not been seen, he would have disappeared entirely.

Rayan had ended up running for Guillet for almost a year, his only skill not getting hooked on what he was selling. It was enough to propel him up the ranks until he was sent, as a favor, to drive for the family. When he'd arrived at the Collections office and seen Mathias, he'd been transported back to the day of Tahir's death. He remembered in the car, as they sped through the city, how he'd been too afraid to look at the man beside him in the backseat. He'd felt a tug as though he were being torn in two, half of him left at the port with his brother, the other half a stranger headed into the unknown to start a new life chosen for him.

It was less strange now. In fact, it was the most constant Rayan's life had been since he'd left his childhood home. Yet here he was, still hiding.

6

Mathias's promotion didn't change much in regards to the work—he'd already managed most of the division's business and construction clients, and any he hadn't were now firmly under his jurisdiction—but it formalized his place as Tony's second-in-command. While this had been obvious to everyone for as long as Rayan could remember, the new title made it official. And Mathias wasted no time using it as an opportunity to jettison the last remaining dregs from his roster. Anything street level went to Sonny, which was about as much responsibility as he could handle. Mathias had even attempted to rid himself of the Russians until Tony—who hated Belkov with a passion—put his foot down.

"So this is less a commercial split and more all the shit you don't want to manage yourself?" Mathias had asked, and the old man had agreed with a snigger.

The two were volatile together, but the Collections head had always been somewhat of a mentor to his boss. Rayan knew part of the reason Mathias had stayed in the division for as long as he had was that he respected Tony. They had a mutual understanding—as long as Mathias made money for him and Tony let him off leash to manage things on his own, they were both happy. Not that anyone could tell.

One late morning, they were on their way to a visit with Hubert Leblanc, a two-bit Quebec businessman who ran a handful of car washes around the city. Rumor was he'd recently started taking in a considerable amount of cash. The man was clearly laundering. For whom, they had yet to find out. It wasn't them—that was for sure. After all, the family had its own ways of making dirty money clean. But Leblanc wasn't being nearly as careful as he should be, and Mathias had enough motivated police personnel in his back pocket to rat out any rival business that didn't toe the line.

There was a loud bang, and the car shuddered, lurching to the right. Rayan pulled over to the side of the road, and they both got out.

"*Tabarnak*," Mathias muttered, kicking the flat with the toe of his shoe. It was amusing that at times like these, his cursing was so very Quebecois.

"I'll call someone," Rayan said, reaching into his pocket for his phone.

He shook his head dismissively, walking over to the trunk. He pulled out the jack and dropped the spare onto the pavement. Then he shrugged out of his jacket, threw it over the hood, and began rolling up the sleeves of his dress shirt.

Rayan stood, phone in hand, as Mathias shimmied the jack under the Mercedes and began to turn the handle, the car lifting with a creak. A not unfamiliar stab of shame hit him as he simmered in his own uselessness. He was more adept at stealing cars than fixing them—one of many life skills omitted from his upbringing.

He crouched beside him. "Let me. I'll never live it down if the office knows I let my capo change a goddamn tire."

Mathias glanced at him with a smirk, a line of sweat already forming across his brow. "Then I suggest you watch closely. You might learn something."

Rayan did as he was told, watching as Mathias unscrewed the flat and yanked it off the hub. He pushed it toward Rayan. "Make yourself useful, and throw this in the trunk."

When he returned, his capo already had the spare on and was tightening the lug nuts. He stood, looking at Rayan expectantly. "Now, bring it down."

Rayan knelt, unwinding the jack in the opposite direction and slowly lowering the car to the ground. He stood to stow the jack with the flat. Behind him, Mathias shrugged on his jacket, grumbling about the fucking Quebec roads. As if the family hadn't been skimming a fat slice of profit off road construction for the past twenty years.

Slamming the trunk shut, Rayan heard his boss's phone start to ring. He rounded the car to see Mathias staring at the screen as it lit up, an odd look on his face.

The number that flashed across the screen was one Mathias knew by heart but had never saved. The phone rang three times before he finally picked up.

"What?"

"It's me." His mother's voice was tight.

Mathias felt himself tense. There was no reason for her to be calling him at this time, on this number, unless...

"He's gone," she said in a low whisper.

A buzzing filled his head, and Mathias leaned hard against the car. "Where is he?"

A small sob came through the receiver before Marguerite spoke. "Hospital Notre Dame, on Sherbrooke."

His mother continued speaking, but he no longer heard her. He lowered the phone from his ear, looking over at Rayan, who was standing before him, eyebrows knitted in confusion.

"Boss?"

"Notre Dame Hospital," Mathias instructed as he pulled open the passenger door and got in. He needed time to think. He couldn't focus on anything, his mind buckling, refusing to cooperate.

His second got in behind the wheel, glancing over at him before slamming the door and putting the keys in the ignition. The drive to the hospital took an eternity, Rayan navigating the car through the city as it filled with midday traffic. But Mathias barely noticed.

His father was dead. He wondered why that information was so difficult to comprehend. He'd been expecting the news for weeks, confident about how little it meant to him.

So what the fuck is happening? Mathias didn't even know why he was going to the hospital. For one last look? Physical evidence that the man was gone from this world?

Mathias felt a sharp pain in his chest, and his hand shot out, clutching the dash to steady himself. There were so many things he'd wanted to tell the old man. How badly he'd fucked him up, for one. How much of his life he'd devoted to the pursuit of being better—or rather, being nothing like his father at all. Instead, he saw it unraveling, sacrifices that amounted to nothing. A man who hadn't cared then sure as hell didn't care now.

It was as though he was being wrenched open, the pathetic little boy clawing his way out, spilling with need, none of the usual tricks working to subdue him. Mathias was so much more than this, but at the moment, it was all of him.

A hand gripped his shoulder. When Mathias looked up, Rayan's face was lined with concern. "What's going on? Are you sick?"

Shaking his head, he brushed away the man's hand, turning to stare out the window as the streets flashed past.

Rayan pulled into the hospital parking deck. Cars were packed into every available spot. They drove from one level to the next, Rayan muttering a string of curses until finally, on the top level, he maneuvered the Mercedes into an uncovered space. Mathias got out and headed to the garage elevator as the clouds darkened in the sky. He was barely aware of Rayan one step behind, following him through the sliding doors to the hospital reception.

"Federico Mancini," he said to the receptionist once they were within earshot. The woman looked up, startled.

"I'm sorry, but you are...?"

Mathias stopped then as though his life was encapsulated in that question. There was no good answer.

"His son," he said finally, the word ringing false.

The woman glanced at her computer, typing away, before giving him a long look. "I'm sorry, sir, but Mr. Mancini passed away this morning."

Mathias gripped the desk. "I know that," he said, his voice curling viciously. "I'm here to see him."

The woman blinked, recoiling, then glanced back to check the screen. "He's in the C Wing, ninth floor, room 908. He should be there for another hour or so until they move him."

Mathias didn't stop to thank her. Instead he turned and headed for the elevator.

As they waited, Rayan spoke softly. "I'm sorry."

"For what?" Mathias countered, looking straight ahead at the illuminated arrow on the wall.

His second fell silent. They rode the elevator through the chaos of the hospital, visitors and medical personnel stepping in and out with each lurching stop. On the ninth floor, they walked through a series of automated doors, the hollow sound of their footsteps projected down the hallway. As they approached the room, Mathias could hear Sofia's thin wailing voice. He stiffened. In the fog of haste, he hadn't considered that his father's family would be there. Mathias wondered who had told his mother. Sofia would have done everything in her power to ensure that Marguerite had not been informed of his father's death. But Mathias knew one thing—his mother had her ways.

They rounded the corner, and Sofia appeared, wrapped in the arms of Freddie Junior, a doctor in a white coat standing to one side. The door to the room behind them was shut, but Mathias could see the number clearly: 908. Sofia looked up as he approached, her reddened eyes widening.

She pulled away from her son and pointed directly at him. "How dare you come here!"

Her shriek echoed through the empty hallway, causing the doctor and a passing nurse to glance up in alarm. Mathias watched Freddie tense beside her.

"Get out!" his half brother spat.

"I want to see him," Mathias said, his voice sounding dull even to his own ears. The doubt he'd felt at the reception desk reared again. He was unaccustomed to this paralysis. The pain in his chest returned.

But Sofia advanced, blocking him from moving any farther down the hallway. "I hope you know he left everything to us—his wife and children," she said pointedly. "You and that woman aren't even mentioned in the will."

"You're not welcome here," Freddie snapped. "You need to leave."

"Careful," Rayan warned sharply, stepping forward, and the man visibly shrank.

None of the usual fury burst forth. Mathias was tired of fighting for something he would never have.

The doctor held up his hands, watching them with concern. "What's the problem here? Family are allowed to see him before he's moved. Are you family?"

"No," Mathias heard himself say. The realization came like a slug to the stomach. He wasn't—never had been. His father had made sure of that. "I'm not family."

He stared at Sofia, his eyes boring into hers. She drew back, fear filling her face. Then Mathias turned and strode past a stunned Rayan and back down the hallway the way they'd come.

Only moments before, he could think of nothing except seeing his father, getting one last look at the man with whom so much was unresolved. Now he needed to get as far away from him as possible. Alive or dead, he'd done nothing but carve a ragged gash through Mathias's life.

7

The journey from the ninth-floor corridor to the car park seemed to take a lifetime. Rayan snuck furtive glances at his capo as they walked. His eyes were dull and his shoulders stiff. The pale sheen to his skin made him appear unwell. Rayan felt a hollow ache as he looked away. Despite Mathias's cool reply to the woman in the hallway, Rayan knew the exchange had cut him deeply.

He hadn't realized the man's father had a wife and a family, one Mathias had clearly not been part of—denied not just his name but apparently any form of legitimacy. Rayan had bristled at the look the woman had given his boss as she stood between a son and his last moment with his father.

Outside, a light rain was beginning to fall. By the time they made it from the garage elevator to the car, they were both damp. Mathias seemed not to notice. He stood by the car, pulling out his cigarettes. He flicked on his lighter, which sizzled in the rain, and tried once, twice, before giving up and hurling it to the ground with a clatter, the unlit cigarette still clenched between his teeth.

Rayan stepped over to retrieve it, pushing back his wet hair before returning to Mathias's side. Cupping the lighter between his hands, Rayan clicked it several times, leaning forward silently. Mathias ducked his head until their foreheads were almost touching, and within the shared shelter, it finally leapt to life. He brought the end of the cigarette to the flame. It took a moment for the sodden tobacco to light. Rayan looked up to see Mathias's face inches from his own, staring at him with a strange expression. The man's mouth parted, letting the half-lit cigarette fall to the ground at their feet.

Rayan felt a jolt run through him. Then the two of them snapped together like opposite ends of a magnet, lips meeting with a force that shattered him. The tension he'd harbored for years, his resistance to this incessant tug, slipped away in an instant.

Mathias grabbed the front of his shirt and pulled him close, Rayan's mouth opening frantically around his. Their tongues met, and Rayan felt the blood rush to his cock. *How is he so warm?* All that coldness and detachment, while underneath it was this. He dug his fingers into the back of Mathias's neck, pushing against him, desperate to be enveloped by this heat.

Then, just as suddenly, they tore apart. Rayan sucked in a shuddering breath and turned away, blinking furiously to get ahold of himself. Mathias stepped back, giving him a wide berth. The lighter lay on the ground between them where it had fallen. Neither of them stooped to pick it up.

Rayan erased the need from his face before turning around, slipping back into the role of unquestioning second. Their eyes met, and he was reunited with his capo's shuttered gaze.

Mathias held out a hand. "Keys."

Rayan fished them from his pocket, stilling the shake in his fingers, and handed them over. Mathias unlocked the car, yanked open the driver's door, and got in. Rayan didn't move. Mathias fired up the engine and, with a squeal of tires, pulled out of the lot and tore down the ramp toward the exit.

Rayan stood there as the rain fell, heavier now, soaking through his jacket, his shirt sticking to his chest as his heart pounded beneath.

Mathias stared at himself in the mirror hanging in the hallway of his apartment. He did not recognize the man looking back. His sodden jacket lay crumpled at his feet. The car keys were still gripped in his fist. Up until this point, Mathias had remained vigilant. He had never sought men out in Montreal.

It had begun as an indulgence while he was attending university in Paris—an itch he'd waited years to scratch. He remembered getting off the plane, feeling as though he'd left the rest of himself behind. The freedom of knowing no one knew him. Mathias was careful to strictly curtail these encounters to when he was out of the country. Even then, it was confined to bathhouses—anonymous, discreet. That way, he was able to compartmentalize, separate the deviation of himself from who he was in the real world. His reputation, his standing in the family, and quite possibly his life depended on that separation.

Rayan had blurred that line. And Mathias had allowed it. There'd been something there—though he could barely admit to it—ever since their first meeting, when the young man's face had captured him, compelling him against his better judgment. But this felt different from the urge that had led Mathias to those faceless men. He didn't just want to fuck Rayan—he wanted to consume him.

With his father gone, a space had opened inside his mind where the old man—a phantom of Mathias's own creation—used to be, reproaching him, voicing his disdain. For what was this but further proof of his deficiency as a son? The man had never known—never been close enough to suspect—yet the voice had always been there. Until now.

Mathias stalked into the kitchen, tossed the car keys on the counter, and poured himself a drink, then another. But the taste of Rayan remained: sweet, wet, wanting. He pulsed with longing, raw with loss, his carefully governed life splintering around him. He did not want to think of his father. He did not want to think of his own ambition, the path he'd committed to. A single thought pierced through his muddied mind. It stuck, unrelenting, spurring him on. Mathias grabbed the keys and headed for the door.

When he heard the knock, Rayan knew who it would be. He'd just stepped out of the shower and shrugged on some dry clothes, wet hair dripping onto the neck of his T-shirt. In the taxi on the way home from the hospital, Rayan had cursed his stupidity. He could only guess what would happen now. He'd exposed himself in a way that there was no coming back from, yet a thought kept returning, one that evoked both hope and astonishment—Mathias had done the same.

Rayan opened the door to find his capo's familiar figure framed in the entrance. He'd abandoned his suit jacket. His tightly combed hair now hung from his forehead. Rayan felt a shiver as he recalled the warmth of the man's tongue. It was so long since he'd last been touched, and it had never felt like that—as though, for a moment, they'd merged into one.

Mathias stepped inside, and Rayan closed the door behind him, waiting for the words that would shatter the precarious life he'd built for himself around this man. For years, his boss had dropped him off outside the building at the end of each day, but he'd never been inside Rayan's apartment. Mathias swung his gaze across the room as if he owned the place.

"How do you live here?"

Rayan was momentarily taken aback. Naturally, his small one-bedroom apartment stood in humble contrast to his capo's top-floor penthouse. But it was the most Mathias had said since the events of that afternoon and was almost comical in its irrelevance.

Their eyes met, and Rayan felt it again—that surge of electricity, blistering and intractable. They closed the distance between them in a matter of seconds. Something had been awakened, and their bodies were simply following through. The intensity of the embrace made him feel as though he was fighting for his life. Mathias was rough, his grip hard, but Rayan matched him. Shirts were shed in a growing fury. Their mouths met with teeth. Mathias grabbed Rayan's shoulders and swung him into the wall, one hand closing around his neck, the other working the zipper of his jeans.

In a series of struggles, they made it to the bed. Everything was moving so quickly that Rayan barely had time to register what was going on. They were possessed— that much was clear. He felt a deep pull of desire. As scary as this was, he fucking wanted it.

Rayan had spent his youth frightened by this part of himself. It had taken longer than he cared to admit for him to gain the confidence to explore, and there'd been far fewer opportunities in recent years, his increased visibility in the family making him overly cautious.

Mathias straddled him, pinning him to the mattress. Rayan's breath caught at the sight of his bare chest lined with muscle. He reached out, his fingers grazing the warm skin of Mathias's stomach. Looking up, he saw the man's eyes clouded with lust. Rayan lifted his chin, and Mathias lowered his lips and kissed him as he had earlier in the rain, the world blurring out of focus.

Breaking away, Rayan pulled open the bedside drawer and fished out a small tube, which he pushed into Mathias's hand. Rayan moved onto his knees as he heard the pop of a cap, a slick swish, and then strong hands found his hips, positioning him for what was to come. He exhaled sharply as Mathias entered him. The sound seemed far away. So little felt real—everything was hot, in extreme close-up. He was agonizingly hard but grateful for the initial sting of pain. It served as an anchor. Without it, he would surely have left his body and simply floated away.

They moved hurriedly, as if time would illuminate a reality neither of them was ready to confront. Mathias's fingers dug into his flesh. His own hands bunched the sheets in fists, grappling for purchase. Mathias brought an arm around Rayan's neck, sinking his teeth into his shoulder. Rayan pressed against him, arching beneath the weight of his capo's body.

Mathias pulled out then pushed back as roughly but hit somewhere deeper. Somewhere that made Rayan's heart stall. He groaned, a low animal sound propelled from his body by force. Mathias was in to the hilt, draped over Rayan's back, breath brushing his ear with each thrust. The thought of being so intimately intertwined with his capo, a man capable of commanding intense fear and respect, made Rayan's skin burn. He lowered his head, exhaling in short bursts as the pleasure built, seizing him. *Fuck, fuck.* He was going to come.

Mathias's hand found his straining cock, pulling it through his fist in a series of quick strokes. It was enough to send Rayan over the edge, and he came hard, stifling a moan through clenched teeth. He felt Mathias bear down on him and heard a growl rumble in the man's chest as he himself finished.

They separated, collapsing onto the bed, heavy, sedated. Rayan tried to string together a single coherent thought, but his mind was foggy, misted over. They lay like that in silence, time crawling as if they were no longer held captive by its rules.

Then Mathias sat up, breaking the spell in one fluid motion. He stood, his broad, muscular back to Rayan and dressed in silence. Rayan turned away, chest tightening. He retrieved his clothes from the floor and tugged them on.

Mathias was already at the bedroom door. "Tomorrow." The word came out thick, a gruffness so different from the usual severity of his voice. He cleared his throat. "There's a job on the South Shore. Be at the office by nine."

And then he was gone.

8

"Paterlini wants to send his son over here for a bit. Get a leg up," Tony said. It was late in the evening, and they'd stayed on at the office for a nightcap. Everyone else had been sent home.

"Silvano Paterlini?" Mathias knew of the man but had never formally made his acquaintance. He was old-school, tending to stick with the same handful of senior mafiosi.

"Yeah, tight with Russo, from the same village in the old country, yada yada. Generally a right pain in the ass."

Despite the prickle of annoyance, Mathias spoke cautiously. "I don't know the kid. What's his deal?"

Tony shrugged and took a long swig from his drink. "Fucked if I know. But I'm putting him on your team. Show him the ropes, teach him a thing or two. Make sure he doesn't get killed."

"No," Mathias said bluntly.

"You owe me, Beauvais. I put in a good word with the boss. Scratch your back and all that." Tony looked at him pointedly. "Besides, he's asked for you. Seems you made quite the impression at the last meeting."

"I don't have time to watch some kid piss himself."

Tony raised an eyebrow. "Now that your boy's all trained?"

Mathias gave him a warning look as he downed the last of his scotch. "Rayan has earned his place."

Mention of his second stirred up a conflicting flurry of thoughts that Mathias quickly quashed. Despite having spent the last few days working in close proximity to Rayan, Mathias found himself avoiding eye contact, barely speaking, as though if he willed it hard enough, everything that had transpired between them would simply disappear.

"And here's Paterlini wanting the same for his kid," Tony said. "Sends a bit of attention our way. Lord knows we could do with the manpower."

"Put him on another team."

Even as he spoke, Mathias realized he was considering it. He'd lost confidence in his ability to keep himself in check. He relied on Rayan too much to have him reassigned but at the same time needed to put some distance between himself and the man. Mathias had allowed him to get too close. He needed a buffer, perhaps in the form of some higher-up's sniveling brat.

"Did it sound like I was giving you a choice?" Tony glowered. "Wise up, Beauvais. The kid's starting Wednesday. Here I was trying to be gracious, giving you a heads-up. Should have just thrown him in the car and told you to shut your mouth."

"Gracious?" Mathias scoffed. "The fuck you think you are, Tony?" He pulled out his cigarettes and lit one. "How much did Paterlini slide you?" He should have known his boss would be off padding his fat pocket regardless of what he had to say about it.

Tony waved him off, reaching across the desk and helping himself to one of Mathias's cigarettes. "The way I see it, with an extra set of hands, you can take on a few more contracts, bump up your weekly take. So it all comes around."

Mathias pulled in a lungful of smoke. *Bastard.* Not only was the old man landing him with some presumptuous daddy's boy, but he was also cranking up his workload. "I want five for my troubles."

Tony scowled. "Fuck off."

Mathias leaned back in his seat and exhaled slowly. "Our pal Paterlini slipped you a nice chunk of change to make sure his boy got what he wanted. Don't disappoint him now, Tony."

"Two."

"Five."

Tony blew a cloud of smoke between them, squinting. "Fine. But no complaints, you hear me? Or I dock your commission next month."

Mathias smirked. "Deal." He didn't need a cent of the money, but he'd be damned if he did Tony a favor for free. His time was worth something at least.

Tony finished his drink and cleared his throat. "Heard about your old man."

Mathias felt a familiar clench in his stomach. He worked hard to keep his face neutral. "Anything interesting?"

Tony gave him a level stare. "You can be cocky all you want, but there ain't no shame in a man mourning his father."

"Who said anything about mourning?" Mathias said with a snicker, pushing away the thoughts of his father. "Good riddance." He stood and pocketed his smokes before Tony could say something more. "So, what's this kid's name?"

His name was Silvano Paterlini Junior, and he was a short, stocky twenty-one-year-old with a nose that flattened across half of his pockmarked face. He had an entitled smirk but was mindful to show Mathias the proper respect when he appeared at the Collections office on Wednesday morning.

"Call me Junior," he said, holding out his hand.

Mathias could think of several other names he'd have preferred to call him. He shook the kid's hand reluctantly, and they walked out to the lot, where Rayan stood waiting by the car.

"Who's this?" Junior asked, cocking his head in Rayan's direction.

His second remained silent, looking warily at Silvano, who sported a gold chain and sunglasses. Mathias had briefly mentioned the favor to Tony on the drive back to the office the previous evening. They hadn't spoken much since the day of the hospital, a coolness settling over their regular interactions. Rayan, to his credit—or more to Mathias's training—had said nothing.

"Does he talk?"

"Exactly. You should take some pointers." Mathias pulled open the passenger door as his second got in behind the wheel. Junior's face darkened as he climbed into the back seat. Rayan started the engine and began reversing out of the parking lot.

"Wait—so the *estraneo* sits up front?"

"Stop the car," Mathias instructed.

Rayan thumped the brake, and the kid smacked his head on the seat in front of him. Mathias turned to look at him.

"Silvano, this is Rayan. He sits up front because his job is to get between me and a bullet. You sit in the back because your papà paid me to babysit. Clear?"

Junior scowled, nodding slowly. Mathias cracked his neck, and they rolled out onto the street.

Rayan pushed Eugene Waith's head into the murky water that filled one of many rusted oil barrels stacked behind the mechanic's workshop at Beaubien Auto Service. Waith's fingers scrabbled at the metal and at the grip around his neck, but Rayan held firm. Mathias studied his second's blank expression. So practiced was he at masking what lay beneath, yet Mathias had seen Rayan's face when he allowed that mask to slip. He could not get the image out of his mind.

Junior stood beside him, grinning. He had the air of a kid who'd been jacked up on sugar all morning. Rayan pulled the man up. Waith coughed and spluttered as he sucked in a wracked breath.

"We can do this all day," Mathias said. "Though I've got better places to be."

Waith owned several automotive repair shops around the city and had borrowed a not insignificant amount of money from the family to open a new garage after the banks turned him down. For good reason, apparently. He was two months behind on interest for the loan.

One month, Mathias could handle. Two months left him looking a fool.

Waith shook his head in panic. "Honest to God, I don't have it, but I'll get it. Tomorrow. Give me until tomorrow."

"I don't want to come back tomorrow," Mathias said, walking toward him. "That's why I'm here today."

He stooped to pick up a discarded crowbar, brushing the dirt from his Armani pants. Waith's eyes widened, but Rayan's grip on his arm held him in place. Mathias swung fast before he could protest and brought the metal bar down on the man's right foot. Waith howled like an animal, his leg collapsing as Rayan kept him upright. Behind him, Junior let out a hoot.

"Where's the money?"

Waith's eyes jumped from him to Silvano then back to Mathias. "In the safe. There's some in the safe. Not everything, but it's all I have. There'll be more. I just need time."

Mathias spun the crowbar, and the man flinched. "Give us the code. Careful—I don't want my associate here to have to go in twice."

Waith rattled off a series of numbers.

"You got that?" he asked Rayan.

His second nodded and let Waith go. Unable to stand on his shattered foot, Waith dropped to the ground with a yelp. Rayan walked past him into the workshop while Mathias lit a cigarette and squinted up at the sky. The sun was barely visible through the dense blanket of cloud.

Junior appeared at his side like a dog. "Can I have a swing at him?"

Mathias shook his head. It was pathetic, the glint in his eyes. A kid brought up on senseless violence. He'd seen so many pass through the ranks. They were always messy and inefficient, getting off on the bloodlust rather than using it as a tool. Violence was an art form. Used well, it could make even the most rigid man compliant.

They waited in silence, Junior kicking at the muddy ground, aiming for Waith's crumpled form. Not for the first time, Mathias resisted the urge to strike the boy. He'd seen the likes of him before in the easy self-assurance of his half brothers.

His second emerged with an envelope in one hand and a clump of purchase books in the other. He stopped beside Mathias, taking in Silvano's antics.

"There's two in cash and another three in prepaid parts," Rayan said quietly in French, aware of Waith's fearful gaze. "Barely covers the first month."

Mathias sighed. It seemed nothing was going smoothly this morning. "Heads up, kid."

Junior looked up expectantly as Mathias tossed him the crowbar. *Might as well get some use out of the jumpy fuck.*

"Have at it."

"Hey, *estraneo*." A hand shot out, grabbed Rayan's shoulder, and yanked him around in the narrow corridor of the Collections office.

Mathias had released Rayan from his duties and disappeared into Tony's office for one of their strategic meetings. He'd been on his way out, quietly happy to have the rest of the afternoon to himself. After almost a year, Rayan was still getting used to life working for the family. The late nights and strange hours of his time at Guillet's remained fresh, having formed a deep groove.

Franco's second, Mikey, stood leering at him, fair headed with a bulbous nose. In the few months Rayan had spent driving for Franco, the man had never treated him like anything but shit. Beside Mikey was Paolo, the thickset kid who'd replaced Rayan after he'd been reassigned as Mathias's second.

"The fuck you pulling? One minute you're some burnout on loan. Now you're shadowing Beauvais?"

Rayan had drawn the ire of many after his capo took him on. As surprised as he'd been to be working with Mathias, there were those within the division who were even more so—men who'd barely known he existed until they felt threatened by the possibility that he'd wormed his way to their level. Rayan didn't have much to do with Franco's jurisdiction. He handled protection money, something his capo had done when their paths first crossed.

"You know outsiders can't get made," Mikey spat. "It's a goddamn disgrace they kept you on."

Rayan said nothing. Speaking would only give them more ammunition. Mikey was right in all respects—Rayan certainly didn't belong in their ranks. He himself didn't know why Mathias had decided to keep him on. He felt no more worthy of his position than they thought he was.

"That's right—you're a quiet little shit. Not too keen on English either. *Es-tu un crétin*?" Mikey dragged out each syllable as though speaking to an imbecile.

Tired of the exchange, Rayan turned and continued down the hall.

"Where the fuck do you think you're going?" Mikey hollered.

Rayan felt Mikey's hand on his shoulder once again, and this time, he swiveled and smashed a fist into that giant nose. The man let out a howl, his hands flying to his face, as Paolo launched himself at Rayan, his tacky signet ring catching him on the temple, breaking the skin. Rayan countered with a knee to the guts, sending the kid sprawling against the wall.

Mikey, blood streaming down his face, had regained some of his composure and was coming at him with heavy, clumsy swings, which Rayan dodged, getting close enough to him to clamp him in a headlock. Right when Paolo was about to slam his knuckles into Rayan's exposed ribs, the door at the end of the corridor flew open, and Tony stepped into the hallway.

"What the fuck is going on here?"

Rayan released Mikey and stepped back, blinking away a drop of blood that trailed down from the cut on his forehead.

Mikey held his face protectively. "Fucker broke my nose!"

"Did he, now?" Tony said glibly. "You starting something, Mikey?"

"No. The guy's a psycho. Tell Beauvais to leash his dog."

"Tell him yourself."

Mikey looked past Tony to where Mathias stood just out of view. He stiffened. "Uh, no offense. I was just minding my business. Kid doesn't know how to stay in line."

"I find out you're making trouble where it's not needed, I'll make it my business," Mathias replied, his voice low. "Understood?"

Mikey nodded.

"Go home, Rayan," Mathias called down the hallway.

Rayan wiped a sleeve across his forehead, stopping the slow drip of blood, then turned and walked out the door into the parking lot.

Mathias picked him up from the office the following morning. "What is it with you and trouble?" he muttered. "You can't be so stupid not to realize you have a target on your back."

Rayan had woken up to a few bruises he hadn't anticipated. He wasn't sure if he should defend himself, knowing his capo did not take kindly to excuses. But if he'd let Mikey and his buddy smash his face in, what kind of soldier would he be? "Should I have let them rough me up?"

Mathias raised an eyebrow. "No. Idiot."

As they drove, Mathias's lips curved into a smirk. "You broke the fucker's nose."

Rayan frowned, failing to mirror his boss's amusement. "They won't accept someone like me."

The smirk had disappeared, Mathias's mouth forming a hard line. "Then you make them respect you. You make them fear you. Acceptance? Overrated."

"Hey, *estraneo.*"

Rayan jolted back to the present. Silvano Junior stood before him, holding out a take-out coffee cup, which Rayan took silently, the heat warming his palm. The man's other hand gripped a second coffee, tiny curls of steam snaking out from the hole in the lid. It was early, and they were at the office, waiting for Mathias to finish up with the Collections boss before starting on the day's jobs. Rayan glanced down the hallway at Tony's door, still closed.

"So, what are you?"

Rayan stared straight ahead. Junior, as he preferred to be called, was young. Younger than him, if he had to hazard a guess. He gathered from Mathias's brief explanation that the kid's father was high up and was pulling a favor, so Rayan was to mind his tone. After a week working with the man, it was already proving challenging.

"Saudi, then?" Junior asked smugly. "Or just another mixed-up Quebec hick?"

"All Quebecois are hicks."

Junior chuckled. "How'd you get to work with him?"

The family employed a great deal of people from all over Montreal—the Algerians, the Haitians, the Chinese—but rarely did it let any of these outsiders into the fold. Rayan had been made painfully aware of this fact as Mathias moved up the ranks. Silvano wasn't the first full-blooded Italian to take issue with that.

Rayan shrugged. "Lucky break."

Junior watched him, sizing him up. Rayan could tell he was growing tired of evasive answers. He had a feeling the kid was used to getting what he wanted. If Junior thought he could mine him for information by ingratiating himself with a cup of coffee, he could get fucked.

The door opened, and Mathias came down the hall toward them. Rayan tempered the immediate quickening of his pulse. As the days wore on, he was finding it difficult to maintain their continued pretense, considering that when he closed his eyes, he could conjure every inch of his capo's naked body.

It hadn't been nothing—he'd felt too much for it to be nothing. The man's mouth had captured his with a force that left him breathless, his hand seeking and claiming Rayan's release. Yet as his capo's frostiness refused to thaw, Rayan was beginning to doubt himself, becoming more and more convinced that Mathias regarded that fateful afternoon as a grievous mistake.

Silvano's presence had only widened the gap that had formed between them. And Rayan had done nothing. He simply carried on, propelled by sheer habit. But there was the twinge he felt when Mathias addressed Junior or requested his assistance while Rayan shadowed. The slow break was harder simply for the space it left for him to wonder about what had once been and what exactly they'd become.

"Here, boss." Silvano handed Mathias the remaining cup as he walked past him toward the door.

Mathias took it wordlessly, the kid trailing behind him like a dog waiting to be praised. Rayan scowled at Silvano's back, tossing his untouched coffee into the trash and following them to the parking lot. As they walked to the car, Mathias absently took a sip, grimacing. He spat out the mouthful at his feet, snapped off the lid, and hurled the liquid into the curbside drain. Then he turned and pushed the empty cup into Junior's hand.

"You put milk in my coffee?"

Silvano looked back at him, wide-eyed and momentarily speechless. Rayan hid a grin. Not that he hadn't also learned this lesson the hard way, but he took a secret pleasure in someone else drawing Mathias's ire. Compared to Silvano, Rayan was in another league altogether.

"The fuck you waiting for?" Mathias snapped. As Junior hurried back into the office, the man leaned against the car, patting down his pockets for a cigarette. "Useless."

For a moment, it was like before, Junior's incompetence uniting them in shared enmity. Rayan smiled ruefully. He'd missed this.

"Something funny?" Mathias asked.

Rayan glanced up to see his capo watching him. He shook his head to clear his thoughts, but something lingered on his tongue, threatening to betray him. "No," he murmured as Silvano returned with a fresh coffee in hand like he was the Savior himself.

Rayan silently reproached himself. He should know how things worked between them by now. Mathias led, and he followed. He would be a fool to think he had any say in the matter.

9

athias couldn't stand it. His skin itched every time Rayan was close. He wondered how long this tension had existed between them, going unspoken, unexplored. They'd both stumbled into it so easily when given the opportunity. Mathias couldn't decide what was more aggravating—having lost control or knowing someone had witnessed the dissolution. He barely recalled the sequence of events that had led to the sudden transformation between them, but he did know there had been no hesitation. Rayan—despite his usual acquiescence—had proven just as impatient as Mathias.

In the years he'd known him, Rayan had appeared to lead an unassuming life. Aside from his early inquiries into the man's background, it was a life Mathias hadn't spent much time considering. But there were signs, carefully hidden, that he was only now beginning to see, perhaps because he'd proven so adept at his own personal erasure.

Mathias paced the floor of his bedroom, sucking with restless vigor on his usual late-night cigarette. When he closed his eyes, he saw Rayan—the slick open mouth, the curve of his back, hips pressed against him.

He stopped, the cigarette clenched between his teeth, suppressing a groan. Mathias couldn't remember a time when he'd wanted—really wanted—to fuck someone so badly it scrambled his thoughts. He had done everything he could to supplant these images with something tamer. He'd gone to a woman in Rosemont, someone he saw when he wanted to steer clear of the family's well-worn establishments. It had only served to highlight exactly what he was missing.

Maybe if it hadn't felt so good... if he hadn't wanted his hands on every part of the man, craved the swell of his cock in his fist... if he hadn't come so hard, his mind emptying for one delirious moment as though he'd been erased. Maybe then, Mathias could bury this reckless lapse of judgment and move on.

Running a hand through his hair, he sat down on the edge of the bed. It was foolish to think adding Silvano to the team would do anything but amplify the deprivation. The distance made Mathias even more insatiable. He resented the way Junior's presence curtailed what had once transpired seamlessly between him and Rayan. And still, his second said nothing. He showed up on time and did his job without question.

Mathias stood to stub out his waning cigarette in the ashtray on the nightstand. *Enough.* He was a grown man, for fuck's sake. He would not be so easily undone.

As Mathias climbed into bed, it dawned on him that perhaps it was restraint itself that was messing with him. Maybe it was simply a matter of getting this out of his system. Enough of anything naturally became its own deterrent as it lost its power. He would shake Rayan's hold over him not through avoidance but by meeting it head-on. When it was done—when it had run its course and he'd tired of the man—Mathias could move past this madness.

Rayan half expected Mathias to say something about Silvano on the drive home. Sitting beside him in the passenger seat, he could tell Mathias was seething after another day of jobs and more of the same. There'd been blood on Junior's knuckles that he refused to wash off, bursting with a manic energy that he'd yet to come down from. The kid had brought his own piece with him that day and carried it around like he was the hero in an action film. It had been a relief to finally drop the kid off at the office, along with their daily takings, Tony smirking away behind his desk and a cloud of cigar smoke.

Mathias pulled the car to the curb outside his apartment building, but Rayan didn't get out. He felt his capo's eyes on him, growing impatient.

"What?" Mathias snapped.

Rayan glanced at him. He had too much to say and nowhere to start. He clicked off his seat belt, opened the door, then stopped. Turning, he spoke into the space between them. "You hungry?"

Rayan was starving. After yet another fitful night, he'd woken later than usual and had to skip breakfast. Then a series of setbacks meant the day hadn't followed its typical pattern. Lunch had been abandoned, and the coffee he'd managed to grab at the office had barely sustained him.

Mathias stared at him, silent. Then he reached out to cut the engine. They stepped from the car, and Mathias followed him into the building. Rayan placed his wallet and keys down on the kitchen counter as Mathias shut the apartment door behind them. He hadn't expected his boss to accept the invitation. He'd anticipated more of the same coldness. But hunger was a powerful motivator.

Rayan would never tell Mathias, but he enjoyed seeing him in his space—standing in the entranceway, walking through the kitchen. He tried not to think of the last time Mathias had been here. Rayan took off his jacket and draped it over a chair then unbuttoned his cuffs and rolled up his sleeves.

Mathias reached into his jacket and pulled out his pack of cigarettes. He paused. There was only one left.

"Rough day?" Rayan baited him, taking a wrapped chunk of roast beef out of the fridge.

Mathias had been chain smoking since they'd picked Silvano up that morning. He gave him a dirty look and returned the packet to his pocket, deciding against smoking his last one. "Chatty, aren't we?"

He was in a bad mood. Rayan sliced thick chunks of bread and spread on a layer of mayonnaise. Mathias took off his jacket and pulled up a bar stool, watching as he carved slices of beef and stacked them onto the open bread.

"He's going to do something stupid," Rayan said, cutting open a dark-red tomato and reaching for a head of lettuce.

"Because he's an idiot," Mathias replied. "Like his father."

Rayan pressed the top layer of bread onto each sandwich and moved them onto plates. He pushed one across the counter toward Mathias. They ate in silence, Rayan standing in the kitchen while Mathias sat hunched over the counter. The sandwich was good, kicking the edge off the gnawing hunger that had a way of jumbling his thoughts. Mathias seemed slightly less agitated after having eaten. He sat back on his stool as Rayan tossed the plates into the sink.

"Are you happy here?"

Rayan looked up at him in surprise. "Happy?" he repeated. *Am I happy?* It wasn't a question he asked himself. Happiness had always felt like a concept that belonged to other people.

"With the job, the work." Mathias frowned, a tweak of irritation tugging at his lips.

Rayan was housed, clothed, fed. Every week, Mathias handed him a brown envelope with more money than he could make use of. Compared to all those years with nothing, what more could he want? But there was something else that chased him—a need for purpose, connection. Something to fill the dark void that descended at night, threatening to overwhelm him.

"Yes," he said finally, not wanting to tarnish his need for a simple answer with the complexity the question invoked.

Mathias did not look convinced. He drummed his fingers against the counter, unsatisfied. Sometimes, Rayan felt he would have an easier time dealing with the man if he wrote up a damn script.

"Though I'd be happier if you'd stop treating me like a fucking leper," he muttered.

Mathias's eyes snapped back to him, and Rayan held his gaze.

"What are you saying?" Mathias challenged him.

"Nothing." He looked away. "I'll grab you a pack downstairs."

Rayan reached for his wallet. Mathias's hand on his arm stopped him.

"I'm still hungry," his capo said, eyes darkening.

Rayan seized the front of the man's shirt, covering his mouth with his own. There was no hesitation. He felt Mathias's hand on his neck, pushing back, as he parted Rayan's lips with his tongue.

"Fuck it," Mathias murmured when they came up for air. He stood and pulled Rayan toward the bed.

"Hnh... fuck—" It came out a muffled murmur as Rayan pressed his face into Mathias's neck.

His skin prickled as Rayan shuddered. He felt the wetness slide through his fingers. It had surprised Mathias how much pleasure he could find in someone else's. He'd never been one of those men turned on by eating out a woman or who jacked it while sucking someone off. He didn't get the point. Sex had always been about his own release... until he found himself fixated on the ways his touch affected this man. The sudden arch of his back, a reluctant groan, the flush of heat along his chest. How Rayan tried to turn away, hide his face, making Mathias all the more determined to see it. It got him off. That and the way he clenched around him, spasming exquisitely with him inside.

Mathias's grip slipped as he let himself give in to what he'd worked so hard to hold back. He came with a sharp grunt, feeling Rayan's fist in his hair and slick thighs beneath his palms, everything else fading, contracting, as the sensation seared through him.

When their breathing slowed, Rayan extracted himself and rolled to one side. Mathias had discovered that Rayan was incredibly sensitive afterward, his body recoiling from the slightest touch. It took him a few minutes to lose his edge, and then he was seductively pliant. It made Mathias want to fuck him again.

They lay side by side, chests rising and falling as Rayan's eyes began to close. Mathias reached out and yanked the pack of cigarettes from the pocket of his discarded jacket. *That's right—just the one left.* It felt like hours had passed since their conversation in the kitchen. He lit up and took a long drag, savoring the taste before exhaling slowly.

Then, from his postcoital nicotine-fueled buzz, Mathias spoke the words he never would have uttered in the light of day. "I'm not the first man you've fucked."

As soon as he said it, a shot of sobriety hit Mathias in the gut. He would be a liar if he said he hadn't thought about it. This thing between them—and he still wasn't sure what to call it—had happened with such intensity that he had yet to give it real-world context.

Rayan opened his eyes, shifting slightly so he was facing him. "Am I?"

Mathias bristled at the confrontation. He had a feeling Rayan already knew the answer to his question. He sat up, crushing his cigarette into the empty pack and reaching for his pants, but Rayan lunged forward, looped an arm around his chest, and pushed him back down onto the bed. He stared at Mathias with a veiled expression. This close, Mathias could see the swelling along Rayan's bottom lip, where he had bitten down.

"The fuck do I care?" his second murmured, their mouths meeting once again.

This time, Mathias stayed. He stared at the ceiling as they lay, spent, on Rayan's bed, the lights from the street ebbing and fading against the exposed concrete. Next to him, Rayan's breathing was quiet and regular as if he were on the verge of sleep.

He'd wanted Rayan to tell him how much he hated the work, his life with the family. It would have made things easy. But as it turned out, lines were beginning to blur. Already, it was becoming difficult to separate the man he sent ahead of him from the man who lay beside him, their sweat mingling.

As if on cue, Rayan rolled over and rose from the bed, rubbing a hand across his face. He disappeared into the bathroom and reappeared several moments later in a T-shirt and gray sweats. "I have cognac, no scotch."

Mathias pulled himself up, giving Rayan a skeptical look. "Here I was thinking this was a dry house."

"Tony's holiday bonus," Rayan shot back, walking to the kitchen.

Mathias snorted. "Knowing him, it's probably cheap." He stood and slipped on his pants then shrugged into his shirt.

On the nightstand was a faded copy of Antoine de Saint-Exupéry's *Terre des hommes*. He'd read it in high school and found it trite, despite the author enjoying a popular resurgence. He picked up the book and flipped through. It fell open on a well-worn page, a place where the spine was heavily cracked, the corner dog-eared. Someone had underlined a passage, pressing hard enough to leave an indent in the paper:

Only the unknown frightens men. But once a man has faced the unknown, that terror becomes the known.

Mathias snapped the book shut and placed it back where he'd found it.

Rayan appeared in the doorway and held out a tumbler of amber liquid. In his own hand was a glass of water. His eyes fell on Saint-Exupéry's memoir, and he picked it up and absently dropped it on top of a pile of books by the door. Mathias glanced around the room, surprised he hadn't noticed before the stacks of books in various corners and along the windowsill. He recalled their conversation about Alighieri. *So this is what he spends his money on?* Certainly not booze and hookers, like the rest of the family's soldiers.

"Favorite of yours?" Mathias asked, tilting his chin in the direction of the pile.

Rayan seemed to weigh his answer carefully. "A gift from my mother."

It was oddly sentimental, a trait he hadn't attributed to the man, who appeared content as his life was blown from one extreme to the next.

His second shrugged. "When I was young, I wanted to be a pilot."

Mathias raised an eyebrow. "If I remember, it's not so much about flying as it is about survival."

"Right," Rayan said, a strange look flickering across his face. "Maybe she knew me better than I thought."

Mathias watched Rayan change shape before him, streaks of color filling in what had been an empty outline. He sat on the edge of the bed, taking a sip of the cheap cognac. "You would've made a shitty pilot."

Rayan laughed. "I figured it was the fastest way out of Maskinongé." He leaned against the wall, observing Mathias. "Tony said you went to university."

"In another life."

"What did you study?"

"Finance, economics." Mathias paused. "Some literature."

"Modern?"

"French."

Rayan smiled knowingly. "Which is why you can't stand Houellebecq."

"That man is rotten." Mathias swallowed another mouthful. It wasn't half bad if you were a newly minted eighteen-year-old looking to get wasted. "What's with the books?"

Rayan stared at the water in his hand, stalling. "I didn't finish school," he said finally. "Thought reading might make up for what I missed."

"What you missed?"

"You know, an education."

Rayan was smart—that wasn't hard to glean from even a passing conversation. If you could pull the words out of him. It was strange to see him discredit himself over something so trivial.

"I've worked with men who couldn't figure out the tax on a bagel," Mathias scoffed. "You didn't miss much."

Rayan brought the glass to his lips, and Mathias watched the mask return. He could tell the man didn't believe him.

10

Tony stopped him on his way out of the office. Rayan was waiting in the parking lot with Junior while Mathias stepped in to give his boss the adjusted figures for the Russian payment they were due to collect that afternoon. He hadn't forgotten—he was going to make sure Belkov paid for his disrespect.

"Kid's complaining he's not doing anything," Tony said, downing the last of his coffee.

"He's done plenty," Mathias retorted.

"Bit of roughhousing maybe, but he wants in on some real action," the Collections head grumbled. "Throw him a bone, Mathias."

"Or he'll run to Daddy?" he snapped. "He's impulsive, careless. It's bad enough having him out on jobs, let alone trusting him with anything important."

"Then give him something low stakes. Tell Nadeau to hang back and let the kid lead for a change—wave his gun around, talk some shit."

Mathias scowled. "This isn't a fucking game."

"Tell Paterlini that." Tony crumpled up his cup and gave Mathias a look, his word final. "In the meantime, give him something to do, for Christ's sake."

Rayan was standing alone by the car when he returned.

"Where's the kid?" he asked.

His second frowned. Mathias knew he shared his distaste for their hyperactive tagalong.

"Said he was getting food."

Mathias clicked his tongue. So Junior thought he'd simply saunter off and keep them waiting? Their eyes met, and Mathias felt it again—the way things had shifted. His body was emboldened, wanting to take liberties against his better judgment— a step forward, the slip of a hand. He thought of Rayan pressed against the car. Despite all his theorizing, nothing had lessened in his want for the man.

Mathias turned toward the street, and Junior appeared, paper bag in hand, taking a bite out of a croissant as he walked. "Nice of you to join us," he said coldly.

Junior shrugged. "I was hungry."

"I don't want that shit in my car," Mathias snapped, pulling open the door and getting in.

Junior got into the back, cheeks distended as he chewed the remainder of the pastry he'd managed to shove in his mouth, the paper bag abandoned. Beside him, Rayan's eyes flicked to the rearview, then he started the engine, and they pulled out.

"What's the most fucked-up thing you guys have done?" Junior asked as they took the ramp toward Laval. "Hacked someone to pieces? Dissolved them in acid?"

He was grinning, leaning forward in his seat, as if this was some sort of schoolyard show-and-tell. Mathias's eyebrow twitched. He didn't know what was more stupid, asking the question or expecting an answer.

He turned to fix the kid with a hard stare. "Why—you wearing a wire?"

Junior blanched. "What? No!"

"Kind of question you'd ask if you were," Mathias said, his voice low. "Are you a rat, Silvano?"

The kid shook his head adamantly.

"Here's a free lesson: you want to get anywhere in this business, keep your fucking mouth shut."

They drove the rest of the way in silence. When they reached Industrial Boulevard, Rayan turned the car down a narrow delivery driveway that led to a series of enclosed lumber sheds belonging to La Fabrique Allwood, a local furniture manufacturer. The Russians had stores in various buildings in the area, and this was their preferred meeting place whenever money changed hands. It was a cut-and-dried operation. His arrangement with the Bratva went back years. Once a month, Belkov sent a couple of his lackeys to meet Mathias with a bag full of cash, and they parted ways without ceremony. Something low stakes, Tony had said. Well, this was as low as it got. Mathias sighed bitterly. Right now it was easier to appease the little shit than it was to create friction with his father.

"Stay in the car," Mathias instructed Rayan, opening the door. "Junior, you're with me." He caught Rayan's look but ignored it.

"Wait, you serious?" Junior said, getting out of the car. "About fucking time!"

The kid walked around to join him, his mouth pulled into a shit-eating grin.

"We'll be in and out," Mathias said to his second, who was watching them with barely concealed disapproval. He slammed the car door and began to walk toward the lumber shed, Junior at his heels.

"Do I get to meet Belkov? Heard he's crazy as fuck," Junior said as they reached the metal sliding doors. "Cuts off the fingers of his enemies and keeps them in a refrigerated box."

Mathias grabbed the handle and pulled it open with a screech. "You're here to carry the cash, not talk."

Junior's face darkened as he passed him and stepped into the warehouse. Belkov's men were already there, one of them squatting while pulling leisurely on a smoke. He stood as they approached.

"Beauvais," the Russian soldier said in a thick accent, giving Mathias a slow nod.

He nodded back. The soldier dropped a black duffel bag onto the concrete floor and slid it over in their direction. Mathias tilted his head at Junior, and the kid stepped forward to pick it up.

"Your boss keep his word?" Mathias asked.

"Twenty extra, as promised."

"Good."

Usually, he would have had Rayan count it, but he didn't trust the kid not to mess up. Mathias doubted Belkov would shortchange him under the circumstances. He was about to tell Junior they were done when he saw the gleam of the kid's gun in the corner of his eye.

The first Russian went down before Mathias fully realized what was happening. By the time he did, Junior had shot the other man and turned his piece on him.

"Always wanted to kill a Russian," Junior said with a sneer.

"The fuck you doing, Silvano?" Mathias said to buy himself time, his mind scrambling.

He was surprised at how calm he sounded. It wasn't the first time he'd found himself on the wrong end of a gun, but never like this, crossed by one of his own. The Beretta beneath his jacket sat heavy against his chest. There was no way he'd get to it before the kid's bullet sent him splattering across the floor.

Junior began to laugh. "Used to things going your way, huh?" He stepped forward, pressing the muzzle of his pistol against Mathias's forehead. "You're not going to like what happens next."

Mathias swallowed the dread that rose to choke him. "Enlighten me."

Junior smiled indulgently. "First, I'm going to blow your brains out. Then I'm going to walk back outside and plug your meat shield right between the eyes."

"And then?" Mathias pressed, trying not to think of Rayan in the car, a sitting duck. "Don't expect me to believe you'd clip a capo for a measly fifty grand."

"This?" The kid kicked at the bag of cash by his feet. He shook his head. "Got nothing to do with money. You're the first of many. But you fast-tracked your way to the top with that little promotion. A year from now, the family will be unrecognizable, a complete overhaul from top to bottom. Not that you'll be here to see it."

Mathias had to concentrate to hear his own thoughts above the rush of blood in his ears. "What's Piero promised in return for you getting your hands dirty?"

Junior's grin grew wider. "Look who's got it all figured out. He'll be pleased you knew. Makes it that much sweeter."

The metal dug into his skin. Mathias fought to control his breathing, not wanting to give the man the satisfaction of knowing he was afraid. He'd always been blasé about death, figuring that in his line of work, it might come sooner than most. But that was because up until recently, there hadn't been anything—or anyone—he thought he'd miss.

"Thing is, there are those of us who prefer things the way they used to be," Junior said, his expression hardening. "Where a son would inherit his father's business, where we'd have nothing to do with your mongrel friend out there, and a bastard like you would never—"

There was a loud bang, and a spray of wetness spattered Mathias's face. For a split second, he was sure it was his own blood. His lungs emptied, waiting for his body to crumple. Instead, Junior pitched forward, the side of his head blown out, eyes rolling back as he fell to the ground.

Mathias looked past where Junior had been standing to see Rayan, gun in hand. On his face was the same expression Mathias remembered from years ago, the day his brother had died—naked terror staring back at him.

Rayan strode toward Mathias, each breath tearing through his chest, heart hammering in his throat. His capo stood, dazed, with blood splattered across the front of his white shirt and along the side of his face. Rayan yanked at Mathias's jacket and ran his hands across his stomach, his ribs, roughly patting him down. He knew what he was looking for, but there was no sign of a wound, to both their disbelief.

Rayan dropped his hands, and the two shared a look, Mathias's gray eyes mirroring his own fear before they shuttered.

"We need to go," his capo said.

Rayan's gaze dropped to Silvano sprawled face down at their feet. "What about him?"

Mathias spat on the ground. "Leave him. Let him rot."

Rayan did what he was told, no longer capable of thought. Apprehensive about Junior accompanying his boss, he had stepped out of the Mercedes to wait. That was the only reason he'd heard the shots—faint, like an engine backfiring. If he'd remained in the car like Mathias had instructed...

Rayan stopped the thought in its tracks. After he left the car, it was all a blur. He could barely recall the moment before he pulled the trigger, registering only Silvano's gun pressed against his capo's head, his own weapon in his hand before he knew what he was doing. No decision, only instinct. One man, he needed. The other, he did not.

They returned to the car, and Rayan pulled out of the empty lot, grateful for the grip of the steering wheel to stop the tremor in his hands. The sky was already beginning to color, the sun ushered out early in streaks of orange, heralding the start of winter. He drove slowly, glancing often in the rearview mirror as though expecting someone to appear.

Rayan could not slow his thundering heartbeat. He glanced over at Mathias, not convinced they were actually in the car, driving away. Alive.

"Mathias," he managed to get out.

"Too close, I know," Mathias muttered, not taking his eyes off the road.

"I thought—" The realization came like a blow.

He felt the car swerve, no longer able to keep his hands from shaking. Rayan pulled over to the side of the road and got out, sucking in the cooling air. He paced along the sidewalk, trying to expel the adrenaline racing through his system. He'd thought he was too late, forced to watch like he had with his brother and hear the thud as his body hit the ground, dull eyes open, staring.

"I'll drive." Mathias appeared beside him, his voice muted.

He seemed to have severed all emotion from their current reality. Rayan had spent years trying to perfect this skill but could only manage a superficial mimicry, unable to fully master the depth of feeling that ruled over him.

"I couldn't forgive myself—"

Before Rayan could finish, Mathias's hand was on his shoulder, his grip hard. "Enough."

The warning was clear. Rayan felt the tension leave him as they returned to the car, replaced by a growing numbness, a black curtain descending upon the whirl of thoughts.

Mathias closed the door of his apartment behind Rayan. As he walked down the hallway, he caught a glimpse of himself in the mirror, the spray of red scattered from chin to forehead. He raised an arm, wiping what remained of the kid from his face with the sleeve of his jacket.

Rayan stood in the living room, watching him silently. After Mathias had relieved him of his driving duties, he'd retreated into himself, not saying another word.

"Stay here," Mathias instructed, avoiding his gaze. He knew if he didn't, something would push itself to the surface, and he could not deal with that right now. There'd been plenty of close calls over the years, but never had he so clearly owed Rayan his life. "I need to make a call."

His second nodded woodenly.

Mathias continued down the hall. He stopped first in the bedroom, shedding the offending jacket and shirt, before moving through to the bathroom, where he splashed searing-hot water on his face then rubbed it hard with a towel. Only when the skin was raw did he stop, throw on a clean shirt, and retreat to his study.

Mathias lit a cigarette, restlessly pacing the room. He took a drag, then another, before finally sitting down at the desk and picking up his phone. Giovanni answered on the second ring.

"Your line secure?" Mathias asked.

"Always," the old man replied.

"Paterlini's kid is dead."

"Junior? What the hell happened?"

"He tried to blow my fucking brains out, for one."

"What?"

"Whacked two Bratva soldiers while he was at it."

There was a long pause.

"Who knows about this?" Giovanni asked.

"You. Belkov shortly, I'd imagine."

They both sat with that, slowly realizing the wider implications.

"He was working with Piero," Mathias said quietly. "Said something about overhauling the family. That I was the first of many."

"Jesus," Giovanni hissed. "The fucker's planning a coup."

"This needs to go to the boss."

Giovanni sighed. "With the kid dead, it's your word against his."

"And his daddy and Russo go way back—yes, I know how this looks," Mathias growled.

"Piero will deny any involvement. The boss won't back you over his son. There's no going back from an accusation like that."

"You want me to stand here and take this?" Mathias asked, incredulous. "Wait until he tries again?"

"He won't. Not right away. With how this has gone down, he'll lay low, wait for things to blow over, before he tries anything. We need to hold our cards tight. And right now, Piero doesn't know what you know."

The old man had a point.

"Until we have more, we treat this as a shoot-out. The Russians fired first, the kid got hit, you finished them off."

Mathias saw the flash from Junior's gun as he shot twice in quick succession. Felt the metal barrel pressed against his head, still hot. "No doubt the same story they were going to tell when I turned up dead."

"Count yourself lucky, then."

It wasn't luck he had to thank. Blinded by Rayan's status as an outsider, Junior had underestimated the man's experience—and his dedication. He wasn't some shiftless lackey content to sit around, killing time. And he'd accompanied Mathias on enough tedious collections to know exactly how long a handoff with the Russians should take.

"I'll send someone to clean up. Paterlini's going to want the body. And some kind of penance, I'd imagine."

Mathias gave the councilman the address, staring at the smoke curling above his head. "And Belkov?"

"When Belkov catches wind his men were clipped unprovoked," Giovanni said grimly, "my guess is it'll start a turf war."

Mathias watched the end of his cigarette burn between his fingers.

"Either way," the old man continued, "it's not good."

No shit. Mathias could feel the blackness closing in around him.

"I'll be in touch." Giovanni hung up.

Mathias picked up the decanter from the corner of his desk and poured himself a drink. The next thing he knew, the room was dark, and several hours had passed. His mind kept slipping, trying to right itself. He glanced over at the decanter to find it empty.

Standing unsteadily, he made his way back to the living room, rubbing a palm across his face to clear the fog. He found Rayan on the sofa, head bent toward his chest, having fallen asleep sitting up. Mathias stared at him. He felt the thoughts coming, no longer subdued, worming past his defenses.

For an instant, Mathias had been sure—had known with absolute certainty—that it was the end. In the blur of disappointments that was his life, he'd wondered what had been worth it. And what had run through his head? Nothing but thoughts of this man.

11

Tony nursed a cup of black coffee in one hand and a cigar in the other, alternating between bringing them to his mouth. Mathias sat across from him, his untouched coffee cooling on the table. They were at Gino's, sitting by the window beneath the buzz of an infrared heater. Nick had turned it on to shield them from the chill that had settled over the city. His boss cocked his head at Rayan on the other side of the glass, standing by the entrance to the deli.

"Tied him up outside?"

"Can't be too careful," Mathias replied.

It had been three days, and he still couldn't shake the paranoia—the feeling of walking on a knife's edge, as though some lackey loyal to Piero was lurking in the lobby of his building, ready to jump him in the parking garage. That was why they were at Gino's and not the office. The more people around to witness, the less likely there would be trouble. The encounter with Junior had rattled Mathias more than he cared to admit, the fact that it was an inside job heightening his distrust of the very people he'd spent years working alongside. He followed Giovanni's logic about Piero lying low, especially in the wake of the fallout. But logic didn't help him sleep at night.

"Let him take a load off," Tony grunted, taking a swig of his brew. "I mean, Christ, he can't sit for a fucking coffee?"

"What was it you wanted to discuss?" Mathias asked, ignoring the question.

It was Rayan who'd insisted on standing guard. He'd been just as jumpy as Mathias these past few days, no doubt gripped by the same fear.

"While the coffee isn't worth it, I have missed seeing you," Mathias said sarcastically.

Tony fixed him with a grim stare. "I don't believe for a second that Belkov's goons took a shot at you, so don't peddle that bullshit with me."

Giovanni had managed to keep things under wraps long enough for them to spin their version of the truth. It was already beginning to circle through the family. But there was no getting past Tony. Mathias should have known that.

The man leaned forward, lowering his voice. "It was the kid, wasn't it?"

"Awfully keen to have him on the team, weren't you?" Mathias said.

"Fuck's sake," Tony snapped, glancing around quickly. "I had no idea—got it?"

In truth, Mathias hadn't been suspicious of Tony. He was a surly old bastard when he wanted to be, but his loyalty to Giorgio Russo ran deep.

"The gall—playing me like that," Tony said.

"You poor thing," Mathias said stonily. "What did Paterlini say, specifically, when he wanted you to take Junior on? You said he asked for me."

Tony exhaled. "What I told you—he thought the kid was aimless, needed some guidance. Thought someone self-made would be the perfect mentor. He mentioned your name."

Of course he did. I was the fucking target.

"How far up does this go?" the old man asked furtively. "Paterlini? Higher?"

Mathias thought back to what Junior had said: "There are those of us who prefer things the way they used to be." An old stalwart like Paterlini, in the boss's pocket, an easy ally in Piero's crusade... the son an extension of the father...

"What do you think?" Mathias asked.

"You're fucking kidding me!" Tony spat.

Mathias held up a hand, not wanting to cause a scene. "Nothing's certain."

"To take his personal grievance this far? I mean, you're not old blood, but you're ranked. It doesn't make sense."

Mathias pushed his cup away, now cold. "It's bigger than that."

"Bigger how?" Tony pressed, eyes narrowing.

Mathias hesitated, not sure how much to reveal. "Kid said I was the first of many."

Tony's eyebrows shot up, and his mouth slackened. "Do you know what this means?"

"I know what it means," Mathias said quietly. "But keep it close. All we have right now is what the kid was stupid enough to tell us."

Tony leaned back in his chair, tossing his cigar in what remained of his coffee. "Stupid, that's for sure. Couldn't even pull off whacking you."

Mathias smirked despite himself.

"No doubt, the man we have to thank for that is freezing his nuts off by the door," Tony said, looking pointedly at Rayan. "Don't let anyone catch wind of that.

Paterlini, like our boy Piero, takes things personal. Your rank offers you some protection, but Nadeau might as well be dog meat."

Mathias understood the warning. He'd already realized the wider implications of this. "Some protection," he muttered.

"You and trouble. I swear." Tony sighed. "You're benched, by the way. Both of you. The Russians are up in arms. Belkov's withholding payments, refusing to deal with us. I can't have you out working with a target on your back."

While it didn't come as a surprise, it still made Mathias's jaw tighten. "How long?"

Tony shrugged. "A couple weeks? A month? We gotta see how far they'll take this."

"I'll go see him," Mathias said. "Smooth things over."

Tony scowled. "The fuck you will. It'll do more harm than good. As far as he's concerned, you clipped two of his men unwarranted. He'll be well within his rights to put one between your eyes." He stood to leave, pausing to toss a few bucks down on the table. "Lay low for a bit. Look out for yourself."

Mathias clenched his teeth, holding back the fury of words that threatened to overcome him.

Rayan woke with a jerk, his body lifting off the mattress. For a moment, he didn't recognize the darkened room and felt his pulse skip, paralyzed by the same fear he'd felt all those nights on the street—the unknown threat looming as he slept, never sure what he'd find when he awakened.

After climbing unsteadily out of bed, Rayan made his way to the window, unfastened the catch, and heaved up the old wooden frame. A gust of freezing night air buffeted his face, and he leaned into it, relishing the feel against his clammy skin. He didn't recall falling asleep. He'd come home in the afternoon, his head foggy, and lain down for just a second. Turning to the clock on his nightstand, Rayan saw it was past ten.

He closed his eyes, hoping to erase the images from his dream. His first kill, Barry Olman, had been several years ago, but the man's face was permanently etched in his brain. The way his eyes had widened to reveal the whites... Rayan remembered thinking about the blood pumping around his body and how his bullet punctured Olman like a pin, allowing it to gush to the floor at his feet. In the dream, the man clawed manically at his ankles, a distorted cry coming from his mouth as Rayan shot him again and again. In reality, Olman had fallen like a stone as though by magic.

If the gun hadn't felt so heavy in his hand, Rayan could have almost pretended he'd had no part in it. It had taken Mathias's hand on his shoulder to snap him out of it. Otherwise, he would have remained there, frozen.

He sat down heavily on the end of his bed. It was an old nightmare, one he'd thought himself rid of. But it had resurfaced after the incident with Junior. Now it came most nights. Sometimes the dead man morphed into his brother. Sometimes Mathias. Rayan would feel the same jolt of terror he'd had at seeing Junior's gun pressed against his boss's forehead. But this time, he would be too late.

He reached for his jeans and a faded sweatshirt then pulled on a pair of sneakers and laced up. Nights like these, nothing helped but to walk the city, the thud of his feet on pavement enough to quiet the incessant hum of thoughts. He grabbed his phone and a handful of cash from the nightstand, slipped into his coat, and locked the door behind him.

Rayan jogged down three flights of stairs and emerged onto the street. He ducked his head against the cold, burying his hands in his pockets as he crossed the road and headed down a side alley toward Saint Denis. From there, he turned onto des Carrières, stalking along the darkened street. Propelled by nostalgia, he crossed the empty parking lot on his right and followed the fence line to where he knew the wire had been cut. Rayan pushed through it and walked down a small slope, the highway roaring overhead. His feet cut across the maze of scrap metal, discarded bottles, and old tires. He'd spent enough time out here to know the terrain from memory.

As he approached the darkened area under the overpass, Rayan began to make out several figures. Some were lying huddled together, trying to sleep through the cold, while two men with their hoods pulled up stood around a rusted-out barrel that had been converted into a firepit.

"Christ! Rayan?" One of them stepped back, staring at him, the glow from the flames illuminating his face. "I thought you were dead!"

Even from where he was standing, Rayan recognized Evan—the paranoid flick of his green eyes, his nose uneven, broken more than once during scuffles he was too high to remember. Seeing him again made Rayan think of Tahir. It was impossible to return to this life and not be reminded of his brother. Tahir had been good friends with Evan, especially when he became one of his regulars.

Rayan had never taken a liking to the various highs and lows his friends on the street peddled. He'd dabbled once or twice but found it frightening not to recognize himself under their influence, afraid he would reveal the self hidden under layers of camouflage. He knew Tahir took the drugs to escape, but for Rayan, everything came back in high definition, as if they amplified his darkest thoughts, pulling them out from within his tightly controlled grasp.

Rayan approached the man slowly, his unassuming appearance allowing him easy passage to the flames. Once he was close enough, Evan slapped him lightly on the shoulder, bloodshot gaze unfocused, slipping from Rayan's face to his shoulder and settling on a point somewhere behind him. He fought hard to remember how he would have acted back here.

"I've been around," Rayan said with a guarded smile, unsure what to say but knowing anything was better than admitting that he was working for the family.

Evan nodded, his head bouncing up and down on his emaciated body, like a puppet. "Right, right. I'm sorry about your brother, man. That was bleak."

Rayan felt the muscles in his face twitch as he tried to maintain the smile. How tightly he and Tahir had been tied. How closely they'd relied on each other for survival. "Yeah."

There was nothing else to say. He felt an overwhelming urge to get out of there, away from the familiarity of the surroundings and the feelings they evoked. Rayan had wanted to purge himself of these memories, not run headlong back into them. He fingered the bills in his pocket, pulled them out, and pressed them into Evan's hand.

"Take care of yourself," he said, not waiting for Evan's reply before retreating into the night, retracing his steps to the road.

By the time he'd rounded the corner to Bellechasse, Rayan knew he was being followed. Two men in black jackets. He continued walking, eyes catching on a half-empty beer bottle perched atop an overflowing trash can. He picked it up as he passed and tipped it upside down, letting the remaining liquid trickle onto the pavement, cursing himself for leaving his gun at the apartment. He never carried it when he wasn't working, always handling it with a level of discomfort. A necessary evil.

Rayan slowed his breathing, hollowing out. He needed his wits for what would come next. The men were Piero's goons, no doubt, perhaps sent by Silvano Paterlini himself, here to exact revenge. Mathias was convinced the boss's son would be too spooked to make a move, but Rayan's experience with Junior had proven just how brazen their kind could be.

He led the men through a series of narrow streets before concealing himself in a doorway alcove. As they passed, Rayan emerged silently from behind, raised the bottle, and smashed it into the side of the taller man's head.

"*Ty che, blyad?*" the man howled, blood streaming from his temple.

Russians? Rayan moved past him, slamming a fist into his partner's face as the man pulled a gun from his jacket. He threw an arm around the man's shoulders, pressing the broken bottle to his throat as he extracted the gun from his grip.

Rayan stepped back, flicking off the safety and leveling the barrel at his pursuers. "Who are you with?"

The man he'd relieved of his weapon held a hand to his neck, breathing hard. "Tell your boss Belkov wants to see him."

"He can tell him himself."

The man shook his head, scowling. "Better if they're not seen talking."

"Why?"

"You know why," the man with the bleeding head snarled, launching a hock of spit at his feet.

Rayan said nothing, looking from one to the other, trying to determine if they were to be trusted. Then he inclined his head in the direction they'd come. "Go on."

The two Russians hesitated.

"Go," he repeated, louder this time.

Slowly, the men turned and walked back down the street, muttering angrily. Rayan waited a moment before pocketing the gun and taking off in the opposite direction. He wound his way through back streets and alleyways before he was certain he'd lost them.

"Ran into the Russians," Rayan said into the phone once he'd returned to his apartment. He placed the Bratva man's gun down on the kitchen counter.

"Define 'ran into,'" Mathias said on the other end of the line.

Rayan glanced at the door to check the dead bolt once again. "I was followed."

Mathias was silent for a moment. "Nothing you couldn't handle?"

Rayan leaned against the sink, wondering if this was his capo's way of asking if he was all right. "You could say that."

"What did they want?" Mathias asked.

"Belkov wants to talk."

"Does he?"

Rayan knew that tone. He knew what Mathias was considering. "Meeting with the Russians is not a good idea right now," he said carefully.

There was a long pause. "I'll be outside in fifteen."

"Mathias—"

"I liked it better when you kept your mouth shut."

There was a click, and the call ended. Rayan swore under his breath. He stared at the gun on the counter, his mind whirring. Then he put down the phone and stalked off to the bedroom to change back into his suit.

12

They drove in silence, the city around them cloaked in darkness. Mathias's first instinct had been to heed Tony's advice and refuse Belkov's invitation. To meet the man on his turf, with things as they were, was brazen, to say the least. Following the incident with Junior, the family was on thin ice with the Russians, and for all he knew, they were walking right into a setup.

Yet his gut told him Belkov knew more than he was letting on, and Mathias was willing to take the risk if it meant getting the answers he needed. *Was Piero courting the Russians?* They were always greedy for more territory and had never been content under Russo's thumb. It would explain the information Belkov had on the boss. The shoot-out was a perfect excuse to provoke the Bratva into war and get rid of Mathias in the process. Then Piero could swoop in with a guarantee of spoils and smooth things over whenever it was convenient, finally getting the respect he wanted from the Quintino, right around the time they were discussing succession plans.

The question was, what had Belkov been promised in return for his cooperation? Two soldiers seemed a high price even for him. *What is Piero dangling that has proven so enticing?*

Mathias had been turning these thoughts over for days, but they'd solidified during the phone call with his second—somewhere between the spike of anger at hearing that Rayan had been followed and the realization that Belkov was forcing his hand. It was better to get it over with before the Bratva boss resorted to other means to get his attention.

Rayan pulled into the parking lot outside Château Suzdal. He took out his gun then checked the chamber, clicked off the safety, and stowed it back in the holster beneath his jacket. He looked at Mathias, his face grim.

"Not a word of this, understood?" Mathias said. He was in enough shit as it was, and Tony had told him, in no uncertain terms, to lay low.

His second nodded, though Mathias could tell there was more he wanted to say. They stepped out of the car and walked around the back of the restaurant to where a tall man with a bloody gash on his forehead was waiting. The man glowered at Rayan, muttering as he led them to the office. Belkov sat behind his desk, with half a dozen Russian soldiers stationed around the room. Rayan's hand moved toward his jacket.

"I don't like these odds," Mathias said.

"Now you want to play fair?" the older man sneered. He barked out something in Russian, and all but one of the men retreated into the hallway, closing the door to the office behind them.

"Igor wants his gun back."

The remaining Bratva soldier crossed his arms with a frown. Mathias watched as his second reached behind him, pulling what appeared to be Igor's weapon from the waistband of his slacks. He stepped forward and placed it on the desk.

"Fair enough for you?" Belkov scowled.

Mathias pulled out a seat and sat across from him. "Knowing you, there's a room of heavily armed gorillas hidden back here. How many M16s did you smuggle in the last shipment? I should know—I collected the tariffs."

"Let's not forget it was you who made the first move," Belkov said, his eyes glinting. "Though from the shit you're spreading, I must have imagined picking up the bodies of my men."

Mathias felt a chill of trepidation. This was a bad idea. Belkov had always been difficult in a manageable way. Applying force usually worked until he reverted to his regular antics. But Mathias had never crossed the man. Like him, the Russian mobster had a reputation for exacting retribution in brutal and bloody ways.

"I'm used to being called a liar, so it's quite funny—don't you think?—when I'm telling the truth." Belkov placed three shell casings down on the desk. "Two of these are from your young friend's gun, which you left behind with his body. Maybe not such good friends after all? My guess is this one," he said, pushing a single spent shell toward Mathias, "belongs to your dog over there."

Beside him, he saw Rayan stiffen.

"Now, I'm curious. Why kill one of your own? And why did I find myself burying two good men?"

Mathias picked up the empty casing and rolled it between his fingers—a tiny piece of metal that had come between him and death. He placed it down, leaning back in his seat. "Why don't you tell me? You're working with Piero after all."

It was a gamble, but Mathias kept returning to how the Russian head had known about Russo's ailing health. Insider information likely gleaned from someone as intent on causing a complete upheaval as Belkov was.

A slow smile spread across Belkov's face. "What gave you that idea?"

Right on the money.

"That meeting was a setup," Mathias said. "What do you gain by getting rid of me?"

The smile disappeared. "Not a setup," Belkov corrected tersely. "But he wanted it to be one. In the end, we couldn't come to an agreement." He frowned. "Seems that didn't matter to Russo's boy."

Mathias remembered the curl of Junior's mouth as he plugged the Russian soldiers. Retaliation. Piero didn't like being told no.

"I'd say it worked out perfectly. You got your excuse to wage war against the family, and I've been benched. Not as satisfying as me being dead, I'm sure."

"*Nyet*," Belkov spat, suddenly angry. "I did not agree to send my men like lambs to the slaughter. You Italians, your old ways are crumbling, disintegrating with all the infighting. But the Bratva…" He pulled his shirt aside to reveal the black stars inked crudely on his sternum. "There is still loyalty among us."

Mathias studied the Russian carefully. He hadn't expected this. "What was he offering?"

"Piero had quite a few—how you say—carrots. We'd take Laval, everything east of Rivière des Mille Îles. No more port fees, no more product blacklists."

"He'd be a fool to give you that much power," Mathias scoffed.

"To gain even greater power, sometimes you have to give some up." He shrugged. "Russo's boy wants to take over, but that is not what big boss wants, no? So he will force the family's hand."

Separate pieces began to click together in his mind, blurred edges coming into focus.

"Aren't you curious, Mathias?" Belkov asked, the slyness returning, "about why I called you here? We have both been crossed. Perhaps we can both get even."

Mathias snorted. "You're just looking for another pawn to use against the family. If I'd been whacked by Piero's little apprentice, you would've been overjoyed."

Belkov began to laugh. "Think. Why would Piero want the Bratva to start a war with his own family?" The old man pulled out a slip of paper from his breast pocket and slid it across the desk toward Mathias. "Because in war, there are casualties."

Mathias picked up the paper and unfolded it. There, staring at him in black ink, was a list of names: *Mathias Beauvais, Giovanni Bianchi, Enzo Carbone, Antonio*

Giraldi, Filippo De Luca. Mathias felt his pulse thud. Loyalists to Russo. He folded the paper and handed it back to Belkov.

"You would have been the first," the Russian said.

The first of many.

Belkov was freely admitting his attempted collaboration with Piero, not caring about the repercussions for Mathias, Russo, and the whole family, yet this was the closest he'd come to glimpsing Piero's master plan. It seemed too elaborate for Belkov to have simply concocted.

"I've known you long enough, Belkov. You're telling me this so you can play us both at the same time."

"Then tell me, Mathias: why does no one know about the hit against you—that it came from inside the family? Why cover that up?"

Mathias set his jaw, refusing to show his hand. It was coming from all sides, the truth twisting and warping around him.

"Perhaps you're biding your time. I can bide my time, too, if the price is right," Belkov said.

They looked at each other, neither averting his gaze.

"Piero's proposal was appealing. I'm not opposed to working with the family to help solve your little squabbles," Belkov said. "But I don't want to back the wrong horse."

What he was proposing was as good as treason. It was also a compelling development.

"I don't know what you're talking about," Mathias said finally, giving the Russian a pointed look.

"Of course you don't." Belkov smiled knowingly, a silent understanding passing between them. Then the man slammed his palms down on the desk. "Come. Let us drink to you coming here today." He pulled out an unmarked bottle of clear liquor and several shot glasses. "To honor my men. Nothing is forgiven, but maybe we can look ahead to what will come."

Mathias observed the Bratva boss skeptically. "How do I know that's not laced with arsenic?"

The older man laughed, sloshing liquid into three glasses. "Give me some credit, Mathias. There are more creative ways to kill a man. And this"—he held up the bottle as though it contained the elixir of life—"is the good stuff." He slid a full shot toward Mathias then glanced over at Rayan. "This one too."

Mathias was about to object when his second pulled out a chair and sat down. He gave Rayan a sidelong glance. The man looked back, giving nothing away. Rayan didn't drink. Mathias had never asked him about it, simply taking it as another cryptic detail he kept close to his chest.

"*Nostrovia!*" the Russian crowed, lifting up his glass as Rayan and Mathias did the same.

The vodka seared his throat on the way down, like battery acid.

Rayan winced, and Belkov grinned. "From my uncle in the old country. He makes it himself."

He poured them another round, and Mathias fought the urge to groan. Once Belkov got started, there was no stopping him. Drinking was the man's signature power play. Fail to keep up, and you showed your weakness. The only way to engender respect was to match him.

"I've always been curious about your boy here," Belkov said, rolling his glass between his fingers. "He's not Italian. What is he, then?"

They all took the next shot, and Rayan placed his glass down on the desk. "Take your pick."

"He speaks!" Belkov cried, topping up their glasses. "Why work for a group with no blood ties? In the end, they owe you nothing."

Mathias recalled Tony's words: "Nadeau might as well be dog meat." He lifted the glass to his lips, concealing his irritation.

Rayan's eyes narrowed. The alcohol had relaxed his usual restraint, his emotions finding their way to the surface. He looked at Belkov then threw back the vodka. "Why work for anyone?"

This made the Russian laugh.

Rayan's movements began to slow. It was clear he was quickly becoming quite drunk. Belkov was already pouring the next shot, filling the glasses so that they overflowed, puddling onto the desk. Mathias began to feel the hint of an encroaching buzz. His second, on the other hand, was attempting to lift his glass without spilling.

"He's loyal like a dog," Belkov said to Mathias as he studied Rayan. "Hard to find loyalty like that in our line of work, Beauvais. You can try beating it into them, but there's always that sliver of defiance."

Mathias stared at Belkov, saying nothing. He knew what he had in Rayan—knew what it was to have complete confidence that his back was covered. But it also ate at him to be the object of that kind of loyalty. There was no line Rayan would not cross for him.

"We're done," Mathias announced after knocking back the round, knowing if he didn't intervene, he would be picking his second off the floor. "I'm not destroying my liver with your Slavic turpentine."

Rayan downed his glass and held the back of his hand to his mouth. For the briefest of moments, Mathias thought he would heave. The Russian mobster threw his shot back with a hiss then launched the empty glass at the wall behind them, where it shattered. They stood, and Belkov leaned forward, holding out a hand.

"Think about it," he said as Mathias took it, sealing an unspoken detente.

He followed his second out of Belkov's office, passing a cluster of armed Russian soldiers smoking in the hallway. So he hadn't been far off. They walked to the car, the moon illuminating the darkened parking lot, an icy wind slicing against his cheeks. Rayan pulled the keys from his pocket and handed them to Mathias, his movements clumsy. He made it to the car, leaning against the passenger door, before promptly doubling over and emptying the contents of his stomach onto the ground. Mathias waited until he was once again upright, wiping his mouth with the sleeve of his jacket.

"Sorry," Rayan muttered.

"Get in."

As they sped along the highway back toward the city, Mathias's mind trawled the conversation, catching on hooks. *Did Piero go to such extremes because he was sure he wouldn't be tapped for succession?* The boss had hinted as much. In the seat beside him, Rayan sat bolt upright.

"Not in my fucking car," Mathias warned, swerving across two lanes and pulling onto the shoulder.

Rayan opened the door and vomited, his shoulders heaving. When he was done, he fell back into his seat, an arm reaching out to close the door with a thump.

Mathias leaned over and pulled on Rayan's seatbelt. "You're an idiot."

"*Oui*, capo."

Mathias smirked and continued driving.

"Think he's lying?" Rayan asked after a moment. "Seemed elaborate, especially for Belkov."

Mathias was accustomed to his second's silence, which gave the impression he observed interactions with a cursory understanding. With the booze stripping away Rayan's usual reticence, it was clear he didn't miss a thing.

Mathias sighed. "If it was anyone else, maybe. But Piero? He's reckless enough to consider it." He took the next exit and wound through the streets of Villeray.

"Why are we covering for him? You almost got clipped."

"You still don't know how this works?"

"The family considers some people more valuable than others," Rayan said, his voice hard. "I know how it works."

The lights changed up ahead, and Mathias slowed the car to a stop at the deserted intersection.

"If I had a dollar for every time one of those old bastards looked at me like I'd crawled out of the sewer..." his second continued, lips curling. "And you. I could kill them for how they've treated you."

Mathias gave him a stony look.

Rayan averted his eyes, chastened. "Everything in my head is trying to come out my mouth," he mumbled.

"Careful with that," Mathias said.

Rayan was an endearing drunk at least. There were worse things. The light turned green, and he sped through the empty streets toward Rosemont.

"How'd you end up with the Russian's piece?" Mathias asked.

"I took it."

"After you smashed up his friend's face?"

"With a beer bottle. I didn't have my gun."

Mathias smiled ruefully, not sure if he was amused or impressed. "What were you doing wandering around at night unarmed?"

Rayan sighed, leaning back against the headrest. "When I can't sleep, walking helps. Takes my mind off things."

"Why can't you sleep, Rayan?"

He turned to Mathias, his mouth a grim line. "Because of the dreams."

Mathias held his gaze until Rayan looked away, staring out the window as they turned onto Saint-Michel.

"What was on the paper?" his second asked into the darkness.

"Names," Mathias replied.

Rayan sat forward, eyes widening. "A hit list... of family members?"

Mathias nodded slowly. There had been another name on the list, below the handful of ranked elite: *Rayan Nadeau*. Proof he'd been getting noticed—the wrong kind of attention.

He parked outside Rayan's building and walked him to the elevator, one hand on his shoulder to steady him. Mathias had thought it an annoyance that the man didn't drink. Now he could appreciate it. Once in the apartment, he steered his second toward the bedroom before heading to the kitchen, taking a glass from the cabinet, and filling it with water.

"That was risky even for you," Rayan murmured when Mathias returned.

He was sitting on the edge of the bed, fumbling with his shoelaces. Mathias handed him the glass, and he took several gulps then placed it on the nightstand.

"Then you shouldn't have come."

"And let you go alone?" Rayan snarled. "That's a mistake I won't make twice."

Suddenly tired, Mathias sat down beside him on the bed, bending over to yank off Rayan's shoes. His second was right of course. Things could have turned out very differently. He needed to go home and collect his thoughts.

When he straightened up, Rayan was moving toward him, reaching for his belt buckle. Despite everything, the surge of desire was immediate, crackling through him like a current. Mathias could almost feel his hand around the curve of Rayan's throat, the firm swell pressing against the front of his pants. He wrestled with the want before easily disarming Rayan and pushing him backward onto the bed. His fingers moved on their own, tracing the scar along Rayan's neck.

"My father's doing," his second said with a half smile. "Didn't like me covering for my brother." The smile disappeared. "'Careful who you stick your neck out for.' His words."

It would have been deep to have left something like this, a mark lingering into adulthood. "Thought you didn't have a father."

"I did once."

Mathias stopped himself, removing his hand from the intoxicating pull of Rayan's skin. He knew if this continued, he wouldn't be able to hold back. Tapping his palm against Rayan's cheek, he got to his feet. "Sleep it off."

His second stared up at him, eyes swimming with vodka yet serious. "If you need something…"

There was that pang again. The lines crossed. The power to make someone cross them.

"I know," Mathias said quietly, turning and heading for the door.

As he pulled the car into the garage beneath his building, his phone rang from where it lay in the passenger seat. He stared at it for a moment before picking up.

"Mathias," Giovanni said. It was clear from his tone that this was not good news.

Mathias leaned back against the headrest, his whole body regretting having left Rayan's apartment. If he'd simply climbed into bed with the man, he would not be on this call—a call with the promise to detonate everything he'd worked toward.

"Join me for a drink."

Mathias was familiar with Hochelaga yet had never heard of Deux dés Noirs. The dank sports bar boasting wall-to-wall zebra-print carpet was the kind of place he would go to find someone who owed him money, not where he'd choose to have a drink.

Giovanni sat in the far corner by the pool tables, his Brioni suit looking out of place among the hockey jerseys and baseball caps. The roar from the flat screen behind the bar was enough to ensure that their conversation didn't travel. On the table sat two drinks, one untouched. The councilman had ordered for him.

"Piero approached the Russians, wanted to make a deal," Mathias said after greeting him, scanning the room out of habit. Junior had really done a number on him.

Giovanni's eyebrows shot up. "That's a pretty hefty accusation."

"Belkov's been getting information from someone with inside knowledge of the boss's condition. I know it's him."

"That Russian bastard would say anything to pit us against each other," the councilman scoffed. "Wait for the family to eat itself from the inside and feast on the scraps."

"Maybe that's what Piero wants," Mathias snapped.

Giovanni shook his head. "Look, I would be lying if I said it didn't seem plausible. Junior, the Russians threatening war... The man's slippery, I'll give you that. Maybe he's got his hands all over this, but we haven't seen so much as a finger. It's still your word against his."

Mathias stilled. He'd been about to divulge the rest of his conversation with Belkov—the list, Piero's willingness to hand out territory like it was candy—but something stopped him.

"It's inconvenient," the old man continued with a sigh, "that you've been caught up in all this."

"Inconvenient?" Mathias repeated, his face darkening. If he closed his eyes, he could still feel the splatter of the kid's blood across his cheek.

Giovanni paused, tapping a finger against the rim of his glass. "Thought I'd give you fair warning so you know what to expect. There's talk of transferring you out of the city."

Mathias froze.

"Not sure if you know Marco Moretti. Oversees family dealings in Hamilton. He's made a right mess of things out there, and they're wanting someone to come in and clean it up."

"Giovanni," Mathias warned.

"I know. But Paterlini's leaning hard on this, what with his son dead and all. Having you around is a painful reminder, and with it happening on your watch—"

"If any other captain had walked away from a hit..." Mathias growled. He didn't need to finish. The precedent was clear: he was entitled to his reprisal. "Yet here I am, cowed by Paterlini's hurt feelings?"

"He lost a son."

"A son sent to whack me, if you remember." Mathias pushed away his untouched drink, aware of the slight.

"That's not the story we've been telling."

"Who else? Who's gunning for this?" he demanded.

Giovanni exhaled loudly, his reluctance telling Mathias everything he needed to know.

"So if Piero can't kill me, he'll make sure I'm pushed out?" Mathias continued.

Giovanni sucked his teeth. "My hands are tied, here. It comes direct from the boss. There's a promotion in it, *vangelista*. You'll be heading a city division."

"You know as well as I do Hamilton is Reapers territory. And the scrap that we do hold, we fight for tooth and nail with Truman."

Giovanni held out his hands. "With you out of town, they're hoping things will settle down with the Russians and Paterlini will be appeased. When the situation is less sensitive, we can look at getting you back."

Mathias stood, pulling on his jacket.

"Mathias, you're young, you're talented," Giovanni continued, assuaging him. "Be patient, stay alive. There's several ways this can go yet."

Mathias dropped a handful of bills on the table, turning to leave without another word.

Mathias stood in the living room of his apartment in pitch darkness. The blinds were drawn, the lights off. He held a full glass of Macallan, not his first. He was past drunk, having started early with Belkov's little game of chicken, and was now entering the realm of false lucidity, as though the world tilting beneath his feet was exactly how it was supposed to be.

He swilled the harsh liquid in his mouth before swallowing. His grip on the tumbler tightened, and Mathias wondered how easy it would be to crush in his hand. There was a dullness about him that he couldn't shake. Perhaps a fistful of glass splinters might wake him up.

The family had always made it clear that there were those in its ranks who were worth more than others. Even Rayan, far on the periphery, knew that, yet Mathias had believed he was capable of moving beyond his station. He was a fool.

He felt a deep rage churning in his chest. It stole his breath, narrowing his vision. Mathias had no choice but to take the fall. And he would stand by and smile through it.

In one fluid movement, he hurled the glass at the wall, where it shattered into tiny shards. The act did nothing to ease the fury pumping through his veins. He picked up the half-empty bottle of scotch from the coffee table and threw it against the glass shelving. All of it came down in an almighty crash. Mathias stepped forward and swiped his arm across the bar cabinet, sending the contents tumbling to the hardwood floor. Throwing his weight against the cabinet itself, he overturned it onto the ground, glasses and bottles spilling out and shattering at his feet.

He caught sight of his reflection in the hallway mirror, a shadow of a man in the darkness. Crunching over broken glass, he strode to the mirror, surprised to find that despite everything, there it was—the same face looking back at him. He raised a fist and smashed it into the glass. His hand came away a bloody mess. He exhaled slowly, looking down at his bleeding knuckles as he gingerly flexed his hand, opening and closing it. Finally, he had something to supplant the fury, the blackness in his head clearing as the pain kicked in.

13

Rayan had heard nothing from his boss for two days. Not that he'd initially noticed through the haze of a punishing hangover. His recollection of that night was hazy, and he had a nagging feeling he'd said something stupid, reinforcing his determination to avoid alcohol altogether. Attempting to keep up with Belkov had not been one of his smarter decisions, but Rayan had been overcome by the need to prove something to the Russian mobster, who had, for the first time, invited him to the table as an equal.

At first, Rayan had given Mathias space, knowing how complicated things had become. But when his capo would not answer his calls, Rayan began to worry. He decided he would go over. The worst Mathias could do was rail against him. At the very least, checking on him would assuage Rayan's fears.

He stood in the lobby of Mathias's building, waiting for the elevator. Once inside, he punched in the private access code, allowing him entry to the top floor. Rayan stepped out into the plush foyer, stopped outside the man's front door, and pressed the buzzer. He waited, hearing nothing from inside the apartment. Figuring Mathias wasn't home, Rayan was about to leave when the door swung open.

"What are you doing here?" Mathias stood shirtless, a towel around his neck, cheeks shaded with stubble. Just below his ear there was a tiny bloom of blood as if he'd nicked himself.

"Checking you're still alive," Rayan shot back, suddenly irritated. His boss didn't appear incapable of picking up the phone. He strode past him into the apartment. As Mathias closed the door behind him, Rayan saw the bandage around his right hand. "Christ, your hand."

His capo ignored him, walking back down the hallway to the bathroom, and Rayan followed. He stopped as he heard a crunch underfoot. The mirror hung askew, the glass shattered. He passed the living room, taking in the chaos. The room, immense and sparsely decorated, had been completely trashed. What looked like it had once been a glass shelf hung haphazardly from a screw on the wall, the rest of it in tatters on the polished wood floor. Pools of liquid drenched the floorboards near an overturned cabinet, and the whole room smelled strongly of alcohol.

The door to the bathroom was open, and Mathias bent over the sink filled with water, his cheeks frosted white. Held awkwardly in his left hand was a razor, its base clenched at a strange angle as he attempted to bring it to his face. Resting on the basin was his bandaged hand, the fingers forced straight.

As Rayan entered, his capo glanced at him in the mirror, his mouth set in a scowl. Mathias was a master of many things, including the impeccable shave. It was strange to see him so out of his element.

He threw the razor down into the sink with a clatter. "What are you looking at?" he growled.

Rayan stepped forward, dropping a hand into the warm water and fishing out the razor. "Let me."

His boss looked at him warily but said nothing. Mathias was several inches taller than him, so Rayan placed a hand beneath the man's chin and tilted his face at an angle. He moved the razor to the base of Mathias's neck and drew it up to his jawline, each stroke slow and methodical. He was aware of Mathias's eyes on him and the tension in his neck as Rayan slid the razor along the contours of his throat. He shook it out in the sink and started on his face. This close, Rayan could feel the steady brush of Mathias's breath, all thoughts focused on keeping his hand steady.

He finished the last stroke, and Mathias wrapped his hand around the wrist holding the razor. The man pushed him against the sink, and Rayan felt the smoothness of his freshly shaven cheek graze his own. Then Mathias stepped back abruptly and walked out of the bathroom.

Rayan found him in the bedroom, getting dressed. "Your hand."

"Martin's seen it," he replied, shrugging on his shirt. "It's fine."

Without a word, Rayan moved toward him and began on the buttons. His capo's frustration filled the room. Mathias's eyes were trained on him as he started at the collar and made his way down. Rayan felt the movement of the man's chest, slow and measured beneath the fabric under his fingers. He was aware of the warmth of Mathias's skin as it brushed against his knuckles. It felt like a feat of restraint not to place a hand on his bare stomach and draw it across the map of muscle that was his chest.

"Since you're here," Mathias said stiffly when Rayan was done, picking up his jacket from where it lay on the bed. "Might as well come for the show."

Rayan blinked. "Where're you going?"

Mathias pocketed his cigarettes, his phone. "To see the boss."

Only weeks ago, the same prospect had been met with anticipation, the promise of something great. And now it was as though he was en route to his execution.

It was rare for Rayan to find himself in a room with the boss. Giorgio Russo was a well-dressed man in his late seventies who wouldn't have garnered more than a passing glance from someone walking by him on the street. Upon closer inspection, however, one could see the diamond embellishment on his Rolex, the thick gold rings that adorned the fingers of both hands, and the perfectly tailored hemline of his custom-made Italian suit.

They were in the VIP room at the back of Le Rouge. The boss had taken his place at the head of the table, an unusual sight in recent months. He looked drawn, his skin pale and waxen across sharpened cheeks. Like Belkov, Rayan had also heard the whispers of rumors—nothing he'd been bold enough to put to Mathias, but there was talk of a worsening illness, an uncertain recovery. Which would explain why his appearances had become few and far between.

Assembled around the table were Giovanni, Tony, and Mathias. Rayan stood by the door with Stefano, one of Russo's handlers, and Giovanni's second, Henri Rossi. He avoided looking at his boss, who had been deadly quiet on the drive over, his silent fury filling the car with a pressure that made Rayan's lungs contract. The drinks had been poured, and they waited for the boss to begin.

"We've found ourselves in an unfortunate position," Russo announced, sitting forward in his chair and wrapping a hand around his glass.

Mathias's expression shifted into a thinly concealed scowl, a curl of smoke rising from the cigarette in his bandaged hand.

"Belkov maintains we fired first, but in all our years dealing with the Russians, when hasn't his story changed to fit their agenda?" The boss looked at Giovanni, who nodded in agreement.

Rayan stared ahead, impassive. Mathias had given him a brief rundown of what had happened before he showed up that afternoon in the lumber shed. He'd also instructed him on what to do with this particular information, the importance of obscuring certain truths. Even so, Rayan knew his capo had left things out and was unsure why he was withholding details.

"I imagine Belkov's attempting to cover his own soldier's misstep," Giovanni said, swilling his drink reflectively. "What seemed an act of open aggression may simply have been a regrettable overreaction. Junior accused the Bratva of coming up short, and one of the men took offense. Words were exchanged, and before the situation could be diffused, the Russian opened fire."

Tony shifted in his seat, a flare of red making its way along his neck. "Look, I'll be the first to admit I pushed the kid forward. Junior was mouthy—might have hit a wrong note with the Bratva. You know how they get. Beauvais made it clear he wasn't ready for the field."

"I'll be frank," Russo said with a sigh, his forehead drawing into a deep groove. "We don't have the weight to back up a call for Belkov's head, and I can't afford an all-out war with the Russians right now. So concessions need to be made. There will be sanctions, a punitive hike in port duties—the Russians can count on that. But Silvano Paterlini's out for blood." Russo paused, taking a sip and letting the information sink in. "And a man who's lost his only child is not overly conciliatory."

Rayan reached for the dull ache of guilt. He had pulled the trigger, after all, taking the life of Paterlini's son. Yet here he stood, remorseless, not because of his hatred for Junior but because the man had been seconds away from taking Mathias from him. Unlike previous times Rayan had used his weapon, this instance had not caused him any regret.

"Paterlini won't stand for this to be swept under the rug. The man has been a loyal member of the family from the early days." The boss looked at Mathias, seeming to weigh his next words carefully. "Rightly or wrongly, he's placed some of the blame on you, Mathias, and refuses to be convinced otherwise. Grief is a polarizing thing."

His logic rankled Rayan. Russo had revealed his own bias—a preference for those whose ties encircled him the tightest. It was clear that Mathias, of lower rank and with limited family connections, had little say in how this played out.

"We need to keep the peace within the family. Especially during this period of..." The boss glanced at Giovanni. "Uncertainty. I'm sure with time, Paterlini will see things more clearly. Then we can revisit this."

Mathias stubbed out his cigarette in the ashtray beside him, pushing down hard until the whole thing collapsed beneath his fingertips. "What does keeping the peace look like exactly?" he asked, his voice low.

"Something has opened up," Russo began judiciously. "Not a bad opportunity, considering—silver lining and all that. We thought it best you spent some time away from the city. Let the air clear."

Rayan's eyebrows shot up in surprise. *We're being pushed out?* His gaze flicked to his boss then down to the man's bandaged hand. *Did he know?*

"Marco Moretti is finishing up in Hamilton, moving back here to care for his elderly mother. The office needs a new head, fresh blood. Figure you'd be an excellent replacement. We'd make you *vangelista* of course. It's a satellite, sure, but you'll be running it."

The information dropped like a dead weight. Russo appeared to be waiting for a reaction. Mathias was entitled to one. He was doing them all a favor by taking this on the chin, allowing himself to be subject to the whims of family seniority, however unhinged. He deserved at least one big outburst, a heated refusal.

But Mathias, in perfect form, remained a stone. "Starting when?"

"Hell, as soon as you can get out there." Russo chuckled. "Who knows? This might prove a decent leg up."

There was a long pause before Mathias spoke. "I appreciate the opportunity."

The sentiment was perfunctory, ringing false. But it was good enough for the men at the table. The boss raised his drink in a toast. "Water under the bridge," he said as the men lifted their glasses.

Mathias downed the contents of his in one swig and stood, providing his obligatory—albeit tight-lipped—thanks to the collection of men, opting against staying for another round and the accompanying small talk. Then he turned and walked past Rayan to the door, leaving him to follow.

Outside, Mathias strode through the parking lot, rolling his shoulders as though trying to shake something. He stopped beside the car, his expression oscillating between anger and frustration. "Make your own way home," he instructed sharply.

Rayan gave a short nod. By the look of him, Mathias seemed wild enough to disappear into the night, untethered to reason, fueled by uncoiling rage. Rayan would have preferred to drive him just to make sure he returned to the safety of his apartment. Then he remembered the room of shattered glass.

"Call," Rayan said flatly, realizing the futility of his concern. "If you need something."

The words sounded familiar, although he couldn't remember from where.

Mathias found himself unable to sleep. He lay in bed, unsure what to make of this new development. The blackness was back, turning his stomach, consuming him. A hard lump of fury had lodged itself in his chest since the meeting with Russo earlier that day. Mathias pulled out his cigarettes and began to smoke, taking long, slow drags. Thoughts flicked through his mind in quick succession. Instead of dismissing them as he usually did, he let them stick. He couldn't seem to shake them loose. A small part of him was already testing the feasibility of retrieving his gun from the safe, driving to Piero Russo's house, and putting an end to him—going through the motions, how each step led to the next. It was simple, with none of the scheming and insistence on the long game. Of course, it would also mean putting an end to himself. There was no walking away from whacking the boss's son as he slept. That was where things began to unravel. Mathias was many things, but suicidal, he was not.

His frustration rose, a tightness that gripped him. He felt a sting as the cigarette burned down to his fingers. Crushing it in the ashtray on his nightstand, Mathias held up his right hand. He tugged on the clasp of the bandage and unwound the fabric to reveal the crisscross of cuts beneath. He needed to distract himself, or things would start to break.

He got out of bed and stalked to the kitchen, where he opened a bottle and poured himself a drink. It didn't so much as take the edge off. Staring at the red light on the stove, Mathias watched it click from *02:32* to *02:33*.

If you need something... He picked up his phone.

Rayan answered after several rings, his voice thick with sleep. *"Oui?"*

Mathias felt a familiar stirring. He'd felt it earlier when Rayan had pressed the razor to his throat, lips parted in concentration.

"Where are you?" Mathias asked, as if he didn't already know.

"Home. What time is it?" Rayan replied, sounding uncertain.

"Two thirty."

There was a pause. Mathias watched the numbers flick from *02:35* to *02:36*.

"Come over," Rayan said as though it were the simplest thing in the world.

Mathias downed his drink, disarmed. He thought of returning to his empty bed and realized that was the very reason he'd called.

He was not kind in his conquest, bridled rage making him rougher than usual. Rayan did not push back at first but soon made his objection clear, cues Mathias purposefully ignored until Rayan slammed the heel of his hand into his jaw, throwing him onto his back on the bed.

Mathias felt his fury drain as he looked up at the clean lines of Rayan's chest, the swell of his cock curved against his stomach. But it was his face, marred by anger yet unable to hide his arousal, that lured Mathias from the blackness in his mind.

"Try again," Rayan said sharply.

Mathias reached up and placed a hand on the man's neck, guiding him back down, kissing him.

"Better," Rayan murmured when they parted.

He lowered his mouth and trailed his lips along Mathias's collarbone then down to his nipples. He reached for Mathias's cock and drew it through his hand. Moving, Rayan mounted him from above, straddling his hips, and resumed their coupling.

Time dissolved as a deep pressure built between them, Rayan slowing, stopping, edging them both, in complete control before continuing, muscles taut as he ground himself against Mathias again and again. He could not tear his eyes from the man, who had one hand around the head of his own cock, his restraint evident in the stiff clench of his jaw. Rayan lowered his chin, a growl escaping from between his teeth. His breath stalled, and Mathias came abruptly, on the other side of release before he knew how he'd gotten there.

Rayan stilled, placing his hands on either side of Mathias as he caught his breath. Mathias realized his fingers were pressed hard into Rayan's thighs and relinquished his grip, sliding his hands around his waist. He rolled the man over, still inside him, and Rayan winced.

"Enough," he said, a hand against Mathias's chest, pushing him away.

The anger now appeased, Mathias felt a splinter of remorse. He had hurt him, and he'd done so willingly. He withdrew, and Rayan exhaled, slumping back into the pillows. Mathias looked down at Rayan's still-hard member and, without a second thought, captured it in his mouth. Rayan's body arched, the low curl of a moan in his throat. He was close, and Mathias finished him quickly, lingering over the tip as he swallowed and let the spent man slip wetly through his teeth.

Chest heaving, Rayan looked at him, eyes wide, face flushed. His lips moved as if to speak but said nothing as Mathias reached for his cigarettes. Lighting one, he was almost sorry at how it masked Rayan's taste on his tongue. They lay beside each other in the darkness, Mathias discovering his mind blessedly blank. As though wiped clean.

"You knew about the transfer," Rayan said.

Mathias closed his eyes with a sigh. *So much for that.* "What does it matter?"

Rayan turned to face him, reaching for his damaged hand and running a thumb along one of the cuts on his knuckles, still fresh. "Seems like it mattered."

Mathias studied him for a moment before withdrawing his hand.

"How much business does the family have in Hamilton?" Rayan continued.

"Not much. Russo likes to keep a foot in the door."

"I've never been out of Quebec."

Mathias stared at the flicker of his cigarette. There was a reason he hadn't told Rayan about the move to Hamilton. He didn't plan on taking his second with him.

Mathias tossed the butt into an empty glass on the nightstand and pulled himself up onto his elbow. "You've never left the province? That's pathetic."

Rayan smirked. "We can't all be so cultured."

But Mathias was already leaning in, the soft graze of the man's lips on his and the thrum as he pushed their mouths apart putting a stop to the questions for now.

The thud of the apartment door woke Rayan. He turned to find the bed empty, Mathias's clothes gone from the floor where he'd tossed them. He rolled onto his back, exhaling loudly. *What did I expect—for him to make me breakfast?* Rayan glanced at the clock on the nightstand. It was just past eight. Mathias had slept over. He hadn't done that before. And he had... Rayan felt a warm shiver at the memory of Mathias between his legs.

He got out of bed and walked naked to the bathroom. As the shower ran, Rayan caught sight of the mark of his capo's teeth on his neck, now a faint red. He brushed it with his fingers, recalling the blackness in Mathias's eyes when he'd opened the door, crackling with the same fury he'd witnessed in the parking lot. Yet the man had surrendered beneath him, the anger fizzling, as if all he'd needed was Rayan to call a stop to it.

He stared at his reflection in the mirror, heart thudding. He'd seen something else in those eyes, barely perceptible, a glimpse into the depths that lurked beneath the icy exterior. *Was it more than just lust?* The thought brought with it a feeble flicker of hope, which Rayan caught quickly and stamped out. He should have known, right from the beginning, how deeply entangled he would become.

14

After the meeting with Russo, Mathias had gone silent, something he was proving surprisingly good at. When he and Rayan were working, there had been a routine, a certainty to their interactions. Without it, Mathias seemed to disappear, only to call out of the blue, as he had that morning, expecting Rayan to drop everything and play nice.

Not that he wasn't relieved to get out of the house. The idleness was making him restless. He hadn't realized how much he relied on work to function. Full days that rendered him unconscious by the end had morphed into long empty stretches of time, allowing the thoughts, never really gone, to resurface with a vengeance.

"How's the hand?" Rayan asked as the waitress placed two cups of coffee down on the table between them.

They were in a small café a few blocks from the office. Despite the jumble of mismatched furniture that crowded the dingy interior, the coffee was decent. When the two of them were sick of the cheap slop Tony served up, they came here.

"Fine," Mathias replied, tapping the side of his steaming mug with his knuckles.

They sat across from each other as customers bustled in and out of the store, drinking their coffee in silent avoidance—a tactic Rayan had become increasingly familiar with. If his capo wanted to tell him something, he would sit and wait.

Finally, Mathias sighed and stood up, the legs of his chair scraping against the floor. "Let's walk."

They left the café, passing Mathias's Mercedes, which was parked outside on the street. Crossing the road, they continued past the metro station before making a left and turning into Parc Jarry. It was late morning, and the park was empty aside from the occasional jogger who appeared on the path ahead. As they walked, Rayan realized what a rarity it was to be out in the city without being on a job. It was strange to see his capo integrated with the outside world.

Mathias lit a cigarette and exhaled into the crisp morning air. As if he'd simply needed the extra time to organize his thoughts, he then spoke. "I'm leaving for Hamilton at the end of the month."

The departure was sooner than expected. The radio silence made sense now. He'd been busy preparing.

"You'll stay here," Mathias continued, his eyes trained forward, not looking at him.

Rayan stopped walking. He'd heard his boss perfectly, but the words were having trouble registering in his brain. Seeing he had fallen behind, Mathias came to a stop.

He turned to face him, his expression unreadable. "Tony needs the help. You'll be assigned another capo."

"No," Rayan said, adamant. "If you're going, I'm coming with you."

Mathias's eyes narrowed. "I don't think you understand—"

"No, I don't," Rayan cut in, anger making him bold. "With everything going on, you need someone watching your back. That day, I hung back when I shouldn't have. Not this time."

"It's not up for discussion," Mathias said, his voice lowering dangerously. "Moretti's leaving his team there. I won't need you."

Strangely, his words didn't sting as much as the thought of staying here without him. Even though Rayan had spent most of his life in Montreal, the thought of leaving felt insignificant. He barely recognized the person who'd existed before the family took over. Without realizing it, somewhere along the way, Rayan had tied his future to Mathias. He'd never harbored thoughts of his own promotion, preferring instead to remain ancillary, watching the man's ascent with quiet pride. It pained Rayan to think of him treading water, attempting to find his footing alone in a new city.

Mathias took another pull from his cigarette and squinted into the sun. "Are we clear?"

Rayan wasn't sure which of the thoughts churning inside his head to address first. Mathias did not want a scene—he wanted a soldier. It was just another order, no different from the countless others that had come before. Rayan didn't fucking like it, but he would do it. That was what he was good at, after all: accepting whatever came his way, content to be a rock in a landslide, tossed about on a whim.

"We're clear," he replied, mirroring his boss's impenetrable reception.

Mathias paused as though trying to read him. "Good," he said finally, continuing along the path.

"Who's going to head Commercial?" Rayan asked when they were back in step.

Mathias's lips curled like he'd tasted something foul. He flicked the cigarette from his fingers and watched it bounce along the pavement. "Nothing's confirmed yet. Tony will find someone. Or take some of it on himself. The man doesn't trust easy."

Rayan frowned, silent.

Mathias was looking at him now. "What?"

"Who're you going to get to replace me?" It was a simple question, aimed at his boss's shoulder so Rayan didn't have to look him in the eye.

Mathias shrugged. "Someone local. Familiar with the city."

The way he spoke, as if swapping Rayan for another was simply a matter of logistics... interchangeable toy soldiers... The thought made his blood boil. "So that's it?" Rayan asked flatly.

He wanted more. He asked for so little, but this time, he deserved more than the party line. He wanted Mathias to acknowledge the reliance they'd built on one another, which had kept them alive in many a hairy situation. He owed Rayan that at least.

"Want me to say something indulgent?" Mathias taunted him. "If there's one thing I've learned from this..." He looked away, his handsome face darkening. "It's that everyone can be replaced. You, me—we're all fucking expendable."

Rayan's shoulders went slack. He felt the willpower that had kept him pliant and obedient drain out of him. "That all for today?"

Mathias gave him a sharp look.

"I'll take that as a yes," Rayan said curtly, turning and heading back the way they'd come.

"Where do you think you're going?" Mathias called out, the warning in his voice clear.

Rayan kept walking.

Mathias called later that evening, when Rayan was back at his apartment, stewing.

"Come for a drink."

He'd been expecting something more along the lines of a harshly worded dressing-down. Rayan was immediately suspicious. "Why?"

"Humor me," his capo said.

They met at a lounge bar on Saint Denis, Mathias ordering a scotch neat, Rayan a black coffee.

"You don't drink because you're religious or because your father's an alcoholic," the man observed.

Rayan stiffened at hearing a name for the drunken tumult he'd lived through as a child. "I never told you that."

"Educated guess."

Rayan stared at him. "I'm not religious."

The truth was, he didn't trust himself, convinced that given the opportunity, he'd disappear down the black hole, like his father and his brother. He'd inherited a set of faulty genes hardwired for addiction.

"How is it you know so much about me, and I know nothing about you?"

Mathias pulled out his cigarettes. "What do you want to know?"

"What's the catch?" Rayan shot back.

Mathias lit a smoke, leaned back in his chair. "Try me."

The questions reeled through his mind. *What were you like as a kid? What is this thing between us? Did you always know you were different?*

"Why did you join?" he asked finally, afraid that if he took too long, Mathias would revoke his offer.

"I had something to prove."

"To your father?"

Mathias blew smoke through his teeth. "My father worked for the family all his life. And he never moved beyond his station. Was never good enough for a title."

Their drinks arrived.

"He must have been proud. His son, a *santista*."

Mathias smiled, but his eyes hardened. "The man couldn't have cared less. In his infinite wisdom, he'd have preferred I do something else."

Rayan felt the hurt he refused to show, his own bitterness softening. "He said that?"

"As he lay dying."

They sat in silence, his capo swilling his drink.

"Do you regret it?" Mathias asked, lowering his voice. "Not walking away back then? Now you have blood on your hands."

There was a familiar clench in Rayan's gut, and for a moment, he couldn't keep his face from betraying how close the question landed.

"There it is—I remember that look," Mathias said, as though confirming his own suspicions. "You're not made for this life, Rayan. I don't know why you're so intent on getting in even deeper."

"Is that why you're leaving me here?"

Mathias said nothing, his eyes shuttering.

"And you're wrong," Rayan said coldly. "I chose this."

"Why?"

His mouth went dry, unable to speak the truth aloud—that after meeting Mathias again at the Collections office, his bearings had recalibrated, placing the man front and center.

"I never pretended to have options. I know how to survive," he said at last.

"When you're done surviving, what then?"

Rayan stopped short. It was as though Mathias had seen right through him. "Now that your father's dead, what's left to prove?"

Mathias stared at him. Rayan felt a sting of remorse, remembering how shaken Mathias had been as they left the hospital. Then his capo snickered.

"You asked why I joined, not why I stayed." Mathias threw back his drink, pulled out his wallet, and dropped several notes onto the table between them. He stood, buttoning his jacket. Then he looked at Rayan. "You coming?"

Mathias led him into the apartment without a word. Rayan walked past him to the living room, which had been restored to its former glory. The smashed cabinet was gone, the shelves removed, and the glass swept. Mathias stood in the hallway, watching him.

"Will you miss this place?" Rayan said.

Mathias shrugged. "It'll be here when I get back."

"So you are coming back?" he asked cautiously.

Mathias smirked. "Would you like that?"

"What does it matter?" Rayan glared. "You'll find a new second, I'll be assigned another capo, and this will all be a footnote."

"Maybe."

Rayan felt his anger flare, mixed with a heady desire. Being this close to Mathias, in his orbit, scrambled his frequencies. Mathias stepped forward, his hand sliding along Rayan's jaw and lifting his chin.

"Maybe not," he murmured.

Then the man's lips were on him, the smoky taste on his tongue. Rayan knew what he would miss. They stumbled through the hallway toward the bedroom, hands tangled in clothes, tearing at one another, unable to wait a moment longer. Mathias threw Rayan down on the bed, tugging off his shirt. Rayan sat up and rolled Mathias over so that he was beneath him. Mathias pulled his face down, kissing him roughly.

With his other hand, he thumbed open the button of Rayan's slacks, unzipping him. The pressure of Mathias's fingers working against his cock made Rayan lose focus, and his capo took the opportunity to flip him onto his back, yanking off his pants. Rayan wrenched at the buttons on Mathias's shirt as the man ground his hips between his legs, eliciting a deep groan.

Mathias lowered his mouth to Rayan's chest, captured a nipple in his teeth, then grazed his stomach with his lips. Everywhere he touched left a trail of seared skin. Rayan pulled Mathias's hardened cock from his pants and ran it through his fist, pressing the pad of his thumb into the slick head as the man gave a low growl. Mathias spat into his palm and reached for Rayan as he arched hard and wanting into his hand. His capo gripped their shafts together, bringing his wrist up and down. Rayan's breathing shallowed, the friction between them sending his arousal surging. When he couldn't bear it any longer, his hand shot out, stilling Mathias's movement.

Releasing him with a knowing smirk, Mathias leaned over to retrieve a clear bottle from the nightstand. Then he grabbed the back of Rayan's knees and lifted. Rayan's face flushed as he found himself so thoroughly exposed. Mathias teased the lubed head of his cock against his opening, and Rayan shivered, clenching his teeth, as Mathias entered him.

"Fuck..." he hissed, and Mathias pulled back. "No—" Rayan clutched at his thighs. "Don't stop..."

Mathias pushed him into the mattress, his strokes measured, deep. He lowered himself so they lay skin to skin, all distance between them gone, bodies fitting together as though they had never been apart. It was a closeness Rayan craved yet could barely stand, overpowering his carefully laid defenses. Incriminating words threatened to tumble from his tongue. He bit his lip, forcing his mouth shut.

The pace increased, and Rayan felt himself slipping, his vision narrowing as his body shuddered in time with each thrust. "Harder," he growled into his capo's shoulder, giving—no longer taking—orders.

Mathias raised himself up and slammed into Rayan, who rolled his head to the side with a groan, anything to avoid the man's eyes on him as he unraveled.

"I need you here," Mathias said, his voice tight with restraint. "I don't trust anyone else."

He reached down to grip Rayan's cock, sliding it through his hand. Rayan felt the swell of release. He sucked in air, gritting his teeth as it took him. Mathias's words scattered in different directions as his mind splintered.

Rayan woke to find himself pressed against Mathias's chest, the brush of the man's breath on his cheek. He lifted his head, knowing how rare the opportunity was to observe him this close, lips parted ever so slightly, face void of all expression. It was uncanny, the transformation he went through. One would never recognize the softened features that appeared on the sleeping man, dark hair splayed loosely across the pillow. It was hard to reconcile this Mathias with the severity of who he was when he was awake.

Mathias stirred and shifted toward Rayan, an arm sliding around his waist. Rayan froze, not wanting to wake him. Mathias settled once again, skin deliciously warm against his own. When he found himself this close to Mathias, he felt as though he'd been granted access to a part of him that few people saw. *Why does he do it, when he otherwise keeps me at arm's length?*

If Rayan could, he would wake every morning beside Mathias. The thought struck him hard in the chest. Immediately, he sought to erase it. He did well when he didn't want things. When he didn't want, he couldn't be disappointed, only pleasantly surprised by what he did get—like this morning with Mathias in this bed, a man he admired and respected, so clear about who he was that Rayan felt like a shadow in comparison. It was what he'd always found so compelling about his capo—how sure he was about what he wanted.

Rayan stared at the lock of hair that had fallen across Mathias's forehead. In the darkness of the room, with the man asleep, he reached over and brushed it back with his fingers.

15

"I need to piss."

Mathias couldn't fault the man. It was a six-hour drive from Montreal, and they'd been sitting in the car, waiting for Marco Moretti to show, for almost an hour.

"Go on."

Rayan pulled up the collar of his winter coat and yanked open the door. He disappeared into the snowy street. Mathias peered back at the run-down office block and rapped his fingers against the wheel in frustration. Not for the first time that day, he felt his stomach thunder in protest. All he'd had since waking were two cups of coffee. That was usually enough to get him through until lunch, but it was now well past noon, and the hunger was making him irritable.

Moretti had offered to meet in Hamilton to walk him through the current setup and make some introductions. The city was a dump, filled with layer upon layer of opportunistic scum and home to many a small-town drug lord. The family maintained a presence here in the hopes of regaining access to former narcotics channels along Lake Ontario—that and because of its proximity to Toronto, the country's financial center.

Unlike Montreal, where the family reigned unchallenged, in Hamilton, their influence was slippery at best. The Red Reapers, a self-proclaimed outlaw motorcycle club led by chest-thumping fascist William Truman, occupied most of the territory worth having. During his tenure here, Moretti had barely managed to hold a seat at the table. The former regional head had taken a questionable approach to maintaining amicable relations with the city's various criminal factions. From what Mathias had heard, Moretti had been far too generous with his cuts, to the point where local thugs were earning more than the family itself.

While Mathias wasn't due to make the move for another two weeks, he figured the more he knew going in, the better. He'd planned on making the trip alone but hadn't completely shaken the feeling that Piero had eyes on him. So Mathias had brought Rayan. The man was still his until the end of the month—not that he'd bothered to let Tony know. Even though the decision had been made, Mathias found himself putting off making it official.

Driving across Burlington Bay, he'd watched his second stare out the window as the city came into focus, dusky eyes reflected in the glass. It was Rayan's first time in Hamilton, the farthest he'd been outside Montreal city limits. Mathias hoped he wasn't expecting much. Both of them had said little on the ride over. He knew Rayan was still sore about being left behind.

That night at his apartment, Mathias had returned from the bathroom to find Rayan asleep. No one slept in his bed but him. He was protective of his home, a final barrier against the world outside. Mathias had waited for the spike of irritation, but nothing came. Unable to think of a good enough reason to wake him, he'd simply climbed in beside him. For someone who asked for so little, Rayan had made a bold claim—unconsciously or not.

Mathias hadn't told his second the whole truth. The situation in Montreal was evolving quickly, and he needed someone on the ground. Someone he trusted with his life. Or so he'd convinced himself. In all honesty, it was the man's name on that slip of paper that had forced the decision. Rayan Nadeau was no one to Piero Russo unless he was connected to Mathias. Bringing him here would only succeed in keeping him a target.

The passenger door opened, and a rich, greasy smell entered the car. Rayan pushed a hot wrapper into his hands. Mathias peeled back the paper to reveal thick slabs of ham and cheese stuffed into a warm croissant. Rayan was already taking a bite out of his. He looked over at Mathias, chewing absently.

"Deli," he said when he swallowed. "Saw one around the corner."

Mathias took a bite, making sure not to let Rayan see how good he found it. He gave a grunt of approval and turned back to watching the building. By the time Moretti showed—over an hour late—Mathias was livid. The man's black Beamer pulled up outside the crumbling building, and he emerged from the passenger side as Mathias and Rayan got out and crossed the road to join him.

"You've got your work cut out for you," Tony had told him shortly after the humiliating meeting with the boss. Mathias didn't want to give him the satisfaction of knowing he was right, but over the last few days, the gnawing anger had turned into fuel, a plan forming to recapture what had been lost. He recalled Belkov's offer. The Russian head had contacts in the city. Mathias would have to start back at square one.

The family's Hamilton office resided in a squat multistory concrete-block building sandwiched between two public-housing towers. From close-up, it was clear things were in a state of disrepair—graffiti sprayed across the walls, wooden boards covering the windows. Stepping around a series of stagnant brown puddles, Mathias walked up to Moretti. The man stretched out his hand, and Mathias took it, finding it slippery with perspiration.

"Welcome to Hamilton," Moretti announced with a grin that revealed his yellowing teeth.

Mathias fought the urge to wipe his palm against the side of his slacks.

"I've brought Cesare with me. He manages the office."

An older man with small dark eyes sidled up beside Moretti, mouth pulled into a scowl. He didn't offer his hand. Cesare was well below his station yet failed to show the proper respect. Mathias was starting to get a feel for the place. It wasn't just the local drug lords he needed to be wary of.

He gestured toward his second. "This is Rayan."

Fortunately, Moretti spared him a hand-drenching shake, instead clapping him firmly on the shoulder. "Let's talk inside," the departing regional head said.

Moretti scaled the front steps and walked up to the building's entrance, fumbling in his pocket for the keys. Mathias felt sorry for whomever would be saddled with this man on his return to Montreal. How a guy like Moretti got to head a regional office was a mystery.

Except, Mathias thought, jaw tightening, *aren't I here, too, accepting my consolation prize?* Perhaps that was how the family managed to keep people in Hamilton—by showering them with undeserved promotions.

His vision tunneled, the realization fixing him in place. That was what this was. The title hung around his neck like a noose. The whole position had been tarnished from its very inception. No doubt, the elite in Montreal were laughing behind his back, just as he had looked down on Moretti. To think he'd worked hard to move up every rung, one step at a time, and now he'd made it to *vangelista* but at the cost of the reputation he'd fought so hard to preserve.

Rayan appeared at his side. "Boss?" he asked quietly.

Mathias nodded, gesturing for Moretti to go first. He couldn't bear to look at the pathetic man's face any longer. They entered the lobby of the building and headed to the stairwell. The place was a mess—peeling wallpaper, scuffed floors. He gripped the banister hard in an effort to steady himself. As Rayan walked by him on the stairs, he caught Mathias's eye, an unspoken exchange passing between them.

The plate outside the door declared it Hamilton Central Contracting. Inside was a disheveled room that smelled of old cigarette smoke. Shelves lined the wall, buckling under the weight of stacks of paper, unmarked folders, and bits of junk. There was a single desk in the far corner, with the rest of the office set up as some sort of recreational space. Chairs were spread out haphazardly, empty beer bottles stacked beside them. Poker chips and playing cards covered a large crate that doubled as a table.

"How many men do you have working here?" Mathias asked, his eyes crawling around the room, discovering one small horror after the next.

Moretti shrugged, shoving his hands in his pockets. "Not sure. There's some coming and going. We've been down the past couple months. Three, four? Cesare?"

Four men running a territory of this size? No wonder they're barely breaking even.

Cesare gave a grunt. "Something like that."

Mathias frowned. The man ran the office but had no idea who worked there. "Where are you recruiting?"

"Most kids who make money like this have a bad reason for spending it."

"You hire dopeheads, and you're surprised they're unreliable?"

Cesare glowered at him, but Mathias refused to look away.

Moretti laughed. "Things are a little different here. You'll learn."

Mathias bristled at the condescension. "I'd like to meet with Truman. When can you make the introduction?"

"Will Truman?" Moretti asked, shaking his head. "I'd stay away from him."

Mathias raised an eyebrow, incredulous. "The Reapers hold the port here. They determine what comes in and out of the city. Why would I avoid him?"

Moretti shrugged. "Our business is on the strip. Porn shops, shake joints, the odd payday lender. The family doesn't deal with the Reapers. They're scum."

"And how much of our business kicks back to Truman? I've seen the books. He's gouging us."

Moretti laughed again. He seemed to think a lot was funny. "Look, Beauvais, this isn't Montreal. We don't run this town. So we play by the rules. Pick up our bit on the side and call it a day."

"The Hamilton division hasn't run a profit in almost two years. Either he's fucking us over, or whatever's brought in is lining someone else's pockets."

The air in the room shifted. The grin was gone from Moretti's face. "What are you implying?"

Mathias had his suspicions. Maybe the reason the region hadn't been profitable wasn't just due to Moretti's blind incompetence. He shrugged. "You tell me."

Moretti's eyes darkened. "They said you were an upstart. You should know by now who's who in this family. Mind your respect."

The earlier swirl of self-doubt dissipated, a single-minded clarity surfacing. "I don't give a fuck who you are," Mathias said stonily.

He was done bowing to the whims of family elite in positions they didn't deserve to hold. Moretti had gotten comfortable doing nothing because his standing meant no one was looking too closely—exactly the kind of man Piero was hoping to preserve in his unspoiled version of Giorgio Russo's organization.

That's how you stagnate. And then someone else moves in.

His lips pulled into a smile. Here he was, the bastard brat of a low-level bookie, having risen to one of the family's highest ranks. He would not rot here like his predecessor. He had a reputation to uphold. Mathias was going to turn this city on its head. He would counter Piero's plan to purge the family of its lack of tradition by building the most unconventional opposition the man could imagine.

"Who were you going to introduce me to?" Mathias sneered. "The pimps on the strip? Your black-rock dealer? I'll save myself the embarrassment."

Moretti's mouth fell open. "The fuck do you think—"

"I appreciate the tour. I'll take the keys. You can go."

The former regional head exchanged a look with Cesare. Mathias knew he was overstepping, but as of last week, he outranked the man. This was his region now. What might have seemed a grievous mistake felt, instead, like the first sliver of control he'd reclaimed since Junior had pressed a gun to his head.

Moretti gave a short bark of a laugh, less amused this time, more sinister. "You're welcome to it. And go see Truman. If we're lucky, you'll end up at the bottom of the lake before month's end."

He tossed the keys over his shoulder as he and Cesare left. They fell with a dull clunk on the filthy wooden floor. Mathias stood, listening to the thump of their footsteps on the stairs and the slam of the building door. A few moments later, tires squealed as they pulled out onto the street.

Beside him, Rayan nudged an empty bottle with the toe of his shoe. It rolled across the floor with a hollow clink. He stepped forward to pick up the keys.

"What next?" Rayan asked into the quiet of the room, handing him the keys.

Mathias almost laughed. He'd gone and obliterated whatever association he had with the departing regional head, and his second remained unfazed, waiting on his next instruction.

Mathias looked around the office, absently crunching the metal in his palm. "I'm going to torch the fucking place."

16

"Jesus." Mathias stepped into Tony's office and shut the door behind him. "What's wrong with you?"

It was clear the past few weeks had done a number on Tony. His eyes were dull and bloodshot, his skin pallid from lack of sleep.

"What's wrong with me? This whole fucking place has imploded. Handing you Commercial was supposed to take a load off. Now I'm down two men—the two who happened to do most of the goddamn work around here."

"Finally figured that out," Mathias said, taking a seat. "Too bad it never reflected in my cut."

"Haven't missed the back talk," Tony snapped. "We've got contracts coming out our ears and no one to collect. Soon, everyone'll be shitting on us, thinking they can take our money and run."

"You'll manage," Mathias said, pulling out his cigarettes and offering them to Tony. The older man took one and let Mathias light it for him.

"You seem perky. When are you leaving again?" Tony asked with a sneer.

Payback. Mathias scowled. "Seems everyone's in a hurry to get me out."

Even though he'd officially been out of commission for the last couple of weeks, Mathias still wore his suit, pressed and all. That was one thing that remained unchanged—no matter how difficult things got, he would not let anyone see him ruffled. He blamed his mother for that. There was strength in vanity.

Tony waved his hand, smoke curling through the air. "I'm talking logistics. When are you out of the city?"

"End of the week," Mathias replied shortly. "They've already pulled Moretti. It's a fucking mess."

"Hey." Tony grinned. "Now it's your fucking mess."

Mathias sucked on his cigarette, unamused. "Who have you got replacing me?" he asked, deciding it was time to address the elephant in the room.

116

Tony snorted. "You wouldn't believe who was gunning for the job."

Mathias flinched even before Tony spoke the name. "Motherfucker," he growled, his jaw tightening.

Tony eyed him warily. "I put a pin in that real quick. Piero couldn't make a dime if he rubbed two nickels together. I'm not letting him near my division."

"Saved by incompetence," Mathias muttered bitterly.

"Is the kid looking forward to the big move?"

"What?"

"Nadeau," Tony drawled. "Kid like that probably never been out of the city."

Mathias exhaled a stream of smoke from the corner of his mouth. "I'm not taking him with me."

Tony's eyebrows shot up. "You of all people should know how hard it is to find good help. You're gonna go through the trouble of training another monkey?"

"I need him here. I need both of you to have your ears open." Mathias thought of the list. Tony's name. He decided against mentioning it. "Piero's gone quiet now, but it's only a matter of time. As soon as succession is on the table, he'll strike."

"If he tries anything—"

"He already has," Mathias said, tapping his ash. "And look what happened. You hear anything, I want to hear it."

His boss nodded slowly. They sat, smoking in silence. Tony was thinking in black and white. Loyalty and treason. When the lines were drawn through the family, alliances would not be so clear.

"Can't say I'm not pleased Nadeau is staying. I need the manpower. And the offer still stands—I think he's up to running his own team."

"No," Mathias said, surprised at his own vehemence. "Nothing too visible. You make him a captain, there'll be talk. We don't need the attention. Assign him to one of the old hands, and get him to do the heavy lifting."

"Don't know how happy the kid's gonna be when he finds out you got him demoted."

Mathias waved him off. "He's a fucking grunt. He'll do as he's told."

"I'd watch it, Mathias," Tony warned, wagging a finger. "You jerk him around too much, and he ain't gonna stay loyal for long."

Mathias tapped his left hand agitatedly against the desk. The old man didn't know shit.

"By the way, one of Belkov's men dropped this off earlier," Tony said, hauling a plastic bag of cash onto his desk. "Enough to cover the month up until now. Wonder who twisted his arm." He glowered at him.

Mathias shrugged. "Maybe he was feeling generous."

Tony thumbed the butt of his cigarette. "I told you not to see him."

"Fuck, Tony. You've got your money, so stop bitching."

"You wait and see how you get on managing your own territory," the Collections head scoffed. "Though the bar is set pretty low. If you were to somehow make money instead of losing it, you'd be doing well. Better than Moretti, at least."

"On that," Mathias began, treading cautiously. "How do I get the Reapers clearance for one shipment a month?"

"What? Into Montreal?"

He nodded.

Tony laughed, shaking his head. "*No bueno.* They're in direct competition with Narcotics."

"They're here already—got their own supply line. Only they're bringing it overland."

"You give them port access, and they'll bring in three times as much and flood the market."

"On our terms," Mathias said. "We skim a cut for every kilo. I know our supply can be patchy, especially when the Feds south of the border get jumpy. We'd ride this during the lulls, still make money, and lower our risk at the same time."

Tony squinted in suspicion. "What are you up to, Mathias?"

"There's money to be made in Hamilton—more than you think." After dismissing Moretti, Mathias had gone on his own tour of the city, familiarizing himself with the lay of the land. "The port might as well be unregulated—offers short sea shipping between the two cities. We can push product into Ontario, widen our scope. But Truman holds all the keys. And we have no clout out there. I need something to bargain with."

"Well, fuck me," Tony said with a smirk. "Why am I surprised you're not sitting back and cooling your heels? Let me talk to De Luca. You grease the wheels with Giovanni. We'll need council buy-in."

Mathias hid a smile. Family politics be damned. Just a whiff of cold hard cash was enough to get Tony off his ass.

It was almost ten on a Sunday morning, and Rayan found himself still in bed. All the downtime was messing with his regular routine. Mathias had left for Hamilton two days earlier after instructing him to go and see Tony at the office on Monday.

He lay under the duvet, the room cold enough to discourage a trip to the kitchen for food. There was the faint stirring of an erection he could coax to life if given the necessary attention. On the bedside table, his phone began to buzz. Rayan reached out and pulled it to his ear.

"I need you to do something."

No longer just a stirring. Mathias's voice—flat, authoritative—had the effect of sending all the blood rushing between Rayan's legs.

"There's a safe in the wardrobe at the apartment," Mathias continued.

Rayan knew the one.

"Code is eighteen, fifty-six, thirty-two, oh seven."

He repeated the numbers, committing them to memory.

"Right. Take out a couple grand, two—no, three—grand. Put it in an envelope. Drop it off at 2087 Saint Urbain." There was a rush of static. It sounded like he was driving. "She hates the envelopes," Mathias muttered, his frustration evident. "Put it in with something else—a bag of fruit or a fucking baguette."

Rayan raised an eyebrow. "Okay."

There was a pause, longer than expected. "I didn't stop by before leaving," Mathias said finally. "Just check in, make sure everything's all right."

Before Rayan could ask who he was checking on, Mathias hung up. Rayan glanced at the blackened screen and tossed the phone onto the bed. He reached beneath the covers, first needing to resolve a more pressing matter.

When Rayan showed up at 2087 Saint Urbain later that afternoon, an older woman opened the door. As he met her pale-blue eyes, it was clear she was Mathias's mother. The man had her nose and the same strong chin. Rayan realized he was staring and handed her the paper bag of apples, not sure whether he should offer an explanation. In the bag, he'd stowed the envelope of cash taken from the fortune Mathias had locked away in his safe. While the stack of money didn't have an effect on Rayan, Mathias's trust in him did. The safe held not only cash but also bond certificates, several foreign passports, identity cards, and title documents. And Mathias had given him the code as flippantly as he would his lunch order. It was pathetic how good that made Rayan feel.

As it turned out, no explanation was needed. Mathias's mother, with what he could only imagine to be a perfect Parisian accent, invited him in for coffee.

"He said to expect someone," she said, busying herself in the kitchen, her long silk dress swaying as she moved.

She wore lipstick and pearl studs. Her hair was arranged deliberately. She looked like she should be holding court rather than making coffee. He watched as she took the envelope from the bag and slipped it into a pile of unopened mail on the counter.

"But I didn't expect…" She paused, turning to him. "You don't look like the rest of them. What's your name?"

"Rayan Nadeau."

"Pleasure to meet you, Mr. Nadeau. I'm Marguerite." She opened the refrigerator door and peered inside. "Do you take milk?"

"No, thank you."

"Where are you from?"

"Maskinongé."

She laughed then. "But you're not Quebecois!"

He smiled, not correcting her.

She filled a kettle with water at the sink. "Did you know he's left the city?"

Rayan nodded.

She exhaled sharply, snapping the lid shut. "I suppose everyone knew but me. All I can hope is that one day, his children will be equally ungrateful."

Rayan could only imagine the woman's disappointment when that particular reparation did not come to pass.

Marguerite set out a plate of lavish pastries that neither of them touched as they drank their coffee at the kitchen table. He had little experience with these kinds of interactions—Rayan had been a child the last time he'd spoken to either of his parents. For the most part, he did what he was good at and stayed silent while she talked about her past, where she'd lived in Paris, and nameless people in a social circle he didn't care to know. Her stories were embellished to the point of implausibility. And then, out of nowhere, she would say something about Mathias.

"I was too needy when he was young. I'd forget about him for days then be distraught all of a sudden if he left my side." She laughed. "I think he preferred being alone—he was always so independent. And just look how successful he's become."

Rayan knew all about that kind of self-reliance born of necessity. He imagined a young Mathias trapped in a house with this fragile woman who talked to fill the silence, her desperation clinging to the air around him.

"Mothers are so hard on themselves, aren't they?" she said with a reserved smile. "What does yours say about you?"

"She's dead." Rayan took a sip of his coffee.

"Oh." Marguerite fiddled with the chain of her necklace. "Was she sick?"

She was lost.

"Yes," he lied.

Mathias's mother frowned, rearranging her cup on the saucer. "Do you know if he went to the funeral?" she asked, her eyes suddenly misty. "For his father?"

Rayan was ashamed to realize he didn't know. He remembered the interaction with the woman at the hospital, how Mathias had denied ties to his father. He couldn't imagine he'd gone after that.

Rayan shook his head, and she gave a sigh, flicking a delicate wrist laden with silver. "They wouldn't let me go, of course. I thought maybe he might." She lifted her napkin and dabbed lightly at the corners of her eyes. "You know, when he was a boy, he wanted to be just like his father."

Rayan gripped his cup, a tightness in his throat, remembering Mathias's words: "The man couldn't have cared less. He'd have preferred I do something else." He wondered if she knew how deep that wish had buried itself and the way it had twisted around her son, shaping him.

When Rayan stood to leave, Marguerite packed everything up—the untouched pastries, the apples—and sent them home with him. By the front door, his gaze fell on a small framed photo sitting on the entry table, the only one he'd seen in the sprawling apartment. Mathias, no older than ten, was unsmiling in a shirt and tie, a school logo emblazoned on his breast pocket. He looked straight at the camera, his features boyish but his eyes cold. Rayan felt a pang, struck by an overwhelming urge to take the picture. Instead, he thanked Marguerite for the coffee and let himself out.

He drove home. Rayan handed the bag of food and a fistful of notes to the man who lived in the alleyway beside his building. Once in his apartment, he changed out of his suit, threw on his sneakers, and headed back out onto the street, not sure where he was going. He zipped his coat up to his chin and disappeared into the crowd.

17

When Rayan reported to Tony on his first day back at Collections, he was surprised to find him sitting in his office, grinning from ear to ear.

"Should I come back another time?" he asked.

"When did you get so mouthy?" Tony scowled. "Sit down, and shut it."

Rayan sat in the chair facing Tony's desk while the old man tossed back what was unlikely to be his first coffee of the morning.

"All right," he said, fixing Rayan with a beady stare. "I have a shitload of work and no one to do it. Mathias has assured me you're not a complete moron."

It was his usual derisive banter, and for once, Rayan appreciated it. At least with Tony, you always knew how little he expected of you.

"You're starting right at the bottom. I don't care what you're used to—it's down in the muck this time around. I need to get through this backlog. Turf fees, defaults, personal guarantees—you're on them all."

Rayan shifted in his seat, concealing a growing annoyance. With Mathias gone, he'd expected something of a demotion, but to be kicked this far down...

Tony stopped him before he could open his mouth. "One month. You do every job I assign you—no matter how dicey—for one month, no questions asked, and you're back on Commercial."

Now the man was getting somewhere.

"I'm bringing Lorenzo Gallo in to take over for Beauvais," Tony continued. "You'll be working under him."

Rayan frowned. Lorenzo was one of the old guard. He'd been in Collections since before Mathias's time. He wasn't exactly a spring chicken. If Rayan remembered correctly, he had retired shortly after he'd joined.

"Don't give me that look. Lorenzo's on the slow side, not used to working white collar, so you're gonna be the brains behind the outfit. Show him how it's done. Let him make a couple calls, but answer directly to me."

"A capo in all but name," Rayan scoffed.

"Optics." Tony shrugged. "Blame your old boss for that. He didn't want you getting too much attention."

Rayan blinked. He knew then why Mathias had left him here. It wasn't because he didn't need him in Hamilton. He was severing their association to throw Piero off the scent. Back in Collections, down at the bottom of the heap, he would once again be invisible. He felt an unfamiliar tug in his chest. Mathias, in his strange way, was protecting him.

"I expect the pay to reflect my responsibilities," Rayan said.

It was ballsy, but he knew Tony would keep him on a second's wages if he could. From the beginning, Mathias had given Rayan his earnings in thick brown envelopes. It was only when he'd overheard Mikey complaining about how little Franco passed on that Rayan realized his capo was padding his cut, doubling what someone in his position earned. It was one thing no one could fault Mathias on— he shared his money. He was scrupulous about earning it, but after that, it was as if all enjoyment was gone.

Tony's face began to redden. "I'll give you fucking responsibilities. I've a good mind to throw you back to Guillet. See how much you'd make running again."

"Then who would you get to do all this work?" Rayan countered, silencing him.

Tony sucked his teeth. "One month, you get bare minimum, lackey's pay. Think of it as probation. You prove to me what you're worth, and then we'll talk." He wagged a finger in warning. "But I see anything I don't like, any little fuckup, and you're down in the dirt for the rest of your career. Got that, kid?"

"Got it." Rayan didn't care about the money. He barely knew what to do with what he already had. But in the family, money was the language of respect, and he wanted it to be clear, from the outset, that was what he expected.

"Good," Tony said, the unnerving grin sliding back onto his face. He leaned over and picked up a pile of contracts at least an inch thick then dropped it on the desk in front of Rayan. "I want these done, cash in hand, by the end of the week."

Rayan's jaw clenched. A stack like that was at least two weeks of work. He flicked through the pages and saw that several were months in arrears. Every job assigned, no questions—Tony was every bit the old bastard he remembered. Rayan thought of how easily he'd been stitched up in one of the crooked deals the Collections boss pushed on their unsuspecting clients.

"Better get busy," Tony snapped.

Rayan stood, picking up the stack of jobs. He knew better than to argue with him. If anything, Tony got more vindictive when he detected defiance. Rayan moved toward the door without another word.

"Nadeau," Tony called out, and the next thing he heard was the jingle of metal hurtling toward his face.

Rayan snapped his hand up and caught the offending object a second before impact. Tony crowed with laughter.

"He said you were quick. Take this—it's yours now. A parting gift from your old boss. Might help get your work done faster."

Rayan looked down at the keys to Mathias's Mercedes in his palm.

Despite the frigid temperatures, the raceway was packed with punters on a Sunday afternoon. The snow had been ploughed neatly to each side of the oval track. If Friday's paycheck hadn't already disappeared along Hess Street or at some of the more questionable establishments downtown, it came here to die.

The family once had a private box at the old Blue Bonnets racetrack in Montreal. Mathias had been there a few times before it closed—the owners had declared bankruptcy after the city refused to bail them out, something Russo maintained he had nothing to do with. The displaced racing crowd funneling into family-owned betting houses was just a happy coincidence. The boss often found himself the beneficiary of happy coincidences.

Glenwood Downs, home to the country's fastest half-mile harness course, was a short drive from Hamilton, sitting on a couple hundred acres of land. Which might have been impressive if Mathias gave a fuck about horse racing. But this was where Giovanni had come to meet him, making a brief detour while in Toronto on family business.

He spotted the councilman in the stands, a tip of his gray fedora signaling that Mathias had also been seen. He made his way through the crowd, scaling several rows of stairs before taking a seat on the bench behind him. This high, the track stretched out before them. Mathias could see the drivers in their sulkies wrangling the horses into position behind the motorized starting gate.

"This is where you want to watch the action, not some glass box with overpriced canapés," Giovanni said, barely audible over the general chatter in the stands. Mathias knew now why he picked the place, and it had nothing to do with the view.

The old man turned his head, catching his eye. "You handled it well. Russo's not a fan of drama. Your composure was appreciated."

Mathias snorted, preferring not to dwell on his public humiliation, however composed it might have appeared.

"If I recall, your father managed some of our race betting in the off-track houses."

"Good for him."

Giovanni's eyes narrowed. "Don't forget where you come from, Mathias."

"Where I come from is a fucking rope around my neck," he muttered.

"Maybe." Giovanni paused. "It's also your meal ticket. Whatever the man was as a father, he came from the old blood. And he's given half to you. It will come in handy—you'll see." The councilman took off his hat and placed it on the seat beside him. "You a gambling man, Mathias?"

"You know I'm not."

"Working Collections, no doubt you've seen the worst of it. I dabble here and there but prefer to rely more on smarts, strategy." He folded his arms, peering at the spectacle before them. "If what you're saying is true, about what Piero's got planned, we're talking open rebellion, a division within the family. We've got ourselves a problem—not enough smarts or strategy going to get us through what comes next. So we nongambling men got to do a little gambling."

Mathias looked past him to the track, where the horses broke into a trot as the pickup towing the mobile barrier led them toward the starting line.

"But you figured that out already, didn't you? De Luca says Tony's been in touch about granting the Reapers port access." Giovanni raised his eyebrows. "Now, that's a big gamble."

"You said it yourself—we need allies," Mathias said. "I'm not picky. And I need the leverage."

"Truman is a loaded gun."

"So is Piero. But Truman hasn't tried to kill me yet."

The pickup accelerated, the wings of the motorized gate folding up as the vehicle moved aside to let the horses and their drivers take off down the track.

"Russo built this business by putting his faith in competence," Mathias continued. "What do you think will happen when Piero clears out those standing in his way? The family will be reduced to a bunch of spectators—men who've forgotten how to work, who run divisions like their own personal slush fund. Everything we've built will be ripe for the taking. Try to keep the Reapers away then, the Russians, the Batos. Montreal will be carved to pieces."

"So you figure, hand them the keys before the castle falls?" Giovanni asked sarcastically.

"Who's talking keys?" Mathias said, his voice hard. "It's a combination. One Truman is too fucking stupid to crack." He watched as a driver in red silks steered his horse toward the front of the pack.

"What makes you think he won't stand back and watch us kill each other?" the councilman asked.

Mathias smirked. "Finesse. Or lack thereof. Montreal has been ours for decades. We have a hand in every pocket of society—judges, politicians, customs, law enforcement. Even if the Reapers took the city, they wouldn't know what to do with it. The powers that be don't want to deal with them. They're sitting on a fortune of untapped product they can't shift through the Hamilton port. Strangled by red tape."

"And that's where you come in."

"If we're going to lose territory, we might as well do it on our terms. And get them to pay for it with their backing."

"You're willing to trust them?" Giovanni asked.

"It's not about trust. It's about what they stand to gain. If it's big enough, they'll do what it takes to cash in. Our numbers in Quebec are enough to crush the Reapers if they revolt—less so if we're divided. But if it comes to that, their numbers would give us a significant advantage."

Giovanni began to laugh. "He underestimated you."

"No," Mathias said grimly. "I'd say he sized me up pretty good when he sent Junior to clip me. But he underestimated what I'd do when that didn't work out."

They listened as the race was called. The winning horses flashing across the giant screen above the track. There was a collection of groans and cheers from the crowd—winners and losers alike.

"It's all well and good in theory, provided I can get Truman to cooperate," Mathias continued.

"Hence the leverage?"

Mathias nodded.

Giovanni rapped his leather-gloved knuckles against the bench beneath him, thinking it over. "I'll green-light the access. But I don't know whether you'll get any traction with the Reapers. Truman doesn't like the family."

"So I've been told."

"Arrangements are being made for when the time comes. There's a place for you in the future of the family, Mathias. Perhaps higher than you expect." The councilman gave him a knowing look. "But honor your blood. When the dust settles, there may be greater tolerance for difference, provided that difference looks the same." Giovanni reached into his pocket and pulled out a small square of paper. He held it up, checking the numbers against the names on the screen. "Would you look at that?" he said, retrieving his hat and standing. "I've picked a winner."

Mathias watched as Giovanni made his way slowly down the stands and disappeared behind the betting kiosks, where a line was already forming, a few queuing to collect their winnings, the majority hoping for another chance to offset their losses and win it all back.

18

"Take those new wheels of yours for a spin," Tony said, dropping a sealed white envelope on the desk in front of him. "I need to get this to your boss."

It was late Friday afternoon, and Rayan had been moments from leaving the office. "He's not my boss."

"Tell him that. Seems to think you're at his beck and call."

He wasn't wrong. Rayan scowled. "What is it?"

"Some good news from De Luca. It'll cheer him up."

So Mathias had pulled a favor with the Narcotics head. Rayan wanted to press further but could tell Tony was being purposely evasive. And knowing the old man, there was something in it for him as well.

Rayan slid the envelope off the desk and tucked it under his arm.

"Tell him this had better work," Tony said. "And that he owes me. But he knows that already."

Rayan wondered what the two of them were planning. In the chaos of the move, he'd heard little from Mathias. He'd figured Mathias was still grappling with starting over in a new city, but now he knew better. When had his former capo taken anything lying down?

As Rayan left the office, he glanced at the clock on the wall. If traffic was decent, he could make it to Hamilton before midnight.

Rayan pulled the car into a spot on the darkened street. Directly opposite stood a high-rise boasting fifteen floors of luxury condos. It was newly built, with a sheer glass facade looking out toward the harbor. He'd been here once before, on his first visit to Hamilton. Mathias had come to view one of the top-floor suites and had paid the deposit in cash.

Rayan hadn't called ahead, not sure what he would do if the man wasn't home. He punched in the number on the buzzer and waited as the intercom rang, his breath coming out white in the cool evening air. After a series of rings, there was a click then a loud beep as the door to the lobby unlocked. He rode the elevator to the fifteenth floor, where he waited for approval before the doors opened and he was released into a lavish entranceway.

"This is a surprise." Mathias stood in the doorway to the apartment, sounding neither pleased nor annoyed. He was in a stripped-down version of his everyday uniform, the top button of his shirt undone, the sleeves rolled up. He looked tired.

Rayan followed him inside, and Mathias returned to the dining table, which was strewn with sectional maps and lists of what appeared to be names and figures. He dropped the envelope from Tony at the end of the table as Mathias picked up his smoking cigarette from the ashtray by his elbow.

"That'd better be what I think it is."

"Tony said it was from De Luca. And that you owe him."

Mathias glanced up, studying him for the briefest of moments before returning to the map in his hand. "You his errand boy now?"

Rayan shrugged. "I'm back on probation. I do what I'm told."

"Nothing new, then."

"Still no second?" he countered.

Rayan had spoken briefly to Mathias the previous week when he'd called to clarify the terms of an old contract. Apparently, Cesare was long gone, and Mathias had dispatched the man assigned as his second after just a day on the job.

The frown on Mathias's face deepened. "I'm working on it."

"Let me come out here for a few weeks, until you find someone."

"No."

Rayan quelled a rising frustration. The thought of Mathias operating on his own in an unfamiliar city made his stomach turn. "You can't keep working like this. It's dangerous."

"Your concern is touching," Mathias muttered, not looking up.

Rayan knew that when he got like this, there was no moving him. It was a bad time, and he was proving an unwelcome distraction. "I'll be going, then."

"Don't be an idiot." Mathias was staring at him, stabbing out his cigarette. "Come here."

Rayan hesitated, meeting his gaze, the wall of restraint they both kept up—the coldness—slipping so quickly. He walked toward him. Mathias reached out and pulled him close. He smelled the same. He tasted the same.

Mathias pushed Rayan against the table, deepening the kiss. Rayan felt his mind slow, his skin flushing with warmth. The want coursed through him as a hand reached for his zipper.

Rayan awoke in a strange room. Most of Mathias's possessions were still in boxes. He wondered if the man's reluctance to move in was part of his resistance to the position, as if unpacking meant an acceptance of his new reality. Mathias was doing what he did best: bending the world to his will. But something was off. Rayan had seen glimpses of self-doubt when Mathias thought he wasn't watching. And there was something else—a quiet fury simmering constantly below the surface. Mathias had been slighted, exiled to clean up some higher-up's mess—cheated of his rightful place in Montreal.

Rayan rolled over to find the bed empty and the sheets crumpled. He dressed and made his way to the kitchen, where he flicked on the coffee machine. From the alcove window, he could see into the living room. Mathias was prone on the couch, one arm dangling off the side, touching the rug, where an empty glass lay overturned.

He wondered how late the man had gone to sleep, noticing the open envelope on the coffee table, its contents scattered. The machine clicked over and began to fill. Maybe it was the smell of coffee or the light slipping in through the open blinds, but Mathias began to stir. He raised a hand to his face and groaned.

Rayan took two mugs from the cabinet and waited as the last few drops of coffee splashed into the pot.

"What time is it?" Mathias asked, kneading his eyes with his fingers.

Rayan glanced at the stove. "Almost ten."

"Fuck," Mathias muttered, pulling himself up and gripping his head. He winced.

He was dressed in a plain white shirt and sweats. He must have come out here once Rayan had fallen asleep. After pouring coffee into both mugs, Rayan picked one up and walked over to the couch, grabbing the pack of cigarettes from the dining table as he passed. He set everything down on the coffee table.

Mathias glanced up, eyes still groggy. Mathias late at night and first thing in the morning had chinks in his armor. Rayan found himself compelled by those small snatches of the man beneath. He leaned in and kissed him. Mathias moved a hand to Rayan's neck, his kisses languid, as though still half asleep. The coffee abandoned, Rayan knelt. He took Mathias out of his pants and into his mouth, his own cock stiffening as he looked up and saw the desire in Mathias's half-lidded eyes, the tiredness and frustration momentarily erased. He couldn't do much about the man's current situation, but he sure as hell could do this.

Still wet from the shower, Mathias hung up his phone, swallowing a string of curses. He turned to Rayan, who was buttoning his shirt in the bedroom. "I have to straighten something out."

"I'm coming with you."

Mathias sighed. *Did I expect him to sit here, staring at the wall?* "Fine," he said grudgingly.

Rayan strapped on his holster, attempting to hide how pleased he was.

As Mathias dressed, he tried to pinpoint what felt different. Like a change in frequency, a shift in the air. The past few weeks had been brutal, a series of setbacks, one after the other. Mathias couldn't remember when he'd last eaten, subsisting on coffee and booze in equal proportions. And then this man had appeared amid a sea of hostility—a city out to get him—and Mathias's lungs had filled, his head clearing, righting him somehow. They fell back into their former roles as if it were second nature.

"I don't know why Russo let this fester so long," Mathias muttered as they drove through the city, relieved not to be stuck in the car with only his thoughts for company. The situation was worse than he'd thought. Moretti—and the family by extension—was a laughing stock in Hamilton, having allowed rival groups free rein for years. "Moretti's been collecting protection money but leaving clients to fend for themselves. Almost everyone's defaulted to paying the Reapers, and anyone who hasn't gets visits from Truman's heavyweights until they eventually come around."

"But this one's still on the books?" Rayan asked as they pulled up outside a cluster of adult stores on the strip, each one indistinguishable from the next.

"For now," Mathias said grimly, cutting the engine. "Joseph Sylvester, the only big player we have left. Hates the Reapers. Prefers to deal with the family. He's already been hit once this week. This keeps up, and he's gone."

A man with a face full of tattoos stalked toward them as they got out of the car, and Rayan stepped forward instinctively. It was one of Sylvester's collection of thugs.

"Second time this week," the man reported with a scowl. "Said next time, they'll leave with the till."

"Where's Sylvester?" Mathias asked.

"Inside."

Together they descended the stairs that led to Foxglove, Sylvester's George Street club. The tattooed man gave a nod to the bouncer standing by the entrance, who pulled open the iron security gate, ushering them inside. Beside him, Rayan's eyes widened. It was several steps farther down the rabbit hole than Le Rouge. Glass windows, like shop fronts, housed performers in different combinations, fucking in various ways. People—almost all men—lined the windows, leering. Despite everything Mathias had seen on the job over the years, even he'd been taken aback by the vulgarity of the spectacle. He and Rayan were led past the punters to the bar, where several men sat around, drinking.

"Mathias Beauvais," Sylvester announced as he emerged from the back room, a martini glass perched between two limber fingers. "Always a pleasure to see you."

He drew out the word *pleasure* in a way that set Mathias on edge. At any other time, in any other circumstance, he would have knocked the man's teeth out. But in Hamilton, Sylvester was one of the family's biggest clients. He owned a handful of clubs on the strip and multiple other establishments across the city. Mathias had to handle him with a mixture of care and intimidation, walking a fine line between respect and derision. In Montreal, Mathias had never had to play nice. His reputation and the weight of the family's presence in the city spoke for him. But here, he could rely on neither.

The slight man's smile tweaked as his gaze shifted. "Who is this?" Sylvester stared past him at his former second with an enamored sparkle in his eyes.

Mathias had almost forgotten about Rayan. "I'll talk to Truman," he said, ignoring the man's question. "Get him to pull back his muscle."

He was hedging. The head of the Reapers had proven elusive. Without an introduction, Mathias was floundering. He had one more card up his sleeve, but he was reluctant to use it.

Sylvester waved him away. "Yes, yes, but first, what is your name, young man?"

Rayan shifted uncomfortably, remaining silent.

"Does he speak English?" Sylvester asked, turning to Mathias.

"Why wouldn't he?" Mathias replied.

Cornered, his former second spoke his name flatly.

"Rayan!" Sylvester trilled. He took a sip of his martini. "You are simply beautiful. Where are you from?"

"Montreal."

"*Enchanté*," the older man simpered, raising a neatly arched eyebrow.

"I don't have time for your shit today, Sylvester," Mathias warned, a surge of anger rising in his throat.

Sylvester laughed, finally giving him his full attention. "I'm sure we can be friendlier than that, seeing as we've been rather disappointed with the service of late."

He raised a hand, reaching for the lapel of Mathias's jacket. Before he could touch him, Rayan shoved the man back, spilling his drink. Sylvester's grin only widened.

"Where have you been hiding this puppy, Mathias?" he murmured. "I will pay you a fortune to let him bite me."

Mine. The word surfaced red-hot, searing through his brain. "Here I was thinking I'd be generous and negotiate this month's fees," Mathias said, keeping his voice even. "But it's generous enough that I leave without breaking your arm."

Sylvester looked at him, the smugness not leaving his face. Mathias had run out of time. He couldn't keep trying to placate with no teeth. "I'll talk to Truman."

Sylvester's lips curled, eyes glinting as though he knew better. "I'm sure you will."

19

The clouds hung low, gloomy. It had been snowing on and off all morning. Mathias eased his new black Bentley into a spot by the river and got out, buttoning his jacket and pulling on his goatskin gloves. A frigid wind blew across the water, buffeting his face as he stepped down the bank. He walked slowly across a powdery carpet of white.

It was a good spot for an ambush, out where no one could hear. He'd told Giovanni he wasn't a gambling man, yet that was all he'd done since coming to Hamilton. Mathias hadn't realized how accustomed he'd become to the security of his life in Montreal. Here, people could turn on a dime.

Not for the first time, he considered Rayan's offer to stay. Yesterday, after Rayan had left for Montreal, Mathias had found a single silver key lying on the foyer table. He'd picked it up and turned it over in his hand before taking out his keys and threading it onto the chain beside them.

Mathias pushed the thought aside. He'd made his choice and would be damned if he backtracked now. But if he wanted to get anywhere, he would eventually have to trust someone. Between the trees ahead, he saw a short man in a faded Blue Jays baseball cap.

The man raised a hand as Mathias approached. "You're alone," he observed, amused. "New town—thought you'd have backup." His accent wasn't as pronounced as Belkov's, but the lilt was there.

"Working on it."

Gurin chuckled. "Not much left to lose, eh?"

Mathias said nothing, caught off guard. The Russian's insight hit close to home. When he'd called Belkov to arrange a meeting with his Hamilton contact, he'd given him a spare account of what had transpired since their last encounter, but he knew the Bratva boss would have taken great pleasure in embellishing the details.

"This guy, too, cashed in his chips," Gurin said, shaking his head.

Beside him, a man lay face down in the snow, his hands bound behind his back, a bag over his head. Mathias saw the sack of river stones the Russian had tied around his ankles. Professionally done—a man well-schooled in his craft. Gurin crouched, pulling up the bag to reveal a face beaten beyond recognition.

"Been subbing powder in our supply. Collecting double." He tutted. "As you know, we hold territory south of the river. Boss tells me he's feeling charitable, wants to cut you in. As a good-faith agreement."

He was being generous in calling it territory. The Russians held onto a narrow corridor from the river that reached just south of the border. It wasn't much on the map but served as one of their key supply lines into the States. Belkov's proposed cut was small but would be an improvement over the pittance the family currently made behind the scenes at the clubs downtown. Mathias had paid Tony under the table to waive six months' worth of port fees for the Bratva in Montreal.

Gurin lowered the bag and stood, gesturing toward the man on the ground. "But Belkov wants to be sure of your good faith."

Mathias leveled his eyes at the Russian. Gurin stared back. *Nothing new.* He cracked his neck with a sigh. He'd been here before, in his early days with the family—a string of tests designed to cement loyalty, weed out the weak. Mathias had employed the same tactics with Rayan when the man first started.

Mathias pulled the gun from beneath his jacket and racked the slide with a click. Then he raised it and fired one shot clean through the runner's head. It was so quick the man didn't make a sound.

"Done with the party tricks?" he asked, stowing his weapon.

Gurin smiled, pulling off a glove and holding out his hand. Mathias took it. "Alexei Gurin."

"Mathias Beauvais."

After the Russian had rolled the body into the river, watching as it sank below the swell of water, he collected the spent shell casing and kicked a fresh layer of snow across the ground. Mathias stood to the side, smoking silently.

"I need an introduction," he said when Gurin was finished.

"Truman?"

"Yes."

Gurin snorted. "He doesn't like the mafia. Still hates Russo for running him out of Quebec."

"I have something to offer. Worth his while."

"I'll see what I can do. He doesn't like the Bratva much either."

"What a fucking team."

Gurin laughed as they walked in the direction of his car. "If you're looking for good men, I know a few who might be persuaded."

"Have a Russian watch my back?" Mathias scoffed. "I'll end up with a knife through it."

Gurin snickered. "Not ours—unaffiliated. Mostly Anglos, the odd pea-souper. They come in handy when we need the extra muscle."

Mathias considered it. If there was one thing he'd found a glaring lack of in this city, it was reliable men. "Send them my way."

Gurin stopped, peering at him curiously. "You're not like Moretti. Rumor is you had a name for yourself in Montreal. Why are you out here, scavenging for scraps?"

Mathias smiled coldly, tapping the ash from his cigarette. "We'll find out soon enough."

The phone drilled into Mathias's semiconscious brain. He rolled over, needing a moment to get his bearings. He didn't remember falling asleep—or even what it felt like to sleep—but his body must have reached a tipping point and shut down on its own. He grabbed his phone from the bedside table and brought it to his ear.

"He's at the Iguana." It was Gurin.

"Now?" Mathias sat up, looking down at the screen to see it was three in the morning.

"Yes," Gurin said. "Says he'll meet with you."

Mathias swore under his breath and pulled himself out of bed. Truman was big dogging him, yanking him around like a trained monkey. Moretti had a lot to answer for.

"I'm heading over."

"Don't fuck this up, Beauvais," the Russian warned before hanging up.

Tossing his phone down, Mathias stalked to the bathroom to take a piss and splash cold water on his face. Despite the early wake-up call, he dressed as he would any other day—crisp white shirt and black slacks. He ran a comb through his hair, slicking it back, and strapped his gun to his chest, fixed in a leather holster beneath his jacket. He took it out and checked the chamber, flicking off the safety.

A half hour later, Mathias pulled the car into a spot outside a plain brick tavern on the outskirts of the city. The building bore no identifying features except for a red skull stenciled in spray paint on the steel double doors. He'd have preferred to meet on neutral territory, but he was confident Truman wouldn't try anything stupid. If his own reputation didn't precede him, the family's certainly did. And Truman had been spooked by Russo before.

Walking through the entrance to the club, he was met by two women in thongs and nothing else. The Iguana was a notorious local titty bar, offering a range of extra services for those who could pay—the jewel in the crown of the Red Reapers' Ontario charter and where William Truman conducted most of his business.

One of the women, eyes dull with dope, asked what he'd like to drink. She tottered over to the bar while the other woman led Mathias through the crowd of patrons. By the look of it, they were mostly members, sporting jackets with the Reapers' skeleton scythe motif. Truman was seated in a booth at the far end of the club, surrounded by his inner posse, a naked stripper splayed across his lap. He was older—in his fifties at least—his face pale and meaty, eyes red rimmed, stomach straining against a leather jacket swathed in weathered patches. Mathias almost laughed. He looked like a glorified boy scout.

The hostess indicated for Mathias to sit opposite Truman and placed his drink on the table between them. Truman waved a hand, and the throng dispersed, the woman slipping from his lap and wandering aimlessly across the room. Mathias left the drink where it was. He had yet to trust anything about the seedy establishment, present company included.

"You came alone." The Reaper leered. "Either you're fucking stupid, or you've got balls. Which will it be, I wonder?" His eyes fell on Mathias's Rolex. "That's a nice watch. What's a thing like that worth? Sixty, eighty K?"

Mathias shrugged.

"You *ginos* like nice things. Think you can swan around, taking what you want, just like the one before." He downed the rest of his drink. "So, you're that shithead's replacement?" He studied Mathias scornfully. "Might be more comfortable with your friends back home. This is Reapers territory. We don't like your kind here."

"Is that so?"

"Take your leather shoes and your nice watch, and fuck off back where you came from," Truman barked, tossing his empty glass at the wall behind Mathias's head.

It shattered, barely missing his cheek. Mathias placed his hands down on the table. In a blur of movement, he rammed the table into Truman's gut, pinning him against the booth. Before the Reaper's entourage could react, Mathias was standing, his gun pressed hard to the man's temple. Blinded by arrogance and accustomed to Moretti's cowardice, Truman had clearly underestimated him—hadn't even bothered to search him at the door. Mathias saw the fear in Truman's eyes, the glisten of sweat on his fleshy face.

"I deserve more respect than that," he said in a low voice.

In the silence that fell over the club, Mathias heard the click of weapons.

"You may have known my predecessor, but it seems you know nothing about me. When we talk business, we keep it civil. Do you neo-Nazi cunts understand the word *civil*?" Mathias felt the man tremble against the barrel. "I don't like to make assumptions, but so far, you're proving me right. Don't fuck with me, Truman, and I won't fuck with you. Now, shall we talk some business?"

The Reaper nodded slowly.

"Tell them to stand down."

Truman raised a hand, indicating for his men to back off. He cleared his throat. "Get the man another drink," he called to one of the waitresses.

Mathias yanked the table back and sat down, placing his gun between them, fingers resting on the handle.

"You've got balls," Truman muttered.

"You've got two million in untapped product languishing on the docks. Port authority won't grant you shipping rights."

Truman's mouth dropped open.

"I can have it green-lit by the end of the week," Mathias continued. "But I want fifteen percent of everything that touches Quebec soil."

"Fifteen percent?" Truman scoffed.

"Fifteen percent of nothing is nothing. Which is what you're making while that stock doesn't shift."

The Reaper scowled. The waitress appeared with fresh drinks. Truman downed his and handed it back to her for a refill. "And who's to say our product won't end up in the river? It's happened before. The mob blocks all port access to Montreal."

"An exception has been made."

Truman snorted. "For what price?"

"Back off our businesses on the strip. No more raids, no more threats. Consider it an olive branch. We have shared interests, and it's in your interest to keep things clean."

"Civil." Truman smirked.

"Now you're getting it." Mathias stood, taking off his watch and tossing it to the man. "Don't think too hard."

Truman caught it with a grin and weighed it admiringly in his hand. "I like a challenge. And you, my ballsy friend, are a challenge."

20

From the twelfth-floor window of the Tour de la Bourse, Rayan could see the first smattering of leaves changing color on Mont Royal. Behind him, Christophe Renault—heir to the Centrale Générale construction empire—swayed in his chair. One eye was already beginning to close, his torn lip dripping onto the collar of his expensive silk shirt, leaving behind a flurry of red. His eyes widened as Rayan turned away from the window, cracking the knuckles of his right hand, stiff from having made impact with the Frenchman's thick skull.

He preferred not to use his hands, but Renault's swanky corner office was sorely lacking in serviceable tools. He smirked at the mental image of setting upon him with a stapler, and Renault recoiled, letting out a low wail. Rayan noticed a darkening stain on the cream carpeting beneath the man's chair.

By the door, Lorenzo hacked loudly, hurling a mouthful of phlegm to the floor at his feet. He stood hunched over, arms crossed, head tilted toward his chest, as though fighting sleep. Rayan eyed him warily. It was best they finish up soon. The old man wasn't known for his stamina.

"We clear?" Rayan's voice was smooth, modeled on his former capo after years of observing him at work.

"*O-Oui*," Renault stuttered. This was a man used to things going his way, but before two of the family's famed foot soldiers, he was proving a fast learner.

"We'll be back Friday," Rayan said.

Renault slumped forward, gingerly lifting a hand to his battered face. Rayan retrieved his jacket and walked to the door, which Lorenzo held open, a cigarette already between his teeth.

"Don't go scaring that pretty little secretary of yours," Lorenzo called out with a chuckle as they closed the door behind them and made their way past the executive's wide-eyed receptionist.

The last half decade had seen the family make a significant profit from providing construction companies like Renault's with tender guarantees for large-scale city projects. With a reach that extended all the way to the mayor's office, it was easy enough for Giorgio Russo to determine who the municipal government entrusted with their multimillion-dollar contracts. And in return, the family enjoyed a sizable kickback. Five percent was standard, but Rayan had worked jobs with cuts as large as fifteen. Renault had gotten greedy, taking on too many projects at once. When construction delays tied up precious capital, he'd started missing payments.

Collections handled these contracts, and all things construction had always fallen to Mathias, so Rayan knew what was involved when it came to a white-collar client like Renault. A touch of friendly intimidation, the odd personal threat—enough to reduce the likelihood and inconvenience of a second visit. Each visit was a lesson in restraint, a psychological push and pull. If you appeared too lenient, it gave the wrong impression. If you got too excited about smashing a client's face in, you had a different set of problems on your hands.

Rayan had learned from the best. When it came to intimidation, Mathias could have taught a master class. But in the last six months, Rayan had taken on far more responsibility than he'd bargained for, and he missed the days when all he had to do was follow orders. With Mathias gone, the job had gained a heaviness he couldn't seem to shake. Before, his loyalty to Mathias had acted as a barrier, a justification for the ruthless nature of the work he performed. Now the brutality ate at him, chafing against something long buried, his conscience resurfacing with a vengeance. Rayan faced each morning with a growing sense of unease, the years stretching before him sullied and empty. He thought of Mathias's question that day in the kitchen of his apartment, Rayan's response tasting more and more false.

Once outside, Lorenzo lit the cigarette dangling from his lips as they crossed Saint-Jacques and made their way to the car. Squat and cantankerous, the man had a face that looked like he'd just come away from a beating—nose squashed and dark circles swallowing his squinted eyes.

"Yuppie piece of shit," Lorenzo mumbled. He took a series of short drags. "If he's doing so well, why borrow from the family?"

True to his word, Tony had returned Rayan to Commercial at the end of his probation period. There had been tension when Lorenzo was called back from retirement to head their team. He'd expressed concern about working with an outsider, especially one who looked like Rayan. Time and Rayan's quiet diligence had brought him around, and they'd managed to establish a working relationship—in which he did all the work and Lorenzo benefitted from the subsequent respect. Tony hadn't downplayed the man's lack of finesse. Lorenzo was old-school, used to frisking dealers for cash and utterly useless when it came to understanding contractual terms—or most simple concepts, for that matter.

"Who knows," Rayan replied absently, pulling open the car door and sliding in behind the wheel.

There was a thump as Lorenzo took his place in the passenger seat. Rayan glanced at his phone. It wasn't uncommon for Tony to send them on dubious errands between jobs. He got a kick out of jerking Rayan around. Tony had never done this with Mathias. But no one jerked Rayan's former capo around. Fortunately, there were no messages for him that morning. Their next visit, in Villeray, was a good way across town, and he couldn't spare the time.

Rayan stared out the window as the car inched forward through late-morning traffic. The weather in Montreal went through a strange resurgence this time of year, remnants of summer humidity returning for a short-lived spell. Then just as quickly, the first icy chills descended, sending the city into virtual lockdown for months on end, forcing people underground to scuttle about like roaches. He hated the winters here. He'd spent more nights than he cared to remember praying he didn't freeze to death.

Rayan watched as a group of teenagers ducked through the rows of backed-up cars in front of them, heading toward Place d'Armes station. They moved with a confidence endemic to their age, naive to the ways in which the world would chew them up and spit them out. One of the kids turned to look over his shoulder, and Rayan started.

Tahir?

The car sidled past, and Rayan found himself scanning the crowd for his face. *No*, he thought as reality grounded him once again. The boy looked nothing like his brother.

It was the age Rayan remembered most, when Tahir was in his late teens. He'd strutted about like he was king of the streets—though the truth had been very different—as his younger brother, Rayan, remained a devoted disciple. Tahir had managed to pull together a motley crew of kids like them. They'd slept under the Saint-Jacques Street overpass or cycled between metro stations when the snow started to fall.

Rayan's eyes followed the boy as he stepped through the revolving station doors and out of view, unnerved by how quickly his brother's face had resurfaced. Turning the car down a side street, Rayan cut across to Saint-Antoine, opting for the longer route. He'd had enough of the traffic.

Mathias scanned Via Roma for the old man. The restaurant was crowded with the lunch rush, and seats were few and far between. The place was an Italian staple, complete with wrought-iron tables and terracotta brickwork crawling with ivy. The weather was warmer than usual for September, and the large French doors had been opened to allow customers to spill out onto the terrace. There he spotted Giovanni, sitting with his face turned toward the sun, an empty seat across from him.

Mathias noted the sleek black Jag idling by the curb not ten feet from where Giovanni was seated, the man's second, Henri Rossi, at the wheel. Parked in the alley behind the restaurant, his own second waited. Jacques Laberge had come highly recommended by Gurin, having worked with the Bratva as hired muscle for years. The man was originally from Gatineau, and the Russian figured Mathias might appreciate working with a fellow Quebecois, considering that the men he'd painstakingly assembled in the new Hamilton office were almost all Anglos.

Jacques had proven proficient, familiar enough with family politics to know when to pull his head in. He wasn't too bright, but you didn't need brains to intercept a bullet. And trivial as it might be, it was a relief not to have to speak English all fucking day.

Mathias made his way over to the table and took Giovanni's hand, shaking it firmly.

The councilman stood with a grin and smacked him lightly on the cheek. "Good to be back in civilization, Beauvais?"

"You could say that," Mathias said wryly.

Giovanni's thin lips tweaked in amusement as he pushed the open bottle of Chianti red in his direction. The man had requested Mathias's presence in Montreal, which meant he had news he couldn't discuss over the phone.

"I've already ordered. The chicken is outstanding."

Mathias poured himself a glass of wine but left it standing near the edge of his plate. Feeling a tickle of perspiration, he shrugged off his jacket and draped it over the back of the chair. They must have been in the thrall of an Indian summer, the temperature set to nosedive at any moment.

"The weather's improved—I'll give you that," Mathias said, breaking off a chunk of bread and smearing it with a thick layer of butter.

Giovanni chuckled. "The weather? You've been out of Montreal too long."

It had been half a year since his reassignment to Hamilton. Every time Mathias came back, he was confronted by the slight that had festered, which reopened whenever he set foot in the city—his city, where he was forced to act like a stranger.

Deciding to let the taunt slide, Mathias took a swig from his glass, unmoved by Giovanni's selection. He'd have preferred something stronger.

The food appeared, and Giovanni winked at the waitress, an older woman who—based on the speed at which their order arrived—knew exactly who they were. The councilman picked up his knife and fork and dove into the dressed chicken breast, mumbling a belated "Bon appétit" between mouthfuls. As Mathias slowly carved into his own piece of meat, he kept his eyes on Giovanni. The man wouldn't be rushed.

"Russo's spent the last two weeks in hospital," Giovanni said finally, letting the information fall on the table between them.

Mathias raised an eyebrow in surprise. Very little got out about Giorgio Russo's condition, what with the city crawling with rivals ready to take his place. He hadn't realized things had deteriorated so quickly.

"What are we looking at?" he asked, lowering his voice.

"Rumor is..." Giovanni paused, weighing his next words. "He won't make it through the winter."

Mathias kept his face blank as the old man studied him intently, gauging his reaction. Then Giovanni took another bite of the chicken, shrugging. "But rumors are rumors, eh?"

His blithe tone hid a clear warning. This information, bordering on sedition, was not to be repeated.

Mathias nodded, taking a sip of wine. Setting the glass down, he dropped his napkin beside the barely touched plate, not hungry. "And Piero?"

Giovanni stared back at him, chewing slowly, the hint of a frown tugging at his gray mustache. "Piero is waiting patiently in the wings. He's recruited a handful of soldiers from within the family and, not unlike us, has made his own arrangements."

Mathias did not give voice to the obscenity that formed on his lips. Instead, he swallowed and reached for his cigarettes, masking the extent to which mention of the man affected him. Giovanni swirled his wine and took a long gulp. He picked the knife and fork back up from his plate, his eyes steely.

"Now, what I want to know is," Giovanni said, slicing cleanly through a chunk of pale flesh, "are we ready?"

21

After they'd finished for the day, Lorenzo headed home while Rayan stayed behind to talk to Tony about a contract he was reworking. He was sitting in his boss's office, going over the daily takings, when the door opened, and Mathias walked in. Rayan blinked, surprised. He hadn't known he was up from Hamilton.

"Beauvais," Tony grunted. "What is it now, I wonder?"

"Giraldi." Mathias mirrored him, reverting to their usual back-and-forth. His gaze flicked to Rayan. "You can go."

Rayan frowned, holding his tongue. Standing, he picked up his paperwork then left the room, closing the door behind him. He considered waiting in the hallway for the men to finish—he still had things to discuss with the Collections head, after all—but decided against it. The last thing he wanted was to be seen as overeager.

Rayan sat down at an empty desk in the deserted office and thumbed through the pages of the contract he was too distracted to read. He'd been hoping to tweak the terms for incumbent councilor Pierre Larrivée, who'd used family money to pad his campaign budget and—now that the election was won—seemed less willing to pay it back. Rayan needed sign off to fast-track a second visit.

He heard the door to Tony's office open and watched as Mathias strode past him toward the stairwell without so much as a glance. Not thinking, Rayan stood and went after him. At the bottom of the stairs, he caught the door before it shut and stepped out into the crisp night air. In his rush, he'd left his jacket inside.

"When did you get here?"

Mathias stopped and turned to Rayan with a scowl. "What's it to you?"

The man continued to his car. He pulled open the door and slid in behind the wheel. Emboldened, Rayan followed, climbing in on the passenger side.

"This is getting old," Mathias warned quietly.

Rayan stopped himself from reaching between them to touch Mathias's face. "What was that with Tony?"

"Russian port fees."

"You came all the way for that?"

Mathias's eyes narrowed. "Focus on your own turf."

Rayan looked at him, the resentment churning in his stomach. "For every time you tell me you're here, there's two other times you don't."

Mathias stared him down. "You're not my second anymore, Rayan. I don't need to tell you shit."

Rayan yanked open the car door and slammed it behind him. He stalked back to the office. When he got inside he threw on his jacket, leaving the contract abandoned on the desk. He didn't care if Tony was expecting him—he would sort it out the next day. He descended the stairs and strode into the parking lot, reaching into his pocket for his keys. Mathias's black Bentley pulled out in front of him, blocking his path.

"Get in," his former capo instructed from the open window.

Rayan pretended to consider, holding himself back for one breath in a feeble attempt at control. But he'd known. As soon as he'd seen the car, he'd known what he would do.

They'd gone from explosive, indiscriminate urge—a race to have their most base needs met, skipping everything else that might get in the way—to more hands, more mouths, a want to savor and make it last longer. Rayan didn't know when the shift had occurred—neither of them had acknowledged it—only that it meant he got more of Mathias, greater reign over his body.

And still, Rayan was held captive by the unpredictable nature of Mathias's presence in the city. He would go weeks without seeing him, sometimes months, only to be startled by the sound of the man's key in the lock or to wake to find Mathias asleep beside him. Needless to say, when they did finally find themselves together, he lost all sense of control.

Back at his apartment, Rayan moved his mouth along Mathias's cock, the desire ensnaring him, dulling his thoughts, straining between his legs. He felt a hand slip beneath his chin, lifting his head. Mathias pushed him backward onto the bed, kissing him hungrily. Rayan buried his fingers in Mathias's hair, relishing the taste of his tongue in his mouth.

Propelled by a growing sense of urgency, he rolled Mathias over, straddling his hips. One hand traveled the length of the man's cock, the other stretching, opening himself. Mathias lurched in his grip, and Rayan saw he was watching him closely, eyes clouded with lust. Fighting the heat rising along his neck, Rayan took him in, concealing a groan as he was filled, his body brimming with pleasure. This was what it yearned for in the time that lagged between seeing him.

On top, he was in control of the pace and the angle, but Rayan found himself unable to surrender. The frustration must have registered on his face, as Mathias flipped him onto his back, driving him into the mattress.

"Ask for it," Mathias demanded. "Tell me what you want."

Rayan's pulse hammered.

"I want you to…" Mathias prompted, grinding into him, a moan escaping through his teeth.

Rayan flushed violently, looking away, distancing himself from his own shamelessness. "Fuck me," he whispered. "Hard."

Mathias's lips curled. "That wasn't so difficult." Then he proceeded to give Rayan exactly what he wanted.

"He pissed himself?" Mathias snickered, pouring more scotch into his glass.

He sat at Rayan's kitchen table in only his slacks, his shirt on the floor by the bed. Propping his legs up on the chair beside him, he looked utterly in control. The beast had been tamed—for the moment.

"First time Renault's given us trouble," Rayan said, recalling the terror on the construction magnate's face. "Maybe he thought we'd go easy on him."

The microwave dinged, and he pulled out a plate of leftovers, the sweetness of shredded lamb wafting through the small apartment.

"Why you insist on making this place smell like a roadside stall is beyond me," Mathias said as Rayan sat across from him, setting the food down on the table.

"There's only so much French peasant food I can take," Rayan said, picking up his fork. It was almost nine, and he hadn't eaten since lunch, other things naturally taking precedence.

Mathias reached over and picked up a chunk of meat with his fingers. He chewed slowly, looking not unimpressed. "Things are going well, then?"

Rayan shrugged. "Is that hard to believe?"

"Working with Lorenzo? Yes."

"I wouldn't say he works. More shows up. Grudgingly."

"Look at you," Mathias scoffed. "A natural leader."

The derision was clear, but Rayan let it slide. The sentiment was one he shared. He hadn't asked for the responsibility. "How's Hamilton?" he asked, regretting the question immediately.

Mathias frowned and took a long swig from his glass. When he put it down, his face was stony. "Fine."

"I've heard rumors about your work with the Reapers. Apparently, De Luca's never seen so much blow come through the port."

"Just rumors."

"Liar." Rayan took a bite of lamb. He wanted to say something but, at the same time, knew what a minefield the subject was. "Jacques still around?" Rayan had met him once at a meeting with Tony that Mathias had driven up to attend. He'd found the man simple, not qualified to protect his former boss.

Mathias stared at him. "Are you fishing, Rayan?"

"He seems slow, unreliable," Rayan said, scooping up a forkful of rice and shoveling it into his mouth.

Mathias rolled his wrist to reveal the faded scar along his forearm. "Happened on your watch if I remember correctly."

Rayan bristled. "Only because you were drunk."

Mathias smirked. "He knows his place. More complacent, less complicated." He gave a low chuckle and reached over to thumb Rayan's swollen lip. He had bruised it with his teeth. "Not what you were after?"

Rayan pushed his plate away, no longer hungry. He felt a familiar prickle of defensiveness. "Just asked if you were working with the man."

Mathias picked up his abandoned fork, stabbed it through a piece of meat, and brought it to his mouth. "If I were you, I'd be more concerned with who's watching your back. Lorenzo isn't exactly quick on his feet."

"He doesn't have to be," Rayan retorted. "Worst I've got coming after me is a shady politician. You, on the other hand..." They both knew Mathias had accumulated powerful enemies before his expulsion from the city.

Mathias studied him, swallowing. "For looking like it was run over by a truck, this isn't half bad."

"Why'd you need to see Tony?" Rayan pressed.

Mathias sighed. "I've been covering Belkov's port fees in exchange for his cooperation," he said, guarded. "We'll need the Russians when the time comes."

Rayan knew little of what Mathias had spent the last few months machinating. He'd deliberately kept him in the dark. But he did know, from the snatches of information he'd managed to assemble, that it involved Belkov, the boss's dwindling health, and a growing alliance with the head of the Hamilton Red Reapers. How each of those pieces fit together, he still wasn't sure.

"You could have told me."

Mathias gave him a sharp look. "Why? I don't need you to sort out my business."

Rayan exhaled, rubbing a hand across his face. The man was right. And what was worse, it only served to illuminate how little he'd needed to be involved. As Mathias had said, he wasn't his second anymore. Rayan no longer had a reason to be kept informed of his former capo's activities.

"Tell me when you're in town," he said, relenting. "I don't need to know why."

Mathias speared another chunk of lamb. "No promises."

It was dark, and Rayan's body was folded into his mother's embrace. He was small again, fitting against her softness, drawing her scent into his lungs—cinnamon and anise. She was saying something quietly, her lips moving in his hair. He smiled and pulled away, staring up at her as he had done as a child.

She ran her hand across his forehead, smoothing his hair. "Where is he?"

Rayan looked at her, confused. "Who, Mama?"

His mother's smile faded, and fear began to gather in her eyes. "Tahir. Where is he?"

Rayan took a step back, then another. His vision narrowed, and with each step, he felt himself growing taller until he towered over the small woman. Rayan looked down and saw he was dressed in his suit. His hands were sticky, and when he opened his fists, they were covered with blood.

"Where is he?" His mother's voice had taken on a shrill pitch, and she was fumbling with her headscarf, pulling it off to reveal her long black hair. She snapped her gaze up to meet his. "Who are you?" she cried, digging her fingers into her hair and beginning to tug. "Where is my son?"

"It's me, Mama."

Her voice spiraled into a mournful howl, her hands latching onto chunks of hair and tearing them from her head. "Where are my sons? What have you done with my sons?"

A child once again, Rayan stood outside the bathroom door of their old apartment—the door, always the door. His brother's desire to protect him had instead cursed him to return to this moment, reliving his own gruesome reimagining over and over again. He no longer knew which was worse—what his brother had seen or what the dreams had conjured. He reached out, against his will, and gripped the cold metal handle, every cell of his body trembling at the thought of what he would find when the door opened.

"Rayan."

There was a hand on his shoulder, jolting him awake. He lurched to the edge of the mattress, away from the man, his chest heaving. Rayan swiped the back of his hand roughly across his face, feeling a wetness on his cheeks.

Mathias was sitting up, eyebrows knitted. "You were talking."

Rayan realized how thoroughly he'd exposed himself. He'd been a fool to think the dreams wouldn't find him while Mathias was here. He cursed the boy he'd seen by the metro, unleashing thoughts of his brother, exhuming the dead.

Rayan turned to get out of bed. A hand gripped his arm. He yanked it out of reach, standing.

"Sit down, Rayan."

He began to dress silently, forcing his hands to remain still.

"I said, sit." Mathias's voice—flat, hard—cut through everything else.

He stopped, lowering himself to the bed, his back to Mathias. There was a creak as Mathias moved behind him, arms encircling his shoulders, pressing Rayan to his chest.

"Breathe for a second, would you?"

He could feel the slow thump of Mathias's heartbeat along his spine and the steady rise and fall of his lungs. Rayan tried to match his breathing, but his pulse slammed in his throat, refusing to cooperate.

Mathias rested a chin on his shoulder, speaking in a low murmur by his ear. "Fibonacci. Each number the sum of the two before." He eased him back into bed, the numbers falling from his lips like a spell. "Three... five, eight, thirteen..."

Arms wrapped around him, Mathias held him as Rayan's mind began to still, his breath finally leveling. He closed his eyes and focused only on that voice.

22

Once the shipments had taken off and Truman was making more money in a month than he had in the past year, Mathias found himself invited into the Hamilton circuit and became a regular attendee at the man's late-night gatherings. While Gurin could barely believe the about-face, Mathias found the constant interactions tedious. William Truman was crude, quick to offend, and a raging drunk yet, depending on how much liquor he had in him, was also proving to be increasingly malleable and almost eager to please.

The more reliant Truman became on the family's good favor, the more influence Mathias discovered he had, which was something he hadn't anticipated. He felt the tables beginning to turn. He'd only wanted to reassert the family's position in Hamilton, but with Truman's burgeoning alliance, it was possible Mathias could stake an even bigger claim on the region.

After reestablishing the local office, he'd recruited a handful of men more competent than the dregs Moretti had left behind. They'd proven efficient at maintaining the family's growing territory, turnover eclipsing anything that had come out of the satellite office in decades.

"So, he's on the ground, and two of my guys are just taking to him." They were at the Iguana, and Truman was regaling him with war stories, one of his regular girls perched on his lap as he pawed at her large breasts. "But his fucking mouth is shut. He's a steel trap. Never seen it get so bloody." He trailed his hand down the woman's stomach and slipped it absently between her legs. Mathias recognized his old watch prominently adorning the man's left wrist.

"Nothing compared to Russo's work." Truman gave a low whistle. "I was there in the nineties, and I saw what he did during the biker war. When that man dies, he'll go into the fucking flames."

"And you?" Mathias raised an eyebrow. "Waiting at the pearly gates?"

Truman chuckled. "Hey, I'm no saint, but there's bad, and then there's bad."

Mathias thought of Dante, the Nine Circles. It was almost comical that they were sitting here, two of the country's most notorious criminals, comparing evils.

"While Russo's alive, there's no getting around your Quebec exile," Mathias said. "But things are changing. One of these days, they'll be different. I'd like to think we both stand to gain, if I can rely on the Reapers' backing."

Truman pushed the woman off his lap. "Get us some more drinks—there's a good girl," he said, palming her ass as she walked away. He leaned forward, face serious. "What are you saying?"

"I'm saying, I may require your assistance," Mathias said deliberately. "Sooner rather than later."

Truman's mouth pulled into a slow grin. "If the price is right, you can count on it."

"It will be," Mathias said, downing the rest of his glass.

On his recent visit to Montreal, he'd met with De Luca about sweetening the Reapers' cut in exchange for Truman's help. Giovanni had also agreed to extend their territory up to the provincial border. But that particular carrot, he would save for a job well done. No need for Truman to get ahead of himself.

"Gurin says you're dropping protection for North End."

Truman shrugged. "You can have it. We're tired of dealing with the Mexicans. It was fun when we took it off Moretti, but it's too much work."

Mathias had become familiar with the man's aversion to hard work. It was an easy virtue to exploit.

The woman reappeared, placing two fresh drinks down before them.

"Come here, honey," the Reapers' boss said, yanking her back to the table. "I didn't say thank you." He leaned forward and spat in the woman's open mouth. She gave him an indulgent smile before continuing on her way.

The disgust must have shown on Mathias's face, because Truman looked at him with a sneer. "Got a wife at home, Beauvais?" He laughed. "On your best behavior?"

"Where I'm from, that means something else entirely," he said carefully.

Truman chuckled. "Girls love that shit. The worse you treat them, the more they like it."

Mathias took a cursory pull from his drink, cheap bourbon and a grueling day contributing to the piercing headache behind his eyes.

"Speaking of, I have a gift for you," Truman announced. Mathias's stomach turned. He could see where this was heading. "In honor of our joint venture, bygones and all that. Fresh off the boat, first-class Euro pussy."

Truman knew only one way to conduct business—in seedy clubs, with bottomless liquor, the same girls offered up again and again. Lap dances, blowjobs, upstairs for full service. The man had a harem he took with him everywhere, offloading women onto his guests like party favors.

"One of our best girls—I don't let just anyone fuck her," he continued. "Consider it good faith, for our ongoing partnership."

What the fuck is it with this town and good faith? The ache in his head intensified, pounding at his temples. It was past midnight, he had business to attend in the morning, and here he was, forced into patronizing one of Truman's handpicked hookers.

But there was little choice in the matter. To refuse the man's gift would be a slap in the face and would set back the progress he'd made. And Mathias needed this to work. They were relying on the Reapers' muscle. Besides, he was surrounded by not just Truman's band of thugs but his own men as well. His eyes flicked to where Jacques sat at the bar, surveying the club's goings-on with mild curiosity. As always, Mathias had to ensure that his authority both as a man and as the family's regional head remained intact.

Truman beckoned over a young woman with white-blond hair, who made her way to their table. "This is Sugar. She'll take good care of you—trust me," he said, leering. "I speak from experience."

Mathias cringed inwardly. Not only did he have to fuck her, but he had to do so knowing the man had been there first.

Truman lifted his drink and clinked it against Mathias's. "Pleasure doing business with you, Beauvais."

Mathias raised the glass to his lips and knocked back the drink to mask the taste of bile rising in his throat.

After instructing his second to wait by the bar, Mathias followed Sugar upstairs to a series of numbered rooms. She was slight with dark eyes and small rounded breasts. Beneath the sheer slip of a dress, he could see the jut of her hip bones. Her arms hung, pale and limp, at her sides.

Giving him a sultry smile, she opened the door to room 7 and waited as Mathias made his way inside. It was only big enough for a double bed and a pair of side tables. She closed the door behind him and locked it with a click.

Mathias pulled out his cigarettes, lit one and took a drag, delaying the inevitable. The girl took it as a cue to totter over and reach for his belt buckle. He grabbed her wrist, stopping her. For a moment, she appeared confused, attempting to hide it with an impish pout.

"Don't you want Sugar to make you feel good?" Her accent was thick, Baltic or Eastern European.

Mathias exhaled roughly, letting her go. He didn't have time for this shit. "Bend over the bed."

His tone must have registered because, despite her earlier efforts, the woman didn't protest. She slipped off her heels, stepped out of her dress, and leaned over the bed, presenting herself in his direction. Mathias finished his cigarette, a coldness spreading across his body. His limbs felt heavy, like dead weight.

He stubbed out his smoke in the ashtray on one of the tables, shrugged off his jacket, and threw it down on the bed next to the girl, who was still poised, watching him over her shoulder. His eye fell on a platter of condoms beside the ashtray, and he picked one up and slipped it between his fingers.

Mathias stood behind her, unbuckling his pants. He thought he would have mustered something by now. The woman's blatant display only served to further his lack of interest. He stared past her, allowing his vision to blur at the edges, and summoned the feel of his fingers in Rayan's hair, finding the curve of his skull. He thought of how the man would press against him, as though even with their bodies fused together, he couldn't get close enough.

Mathias unwrapped the condom and slid it along his hardening shaft. The morning of his last visit, he'd found Rayan in the shower. Pushing his slick body up against the tiles, Mathias had held Rayan's wrists behind his back, preventing him from touching his cock—claiming dominion over him, his pleasure, his release.

He entered the girl in one thrust. Pressing down on her lower back, he moved fast, thankful for the layer of latex between them. She began to gasp and moan.

"Quiet," he instructed sharply, and she fell silent.

Mathias focused on the contact his hips made with her ass, the friction of his movement inside her. Every time he got close, something about the encounter would jar him, and he'd lose it, having to reach deeper within himself to invoke the necessary response. He wondered if it had always been so much work. Maybe he'd become spoiled, more familiar with the effort of holding himself back than forcing himself through. In the beginning, his separation from Rayan had proven a useful tool, but lately, Mathias found himself less willing to draw him into places like these—to allow his desire for Rayan, set on a hair trigger, to share the same space as the company he reviled.

They continued in silence until Mathias came perfunctorily, relieved to be done and end their brief interaction. After throwing the used condom in the trash, he buckled his pants and picked up his jacket. The girl sat on the bed, curling her legs beneath her as she watched him.

"What's next, baby?" Sugar smiled lazily, looking at him with half-lidded eyes. "You got me all worked up."

Mathias reached into his pocket and pulled out a stack of bills. He peeled off a handful and placed them down on the side table.

"That one's on the house," the girl teased, raising her arms and stretching out across the bed. He saw the dilated pupils and the smudge of darkness under her eyes. Around her neck and thighs lingered the shadow of bruising, barely visible in the low lighting.

"My regards to Truman," Mathias said, turning toward the door. He felt the girl's eyes on him as he stepped out into the hallway.

At his apartment, Mathias collapsed onto the bed, fully clothed. His skin crawled, his stomach heavy. He needed to wash the woman off him, but he couldn't bring himself to stand.

He pulled out his phone and stared at the screen. Despite the late hour, his thumb moved on its own, punching in the number from memory. He hovered over the call button but regained enough sense not to dial, dropping the phone onto the bed beside him. Mathias realized he'd only wanted to hear the man's voice—how he hesitated before speaking, as though juggling multiple threads of thought. He often felt the real Rayan existed far beneath the surface, and what he did let people see was a carefully managed version of what they expected. But recently, the shroud had begun to lift, frustration, possession, and that disarming softness breaking through.

There was a buzz as his phone started to ring. He picked it up, stiffening when he saw the number on the screen.

"Sorry, it's early."

"It's late."

"Right." Rayan laughed softly. "Figured there was a chance you were still up."

"Unfortunately." Mathias pulled himself up, unable to shake the eeriness of the coincidence.

"I spoke to Hassir, who works for Ahmad. He said the Algerians are pulling out of the port because of competition with Truman."

Mathias had a feeling that might happen. But the family's cut with the Algerians paled in comparison to what they were bringing in from the Reapers' shipments. "I'll discuss it with De Luca. There might be a way to alternate the timing. What else?"

There was a pause. "That's it."

"You called me at two in the morning with that hot tip?"

"What else?" Rayan countered. "It's cold as balls. There's a drunk kid hurling in the gutter outside my building."

Mathias snickered. "Why are you up? Can't sleep?"

Another pause. Rayan didn't talk about the dreams, but Mathias had watched the man tremble, muttering in a language he didn't understand. When he'd woken him, Rayan had startled like a cornered animal.

"You know there are pills for that," Mathias continued.

"I know." Rayan's tone was surly. "What's your excuse?"

Mathias recalled the woman, the ugly slap of their bodies meeting. He closed his eyes. "How cold?"

"Two below."

"That's nothing."

Rayan hated the cold. Mathias always noticed a change in him when the weather turned, a kind of steely trepidation.

"There might be something else," Rayan began cautiously. "But I don't know how much you should read into it."

He stood, walked to the window, and pushed back the blinds. Lake Ontario stretched before him, the water black and glistening. "Go on."

"Tony was called in to see the boss this morning. He came back to the office, looking grim."

Mathias sighed, surprised by the twinge of sadness he felt. Giorgio Russo had carved his place into the annals of Montreal history. It was hard to imagine what the city, and the family, would look like in his absence.

"It's close. Giovanni thinks only a matter of months."

"What happens then?" Rayan asked quietly.

Mathias stared out the window as the lights flickered across the harbor. "We wait."

23

The sky was gray and overcast, lending a solemn air to a solemn occasion—the weather itself bending to Giorgio Russo's iron will. It had made the front page of the *Gazette*—"Montreal Mob Boss Dead." In the end, the man had accomplished what few crime bosses managed: death from natural causes.

As they filed out of the Chiesa Madonna della Difesa, bells pealing overhead, Mathias glanced up at the clouds, which threatened rain. Built by Italian immigrants in the early 1900s—and boasting a remarkable portrait of Benito Mussolini behind the main altar—the church remained a historic landmark in the city's Petite Italia neighborhood. It had played host to many a high-profile family funeral, but nothing quite like this.

Ahead of him, Mathias could see the bronze casket being carried toward the hearse, Russo's wife and son trailing behind, arm in arm. The front of the church and the street outside teamed with mourners, members of the family and unaffiliated alike, here to pay their respects to the man who had governed the Montreal underground for over half a century.

Despite what he knew about the boss's declining health, Mathias had still been stunned to receive the call from Giovanni informing him of his death. The councilman had predicted he wouldn't make it through the winter, but to not have even lasted the month, he must have been hiding the truth about his condition from them all. Mathias watched as Russo's family climbed into a black limousine and pulled out behind the hearse, headed for the cemetery. A procession of cars began to form behind them, snaking down the street. If one didn't know better, they would think this simply a grieving Italian family sending off their much-loved patriarch. It was hard to miss the cops on standby, though, and the flash of cameras as the national media came out in force. Across the street, the municipal police were lined up as if watching a parade, trying to catch sight of new faces and gauge shifting alliances—any hint of what was to come.

Mathias didn't join the procession to the cemetery. Earlier that morning, he'd paid his respects to the boss in a smaller visitation held at the family-owned funeral home. There, he'd taken Piero Russo's hand, formally offering his condolences before a gathering of the group's elite, the two of them looking at each other, giving nothing away as they performed the required courtesies. Mathias didn't think Piero was brazen enough to knock him off at his own father's funeral, but it was anyone's game at this point.

After the news went public, there'd been little chance to regroup. Mathias had worked swiftly to put the final arrangements in place but could do nothing before receiving word from the Quintino, who'd so far remained silent. Giovanni had assured him it was simply a matter of tribute, to give the weight of Russo's passing time to settle. It made Mathias uneasy. Time was the one thing they couldn't afford to lose.

"Even my ma back in Hull has heard of Giorgio Russo," Jacques marveled as they watched the crowd disperse. "It's like being part of history."

He was as bad as the reporters clambering for a spot behind the police blockade, turning it into a spectacle. "Man's not even in the ground, and you're looking for a souvenir? Have some respect."

He started back to the car, taking out his cigarettes, Jacques falling into step behind him. Mathias lit one, spotting a familiar face approaching them.

"Thought you'd be at the burial," Mathias said to Giovanni as they came to a stop. He offered the old man a smoke and lit it for him.

"I'm on my way, waiting for the circus to pass." Giovanni looked sourly at the police presence on the other side of the street. "We're giving them something to talk about."

"Good," Mathias said. "They need something to do."

Tony sidled up beside them and slapped him on the back. "Sad day," he announced soberly. "I've known Giorgio Russo forty-three fucking years. Longer than I knew my own father."

Mathias nodded. "He was a great man."

The Collections boss accepted a cigarette, and the three of them stood, smoking silently.

"The council wants to see you both tonight," Giovanni said quietly, keeping his face neutral. "There are things to discuss. The regular spots aren't safe. Assume, for now, nothing is safe. There's a house on Maisonneuve West, 4151. Be there at six."

He peeled off without waiting for a reply. Mathias noticed Giovanni had several men stationed around him who followed as he walked, escorting him to his car. The man wasn't taking any chances.

"Well…" Tony sighed, the smoke curling above his head. "There goes my evening plans."

"You can sit around, counting your money, tomorrow, Tony."

The old man scowled. "You're as cocky as ever. Figured six months kissing Truman's ass would've knocked you down a peg."

Mathias smirked. Tony tossed his cigarette to the ground and crushed it with the toe of his black leather shoe. "I'm off," he announced, glancing across the parking lot. "My ride's waiting."

Mathias followed his gaze to see Rayan standing by the Mercedes, eyes trained in their direction. "Take him with you tonight," he said, his voice low. "For protection."

Tony snorted. "Don't get him involved in your little game of leapfrog. He's a good fucking soldier. I don't have another man in my division decent enough to replace him."

"Look out for yourself, is all I'm saying."

"Would you believe that?" Tony chuckled, giving him a scornful grin. "Almost fooled me into thinking you gave a damn."

Mathias watched as Tony made his way across to the car and Rayan got in behind the wheel. He thought of the list, recalling Piero's hardened stare as he shook his hand mere feet from his dead father's body. Tony had no idea. Rayan was already involved. They were all involved. Now they just had to make it out alive.

Stamping out his own cigarette, Mathias turned to Jacques. "Let's go."

The mood at the Collections office was muted when they returned from the funeral. Tony sent everyone home, figuring it was a lost cause trying to get a decent day's work out of them. Rayan stayed behind. On the drive back to the office, Tony had requested that he escort him to a meeting later that evening.

While Mathias had remained cryptic about what would happen in the aftermath of Giorgio Russo's death, Rayan couldn't imagine that the meeting involved anything besides succession. As an outsider, he hadn't been allowed in the church for the service, but as far as he knew, nothing had been formally announced. An unofficial ceasefire hung over the city while funeral arrangements were made, the family and the remainder of Montreal's criminal factions waiting with bated breath.

He sat in Tony's office as the man opened a dusty bottle of brandy rescued from one of the filing cabinets. He poured two glasses and eased into his chair with a heavy sigh. "I was gonna say the older you get, the more people you know start dropping dead. But then I remembered what business we're in. Age ain't exactly a factor."

Tony raised his drink. "To Giorgio Russo."

They clinked glasses, and Rayan took a cursory sip, not wanting to offend, then placed his glass down on the desk between them. He wasn't sure how he felt about the boss's death. Russo had always been a remote figure, something of a Montreal celebrity—although the authorities certainly wouldn't admit to that. He'd come to Canada with nothing and built an empire that spanned multiple provinces, spilling over the southern border into the States when RICO crippled the American-based Nostra. Rayan could respect his ambition and tenacity yet found himself unable to ignore the trail of blood Russo had left in his wake—the nameless scum he'd stepped over, his brother among them, to ensure that his position in the city remained unchallenged.

Tony, loosened by nostalgia and the liquor, told stories of his early days with Russo. Sitting across from him, Rayan found it difficult to imagine a younger, scrappier version of the man featured in these tales. Close calls with the Mounties, going head-to-head with the Red Reapers during a years-long turf war. He felt a renewed admiration for the Collections boss, who had remained a reliable cog in Russo's machine over the years, pivoting from his youth in the field to building a profitable division that held up many of the family's other interests.

"That's when I met the upstart, your old boss." Tony smirked. "You should have seen him waltzing in here, demanding I give him a job. All the other divisions had turned him away. Some *goomah*'s bastard with a degree. Can you imagine? I tell him to fuck off, that he'd be better off downtown working for some finance company—crooks all the same, mind you. He refuses. So I figure I'll teach him a lesson, scare him off. I send him out on the dirtiest fucking jobs imaginable. But he does every damn one. I had people coming in here, begging to pay—that's how scared of him they were. Never met a man who didn't hesitate before his first kill—except Beauvais."

Tony shook his head ruefully. "It's impressive, actually, how well he's severed the human from him. Like he was born for this. You would know—worked with him long enough. Under the skin, all that's left is cold, hard ambition."

Rayan swallowed his dissent, remembering how Mathias had held him that night, stiff with fear, fighting for breath. Tony was wrong—there was more to him than that. Mathias was more fragile—more wounded—than he would admit to even himself.

"Always figured that's why he took you on—fellow underdog and all. Another *fuck you* to the old guard who doubted him." Tony knocked back the rest of his glass. "Well..." He rose from his seat with a grunt, retrieving his phone and keys. "We'd better see what the suits want with me."

Rayan stood and stepped into the hallway to retrieve his jacket. They made their way through the empty office and down the stairs to the back entrance. He held open the door as Tony strode past him into the car park. The old man was steps from the Mercedes when Rayan heard the shot fracturing the quiet evening air and sending Tony pitching forward, first to his knees then face down on the concrete.

Rayan turned in the direction of the sound, pulling back instinctively. The second shot came too quickly, likely meant for his heart but instead puncturing his right shoulder, just below the clavicle.

He felt the impact but not the pain, throwing himself behind the car as his vision tunneled. He tried to reach for his gun, but his right arm hung useless at his side. Rayan heard footsteps approaching and yanked at his holster clumsily with his left hand, managing to free his weapon, his thumb scrabbling for the safety.

Come on, come on.

The man rounded the side of the car, and they both fired. Rayan heard the stranger's bullet ricochet by his ear, almost tearing through his cheek. His, on the other hand, found its target, embedding deep in the man's chest, sending him toppling backward. Rayan fired again at the twitching figure on the ground, then once more to be sure, and watched as the man's fingers stilled, weapon falling out of reach. His own gun slipped from his grip, too heavy to hold.

All thoughts were drawn to the pain that had clawed out from under the adrenaline and was now splintering through his body. He howled, smacking the back of his head against the car, pulling air through his teeth.

"Tony!" he yelled to no answer.

He knew the man was dead. Rayan looked down, the ground beneath him a liquid black. In his pocket, his phone began to vibrate. He reached for it, but the life was leeching from him, mixing with the blood pooling on the pavement.

Then everything went black.

24

Mathias lowered the phone from his ear, Giovanni's eyes on him. First Tony, now Rayan—they weren't picking up. Sitting around the meeting table at the safe house on Maisonneuve, the Quintino were assembled, waiting silently.

Something was wrong. Biding their time, they'd waited too long. Standing, Mathias grabbed his jacket from the back of the chair, Giovanni following suit.

"Stay here," Mathias warned.

"The fuck with that," the councilman growled. "I've known Tony since you were in diapers."

"And if you're next?" Mathias hissed. "The family will be torn to pieces without a head. All of this—for nothing. Stay here."

Giovanni scowled, clearly conflicted. But they both knew the stakes. He turned to his second. "Henri, go with him."

Mathias descended the stairs quickly, passing the men Giovanni had stationed by the front door. He strode out to the car, Jacques and Henri one step behind. "Start at the Collections office," he said, slamming the passenger door closed while Jacques started the engine.

As they drove, he tried Rayan again, a knot forming in his chest. He felt the panic encroaching and knew he needed to disassociate, keeping his head clear to tackle what would come next. Yet all he could think about was his apartment a month before, with Rayan lying beside him in the dark, his face so close Mathias could see the sliver of light from the window reflected in his eyes.

"What would you be if you'd never joined?" Rayan had asked, his voice a low murmur as though not expecting a reply.

"That's a stupid question."

"Is it?"

"And you?" Mathias countered. "Don't say 'pilot.'"

"Would I still have met you?"

"It's your fucking construct."

There'd been the pull of a smile at Rayan's lips, and he'd said nothing further.

Mathias should have gotten Rayan out when he had the chance, but he'd been greedy—had wanted him too much.

Jacques turned into the parking lot behind the office, and Mathias saw the body, face down, unmoving. His blood froze. He reached for his gun, opening the door before his second could stop the car.

"Boss, you can't go out there!" Jacques cried, but Mathias was already sprinting to the figure and crouching to find a pulse.

"Christ, Tony," he whispered, taking in the man's familiar features, the skin already cold.

He heard the shuffle of footsteps as Jacques and Henri approached, weapons in hand, glancing around nervously. Mathias stood, heart pounding in his throat, unable to register the slug of grief as his eyes scanned the lot for Rayan.

"Henri, stay with Tony. Call for backup," he ordered. "Jacques, with me."

Did Rayan leave to get help? No. Mathias had seen the Mercedes when they'd pulled in.

Gun drawn, he began to walk toward the car. There, barely visible in the shadows, was a shoe. Mathias raised a hand, signaling to Jacques before rounding the car.

The shoe belonged to a man on his back, eyes still open, a series of holes through his chest. Mathias's gaze fell on another figure, who was slumped against the car. Rayan's eyes were closed, white shirt blackened with blood. Mathias's breathing slowed, and he lurched forward. Dropping to his knees, he put a hand to Rayan's neck and felt a pulse. Mathias yanked off his jacket and pressed it against the wound on the man's shoulder. Jacques appeared beside him, helping to pull Rayan up, and together, they carried him back to the car. Henri was kneeling beside Tony, speaking quietly into his phone. He glanced up, taking in Rayan's limp body, and gave a brief nod.

Mathias didn't respond, his mind narrowing to a single focus. He hauled Rayan into the back seat with him while Jacques got behind the wheel.

"Drive," he snarled.

The warmth soaked through his shirt, sticking to the skin. Rayan's head rested against his shoulder as Mathias gripped the jacket, keeping pressure on the wound.

"Hold on." He pulled out his phone with one hand and dialed Martin's number. "The apartment on René-Lévesque," Mathias instructed his second. It was the only place he could think of. He knew Martin had a clinic somewhere in Brossard, but it was too far. "Faster!" he barked.

Mathias felt the ring of the phone in his chest. He was unable to tear his eyes from Rayan, who looked paler by the second. *Pick up, pick up, you fucker.*

Finally, the doctor answered. "Is he conscious?" Martin asked after Mathias had briefed him on Rayan's condition.

"No."

"How long has he been out?"

"I don't know."

"Can you get him to wake up, even for a minute? It will give us an idea of how much blood he's lost."

"Rayan," Mathias snapped, jostling him. "Get up."

He didn't move. Mathias felt his palm grow damp as more blood soaked through the jacket. His chest tightened in panic. They might not make it to the apartment.

"God dammit, Rayan!" he growled. Pressing the phone between his ear and shoulder, Mathias raised his hand and struck the man hard on the cheek. Rayan's eyes rolled open, and he lurched in pain, his body stiffening.

"He's conscious," Mathias reported into the phone, hiding the relief in his voice.

"Try and keep him awake. I'm leaving now—will be there shortly."

Rayan was writhing in his grip, teeth grinding in agony. His eyes kept losing focus, his breathing so irregular it was almost as if he wasn't breathing at all.

"Hang on. Do you hear me?" Mathias demanded. His voice seemed to make it through the clamor.

Rayan stilled, pulling himself back. "Tony's hit," he choked out, barely audible.

"I know," Mathias said quietly. He had yet to fully register that fact. That was something for another time.

"Mathias," Rayan murmured.

"Focus. Stay awake." Mathias's voice was urgent, constricting with fear. He'd never been so powerless, standing on the precipice, about to lose everything.

"I..." Rayan started, eyes fixing on his face before rolling back.

Mathias heard the blood rush in his ears. This couldn't be it. He wouldn't accept it. Through the window, he saw the lights of the bank across the street from his building.

"Pull into the underground lot. Park by the elevator," he told Jacques. He would not let Rayan die.

They brought him into the apartment and laid him down on the kitchen table. Minutes later, there was a soft knock at the door, and Jacques let the doctor in, an assistant trailing behind with a large case of equipment. Martin pulled on his gloves. The woman set up a standing lamp as the doctor removed Mathias's sodden jacket from the wound and cut away Rayan's shirt.

"Hold him down," Martin instructed.

"Give him something for the pain," Mathias growled as he reached across Rayan's chest and pinned the man's arms to his sides to stop him from moving. Jacques appeared at the end of the table, taking hold of his legs.

The doctor shook his head. "No time to take effect." He placed a silver tray down on the table and retrieved a scalpel and a set of narrow forceps from his carrying case. "I need to get in now, assess internal damage."

From the lamp, the woman hung a bag of blood attached to an IV. She took the needle and inserted it into Rayan's wrist as the doctor bent over, easing the forceps into the hole in the man's shoulder.

Rayan tensed beneath him, an animal cry tearing from his throat. Mathias held him down, teeth clenching. The doctor's forehead creased in concentration as he pressed deeper into the wound. Rayan's eyes opened, staring blindly at Mathias, his face twisting in anguish.

He could say nothing. There was nothing to say. Mathias could only look back at him, knowing it wasn't enough. There was a clink of metal as the doctor dropped the bullet into the tray. Glancing down, he saw that Rayan had slipped away again, his body going slack in his grip.

"It's surprisingly clean. Missed the bone, so there's minimal fragmentation," Martin murmured. "But we need to get this bleeding under control." His assistant passed him a handful of gauze pads, and he began to pack the wound.

Only then did the woman take a sack of morphine and hook it up to the IV. Mathias felt the relief as if it were his own, realizing how afraid he was of the man's eyes opening once again, revealing the pain within. The doctor dismissed him and Jacques as he and his assistant worked to clean and bandage Rayan's shoulder.

Mathias stepped back, hands curling into fists to still the shake. His phone began to ring in his pocket. He knew who it was. He knew on the other end of the line was a looming crisis that needed his attention. The board had been hurled to the floor, the pieces sent flying. But he could think of only one. His shirt stuck to his chest with a growing coldness.

Martin turned to him, his expression grim. "He's stable for now."

Mathias pocketed his phone after listening to Giovanni's message. Once the doctor had finished dressing the wound, they'd moved Rayan to the empty bedroom in the apartment. Mathias stood in the living room as if stuck between two realities. He needed to go. He couldn't allow it all to fall apart now—not after everything that had happened. At the same time, the thought of leaving Rayan bleeding and unconscious, his fate unknown, was as impossible a task as doing nothing.

Martin appeared in the doorway, shrugging on his coat. "He's sedated. The bleeding has slowed, but Camille will continue administering transfusions. He lost a lot of blood. She'll call me if there're any concerns."

"You're staying." It was a command, one he expected the doctor to follow.

Martin sighed and clasped his hands, carefully choosing his next words. "Mr. Beauvais, I'm afraid I can't stay longer than I have. The man is stable. Camille will remain with him overnight to monitor his vitals and administer pain medication, but there's not much more I can do. As I said, call me with any concerns, and I'll—"

Mathias grabbed him by the front of his shirt. "And if he dies?"

"That's always a possibility, Mr. Beauvais," Martin said slowly. "But short of admitting him to the hospital, I think you should take your chances with him here."

Mathias released the man, the strength sapped from him.

The doctor straightened his coat and gave Mathias a quick nod. "Call me if anything changes." He stepped into the hall, letting himself out.

Standing outside the door to the spare room, Mathias cracked it open to reveal Rayan lying motionless in the dim light, a thick swath of white wrapped across his chest and around his shoulder. The doctor's assistant glanced up, but Mathias said nothing, simply closing the door. His phone began to ring again, but he couldn't bring himself to answer. Mathias no longer trusted himself on the phone. He needed to see Giovanni in person.

He'd completely forgotten about Jacques until the man stepped out from the kitchen as Mathias made his way back down the hallway. "He's gonna pull through?"

Mathias found his presence an imposition, and the question even more so. He nodded curtly.

His second appeared momentarily relieved. "What should I—"

"Stay here," Mathias instructed, moving to the front door. "Wait for me to come back. Don't let anyone in." He reached for his jacket, but it wasn't on the coat hook. It lay instead in a bloody clump on the kitchen floor.

"Boss," Jacques said. "Your shirt."

Mathias looked down at his shirt as if seeing it for the first time. He placed a palm on the wall to steady himself, suddenly overcome. He grasped for anger, only to discover it missing. Instead, he found a jarring blankness. If he was to be the leader they were expecting, Mathias couldn't arrive in this state—fear lingering on his face and his greatest weakness painted in blood across his chest. Wordlessly, he walked past his second to the bedroom to change.

25

When Mathias stepped into the sitting room at the safe house on Maisonneuve, it was like waking from a dream, as though the events of the past few hours were simply an illusion and he'd been transported back to the start of the evening.

The Quintino had left—hastily, by the look of the unfinished drinks dotted around the table—disappearing into their various bunkers once the news had reached them. The seat meant for Tony remained empty, the glass untouched. Giovanni stood at the head of the table, smoking. Neither of them said anything.

A wave of exhaustion caught up to Mathias, flooding his body. He gritted his teeth. This was only the beginning.

"Henri called it in," Giovanni said finally, breaking the silence. "We've moved Tony somewhere safe."

The image of his former boss face down in the car park flashed through Mathias's mind. He pushed it down, out of reach.

"Nadeau... did he make it?"

"For now," Mathias said, the blankness yawning, swallowing his insides.

"That's something, at least."

Something.

"Piero's formally announced his succession, denouncing any verdict by the Quintino. He's sending men to the other groups in the city, demanding their loyalty," Giovanni said, tossing his cigarette into a half-full tumbler of scotch. "I've instructed the council to lay low."

Mathias reached out, his hand closing around Tony's abandoned glass.

"Tony was a declaration of war," Giovanni said, his voice hard, lined with grief.

Mathias lifted the glass and hurled it against the wall. He gripped the edge of the table and upended it, sending everything to the ground, broken glass scattering across the hardwood floor like marbles, the anger finally working its way through his blood, saving him from the void.

The councilman met his furious gaze. "You've waited long enough, Mathias," he said quietly. "Consider yourself off leash. How soon can the Reapers get here?"

"They're on their way." Mathias had called Truman on the drive over, and he'd sounded unnervingly enthused.

If Tony was the target, had Rayan simply been caught in the crossfire? He doubted it. Piero would have had the two of them in his sights because of their proximity to Mathias, ensuring that it was personal—a knife to the gut.

"We were due to discuss this earlier. Might as well get it settled now," Giovanni said with a frown. "Russo did not name his son as successor. Leadership passed to the Quintino, with the express purpose of selecting the new family head. The council was in the room when Giorgio relayed his last wishes. Piero, too, but he'll deny it. He's already refuted any ulterior claims as mutiny."

"And the council's decision?" Mathias asked.

"The Quintino have elected me as the new *capomandamento*."

A look passed between them. It was as though months of furtive discussions had culminated in an outcome that was both predicted and at the same time astonishing. There was no man better suited for the position. He walked to Giovanni and kneeled as the man extended his arm.

Mathias brought his lips to the signet ring on his right hand. "I swear to be faithful, *capomandamento*," he pledged, as he had to the boss before. Mathias had been younger then, with blood already beneath his fingernails—a small price to pay for entrance into a family where he was more than an omission. "If I betray, my flesh shall burn."

Then Mathias stood, touching cheeks with the old man, cementing his loyalty.

"I'm sure Tony would've had a few choice words to say about this," the new boss remarked, fixing Mathias with a look of cold-blooded fury. "Make the fucker pay."

The empty parking lot beside the Resto Lafleur in Pointe-Claire was as good a place as any to stage a gathering of the country's three largest criminal organizations. It had been Truman's suggestion. He'd traveled up with twenty of his men and set up camp in the lot between the fast-food chain and a neighboring steel-distribution center, awaiting instruction. Mathias had arrived to find the Reapers milling about their bikes, stuffing their faces with burgers and poutine.

Belkov had reluctantly agreed to join them, making his distaste for William Truman clear over the phone. But the Russian was willing to put that aside for the pleasure of long-awaited payback. He had Silvano Paterlini's name on a bullet and, as promised, had proven extremely patient while waiting for their collective gamble to pay off.

As they waited for Belkov to show, Mathias eyed the group of soldiers Giovanni had assembled. Loyal to Russo and his final wishes, they had heeded the call of the Quintino, pledging their allegiance to the new boss. De Luca was in attendance, along with several familiar faces from Narcotics. So, too, were Franco, Sonny, and the rest of the Collections team. Domenico Lombardi, the Bettings head who'd recently pushed back on Piero's unending line of credit, was noticeably absent. Mathias heard he'd been whacked on the way home from his *goomah*'s shortly after Tony's hit. Many of the men here had targets on their backs, had heard about Tony, and wanted to strike first.

Mathias was exposed without Jacques, but there was no way he could leave Rayan alone. There was still a chance Piero would send someone to finish the job. He took out his cigarettes, realizing how much he needed one to suppress the tremor beneath his skin. He'd spent months planning, orchestrating his revenge, only to be outmaneuvered from the start. He was barely functioning, acting on pure instinct, the remainder of him retreating within.

He watched as Belkov pulled up in his black Lincoln Town Car, followed by a second identical vehicle, out of which scrambled a team of thick-necked Russian soldiers. The man stepped down from the car, his driver shadowing him cautiously, taking in the surrounding activity.

Belkov appeared unusually sober, his eyebrows creased into a frown, mouth wrapped around a thick cigar. It had been a while since Mathias had seen the Bratva boss in person, most of his interaction with the Russians having gone through Gurin. Mathias couldn't say he missed him as he steeled himself for the antics Belkov's presence would provoke.

Truman strode across the parking lot toward them, a cigarette in one hand and a half-eaten cheeseburger in the other. The three men stepped away from the growing assembly of soldiers, eyeing one another warily.

"I take it you're all aware of the situation," Mathias began.

"Can't say I'm too sad about the big man croaking." Truman grinned, taking a bite out of his burger. "Looks like the apple don't fall far from the tree."

"Surprised you managed to put two and two together," Belkov sneered.

Truman paused midchew, his face darkening. "The fuck you saying, Russki?"

"Shut it," Mathias snapped, his patience down to a sliver. He was done with the man's childish temper—done indulging his boorish behavior. It was time for Truman to step up and show what he was worth. "We divide and conquer. I've got eight names. Smoke them out—no questions. They've made their beds. There's no coming back from this. Belkov—Paterlini's yours. No one touches Piero but me. Any intel, pass it along. The quicker it's done, the quicker we clean up the mess."

"And the other factions?" Belkov asked.

"If they've turned, we make an example. But when Piero's men start falling one by one, they won't stay that way for long." Mathias pulled two slips of paper from his pocket and handed them to Truman and the Russian.

"Now you have your own list," the Bratva boss remarked wryly.

The irony wasn't lost on Mathias.

"Names and addresses—where they live with their wives, where they keep their mistresses, grandma's room at the nursing home. You turn over every stone. Hunt down each one."

Giovanni had not spent the past six months idly. While Mathias had been greasing the wheels with Truman, stamping down sedition in Hamilton, the old man had built up a database of information on all of Piero's loyalists.

Truman tossed his unfinished burger onto the pavement, glancing at the paper briefly before shoving it in his pocket. "Easy enough. I thought you had a challenge for me, Mathias." He laughed. "Been a while since I've gone headhunting." Truman turned and strode toward his men, who were gearing up on their bikes. "We're moving out, shitkickers!"

Beside him, Belkov looked on with scorn. He muttered something in Russian, rocking back on his heels. "They make too much fucking noise."

"Works in our favor," Mathias replied, pulling on his cigarette, the smoke rising white against the blackened night sky. "The bigger the distraction, the more cover it gives us."

"Look at you, Beauvais. Thought of everything." The Bratva boss slipped his hands into his pockets, fixing Mathias with a disquieting stare. "Heard they shot your dog."

Mathias's jaw clenched.

"That part of the plan too?" Belkov asked.

Mathias stared back, refusing to let the man see how his remark had rattled him. The mask hung on by a thread. All of him was hanging on by a thread.

"You hold up your end, Belkov," Mathias said in a low voice, "and I will mine."

Mathias sat beside the makeshift hospital bed Martin had put together in the spare room of his apartment. Jacques was asleep on the living room couch, and the doctor's assistant had excused herself to make coffee. Rayan lay beneath a thin sheet, his chest bare except for the layers of thick padding that encircled his right shoulder. His skin was alarmingly pale, the sheet rising and falling as he took long, labored breaths. Even in sleep, his face flickered in pain. Mathias glanced up to check the bag of morphine on the standing IV.

It was now the early hours of the morning, but Mathias was having trouble leaving the room for his own bed. After briefing Truman and Belkov, he and a handful of soldiers had crawled the city from Saint-Marie to Longue-Pointe for clues as to Piero's whereabouts. An eerie silence had descended over Montreal. Everyone seemed to be ducking for cover, afraid of getting drawn into the conflict.

He laid a hand on the inside of Rayan's forearm and traced the line of muscle to where the bandages began. Staring down at his softened features, Mathias wondered how lasting the damage would be. He reached for the man's hand and felt it shudder, the fingers gripping his.

Rayan's eyes fluttered open, his mouth creasing into a grimace. "You're here." He spoke with considerable effort, his voice sounding as if it came from far away. He was barely lucid, cloudy with morphine.

"I'm here."

Rayan managed a weak grin. "Good."

They sat in silence, Mathias waiting for him to drift off once again.

"I saw him," Rayan murmured.

Mathias frowned. "Who?"

Rayan blinked as if he'd forgotten Mathias was in the room. "My brother. Said it's not so bad."

A weight pressed against Mathias's chest. When he'd first seen Rayan on the ground, blood pooling beside his body, he had been confronted by an image of the young man, whose death still managed to play out clearly in his mind.

"I used to think I wouldn't mind it," Rayan said, staring at him with a strange intensity. "Then I met you."

Mathias froze, the words lodging in his head. He looked at the battered man and felt the thud of his pulse beneath his fingertips. "Tell me about him."

"Tahir?"

Mathias nodded. In all their time together, they'd never talked about his brother—never acknowledged what they'd both seen.

"I idolized him. He looked out for me, and I did everything he asked," Rayan said. "Sometimes I wonder how different my life would've been if I hadn't."

Mathias said nothing, his gaze falling to the faded scar along Rayan's throat.

"In a way, he had it coming," he continued. "He was reckless. We were homeless. Our days were numbered..." He flinched, not quick enough to wipe the pain from his face.

"You need to rest."

Rayan took a shuddering breath. "I should have gone first, made him stay at the office—"

"Don't insult the man," Mathias cut in. "You think you could convince Tony to do anything?" But the thought pierced him. If Rayan had gone first, would he be here right now?

Rayan closed his eyes once more, his face slack with fatigue. "I know what he meant to you."

In all the chaos, Mathias had avoided thinking about Tony. He felt the ache finally enclosing. In his own father's absence, the old man had taken him in like a bothersome wayward son. He'd vouched for Mathias when no one else would and seen his potential despite the marks to his name. And Mathias had never thanked him for it.

He watched as Rayan slept. Sleep didn't come easy for him. Mathias wondered how much he was to blame for that, and for all of this. Rayan did not belong with the family. He never had. The man had no interest in money, status, or power games. He was a good soldier, but only practice had taught him that. Mathias didn't spare a thought for those who fell on the wrong side of his gun. Rayan remembered each one.

He felt a hollowing as the truth closed in. Rayan stayed because of him. He wouldn't leave so long as Mathias needed him. Yet while he remained with the family, Rayan would always be in the firing line, his life forfeited.

Rayan had become a liability to Mathias—to his ability to function and fulfill his obligations. He'd encountered many situations over the years, some far more treacherous, but never had he felt fear like when he'd pulled into that parking lot. Mathias had nearly lost himself, paralyzed with indecision, his mind shutting down. He could not risk being this immobilized again.

He leaned forward, brushing Rayan's hair from his forehead. Then he gently extracted each of Rayan's fingers and moved his hand away from the warmth, the life that pulsed through the man's body, distancing himself from the fear.

26

"It's like a fucking homecoming," Truman crowed as they stood smoking outside the lumber sheds at La Fabrique Allwood, waiting for Belkov to emerge.

They were in Laval, back on Industrial Boulevard, the shadow of that fateful afternoon with Junior still lingering even a half year on. The Russian was theatrical like that, bookending experiences, finishing them where they started. The place set Mathias's teeth on edge. He thought of that day often and how differently things might have turned out.

"Been years since I've set foot in the city. The broads, I swear." He whistled. "Like they all flew in from Paris."

"Don't get too comfortable," Mathias cautioned absently, more focused on what was happening inside the shed than on the man's appraisal of Quebec women.

Truman laughed. "Yeah, yeah. But we came through, eh?"

The eight men on their list had been whittled down to two, Mathias's gamble on Truman paying off. Belkov and his men had proven equally efficient. The municipal police were scrambling. The Red Reapers hadn't been seen in Montreal for decades, and their reappearance coincided with the passing of notorious mob boss Giorgio Russo. When it came to family infighting, the cops usually kept a wide berth, but it had been five days, and the bodies were still piling up.

Information swirled through the underground. The Russians and the Reapers were working with the family establishment, all of them vying against Piero's claim to leadership, acting as a deterrent to the remaining groups, who had yet to choose a side. In the melee, they'd lost a couple of De Luca's men when Filipo Abruzzo—Piero's longtime crawler—holed himself up in his third-floor apartment and started taking shots. They'd gotten to him in the end, but not before the two soldiers had bled out on the sidewalk.

"You came through," Mathias agreed. "And there will be spoils."

"You'd better fucking believe it." Truman grinned, sucking on his cigarette.

Belkov appeared with blood speckled across his gray suit jacket, a giddy smile on his face. He'd been the one to smoke out Silvano Paterlini, so Mathias had given him first rights—provided he kept the man alive. Piero was still proving elusive. Any clues they were able to extract from his loyalists quickly led nowhere. Mathias had trawled the city, exhausting a shared trove of safe houses, only to turn up nothing. He was banking on Paterlini squealing. The old man was high enough in the family hierarchy and close enough to Piero to have the greatest insight into his master plan.

"I told you I was patient," Belkov announced, joining them as the sky became mottled with heavy gray clouds. "It was a long wait but worth it. Blood for blood. Tastes sweet."

"I said talk to him, not tear him to fucking pieces." Mathias scowled. "Tell me you got something."

"I got more than something," Belkov said with a smirk. "Says Piero moved Tony to the top of the list. He knew the Quintino were about to make their announcement and wanted to set an example."

Mathias brought the cigarette to his lips, swallowing the anger.

"Russo's boy has a safe house Paterlini knows about, in Hochelega. He's hiding right under our noses. And don't worry—Senior's still alive." The Russian snickered. "Didn't want to end things too quickly."

Mathias nodded, the information slotting into his head, revising the course of action. If Paterlini wasn't bluffing, they almost had him. "If that's the case, I'll go pay my respects." He signaled for Jacques, and the two of them walked toward the shed.

"Don't forget, he's mine," Belkov called to his retreating back.

Inside, Silvano Paterlini was chained to the exposed steel framing on the far wall. Several Bratva men stood off to one side, more animated than usual, high on bloodlust. The Russians had taken to the old man, intent on ensuring that their reputation remain unsullied. And they certainly had a reputation—even Mathias appeared tame in comparison.

Bloody and bruised, Paterlini stared at him through the slits of his swollen eyes. From where his wrists were shackled, his hands appeared, each missing a finger, the stumps sloppily cauterized to make sure he didn't bleed out. Letting him die would be far too compassionate. Mathias did not envy the man. Junior's bullet through the head seemed charitable compared to what awaited his father.

Beside Paterlini sat a black toolbox, open to display an array of instruments, several of them bearing the marks of recent use. Belkov had left it out so the man could see what was to come and sit with the knowledge that the task wasn't yet complete. But still, Paterlini stared at Mathias, summoning as much composure as a man dangling at the precipice could muster. The old bastard was tenacious—Mathias would give him that—enough of his life spent with the family to know how to keep his shit together. After all, nothing was more pathetic than a blubbering mess.

Mathias crouched before him, taking another pull from his waning cigarette.

"You'd get that Slavic fuck to do your dirty work?" Paterlini spat, words slurring between cracked teeth. "You're more pathetic than I thought."

"But you knew that already," Mathias said, exhaling a plume of smoke into his face. "Half-breed son of a whore sullying the family name. Isn't that why you sent your boy to whack me? Not too quick, that one. I would know. Saw his brains myself."

Paterlini shrank.

"And I'll do you one better—it wasn't me who pulled the trigger," he continued. "That honor goes to the *estraneo* with more talent in his little finger than your son inherited from a long line of inbred Italians. A line that ends here, with you."

Watching Paterlini's eyes widen in horror, Mathias flicked his cigarette at the man's feet and stood. He walked out of the shed into a shower of rain, the clouds opening up above a city roiling with death.

"He's all yours, Belkov," Mathias said as he strode past the Russian to his car. "Clean up when you're done."

Jacques drove toward the address in Hochelega, where Truman and a handful of his men would meet them. Mathias pulled out his phone as they sped through the city. He listened to the click as Giovanni picked up.

"We've tracked him down," Mathias said.

"Good," the boss replied.

"When we get there...?" Mathias stared straight ahead as his second turned onto Rue de Rouen. He thought of Rayan limp in his arms, Tony face down on the concrete.

"Scalp him." The old man hung up.

They parked a street over from the safe house and walked through the narrow alleyway that connected the triplex to the neighboring road. Mathias kept a lookout for scouts, despite the fact that Piero's army of loyal supporters had dwindled over the past few days. The few remaining were willing to keep him safe.

As he and Jacques neared the basement entrance to the apartment, Truman appeared across the street, shielded by a bus shelter, eyes on them. The Reapers would stay outside and cover the perimeter in case Piero ran. Mathias knew enough about the man to consider that a serious possibility.

"We break off, go room by room," Mathias instructed his second. "If you find him, hold him until I get there."

Jacques nodded, his hand slipping beneath his jacket. He gave Mathias cover as he pulled out his gun. They would have to move fast. He raised it and shot the lock on the door. His second threw himself forward, slamming his shoulder against the panel and sending the door flying open.

Mathias followed Jacques inside. The place was eerily quiet. The hallway split off in two directions with the stairs to the second level set in between. He heard the thud of footsteps approaching from the right, and Jacques surged ahead. Over his second's shoulder, Mathias saw the blur of a face he didn't recognize—thick jaw, beady eyes. The man lifted his weapon, but Jacques fired first, throwing him back against the wall, where he slid to the floor.

His second crouched to retrieve the fallen gun, and Mathias stepped over the soldier's body, continuing along the hall to where it opened into a darkened foyer. He felt the rush of a bullet whizz past his head to embed itself in the plaster behind him. *Fuck.*

Mathias ducked behind a large wooden cabinet by the foyer entrance. He was sorely off his game, the events of the last several days corroding his instincts. Jacques retreated, doubling back down the hallway to emerge on the other side of the stairs. Mathias could just make out the open door of what looked like a study. That was where the shot had come from.

"No surprise the old fucker sent you." Piero's voice cut through the silence of the empty apartment. "That hack, Bianchi, has been waiting years for my father to die. And now the vultures descend."

Mathias shifted, attempting to get a better view of the room. Another shot sounded, shattering the cabinet door. Glass tinkled around his feet. He watched Jacques—gun in hand—stalk along the wall opposite him, making his way slowly toward the room where Piero was camped out.

"Caught up with our good friend Paterlini," Mathias said, goading the man to keep him talking as his second inched closer. "You're lucky it's me and not Belkov who found you first."

Silence from Piero.

Jacques had reached the doorframe and gave a nod in his direction, readying himself to enter. Mathias nodded back.

His second flew into the room, and the sound of a struggle erupted, then a single shot. Mathias sprinted to the study and found Jacques wrestling Piero to the ground, the man's gun falling from his grip. Mathias kicked it out of reach, raised his own weapon, and smashed it into the side of Piero's head. He dropped to the floor with a thump, blood streaming from his temple.

"Get him up," Mathias ordered.

Jacques pulled Piero to his feet, holding his arms behind his back. The man spat at him, and Mathias raised his gun again and cracked it against his cheek. Piero grunted, panting, glaring at him as the blood trickled from his nose, ready to tear him to pieces with his teeth.

"How does it feel?" Mathias asked, pressing the barrel hard against Piero's forehead, recalling the paralyzing fear that had gripped him as Junior stared him down.

"You're not going to shoot me," Piero sneered.

Mathias noticed the shadow of stubble along his jaw and the dark circles beneath his eyes. So they'd spooked him. He'd been holed up here, hiding like a rat.

"Why's that? I've done far worse in my time." Mathias's expression hardened. "And I'd say you've given me plenty of reason."

Piero shook his head, the smirk wavering. His eyes darted from the gun to Mathias to the doorway as if hoping someone would save him—perhaps the man growing cold in the hallway. "I know how much you admired my father. You wouldn't kill the boss's son."

Mathias snorted, his mouth curling. "Giorgio Russo is dead. I don't owe him a goddamn thing."

He'd thought about this moment for the better part of a year, imagining how he would exact his revenge for all those months of humiliation. But now that Mathias was here, he felt nothing. Too much had been taken for him to get even. He needed for all of this to be over.

He racked the slide on his gun with a click. Before him, Piero recoiled, paling. "You would side with fucking Truman and Belkov over one of your own?" The man's voice rose in disbelief.

"Have you forgotten, Piero?" Mathias's eyes narrowed. "I'm not one of you." How bitter that had once tasted. "And this fantasy of the family resembling your idyllic Italian village?" He yanked the front of Piero's shirt, forcing his gaze to meet his own. "Take a good look at my face," Mathias said in a low voice. "Because one day, this bastard's going to be leading it."

He felt cold metal beneath his finger and saw Piero's eyes widen in terror.

"How's that for legacy?" Mathias pulled the trigger before the man could respond.

Piero toppled backward and came to rest on the ground as blood snaked out from behind his shattered skull, pooling on the scuffed hardwood. Mathias spat on the floor by his feet.

"That was for Tony," he growled, barely able to get the words out, he was so overcome with anger. "You entitled fuck."

27

"Mr. Nadeau has not been taking his pain medication," Dr. Martin said at the beginning of his weekly checkup call.

Mathias stood in the bedroom of his apartment, staring out the window at the city below, a rare moment of respite amid the frenzied activity of the past fortnight. He came back to shower, eat, and fit in a couple hours of sleep before he was needed again for meetings with family elite—endless fires to put out. He'd made efforts to keep his distance from Rayan, with the doctor's calls the only update on his condition. Not for the first time since Rayan's injury, Mathias noted how difficult a patient he was.

"I noticed the bottle was full on my last visit."

Mathias clicked his tongue in agitation. "What is he supposed to be taking?"

"Two tablets of Percocet twice a day."

He looked down at the cars streaming along René-Lévesque. They slowed, the crowd of pedestrians surging onto the road—young women, men in suits, mothers pushing babies. Small, insignificant, completely out of touch.

"I'll take care of it," he said finally.

Later that day, he found himself with an elusive free afternoon. Jacques was starting to sag on his feet, so Mathias had dismissed him early. He remembered that not everyone functioned well in chaos. That ability seemed unique to him.

He drove to Rayan's apartment, a route familiar enough that he could do it in his sleep. Once Rayan had been able to stand on his own, he'd insisted on recovering at home. Mathias had seen him only once since then, in part due to affairs that needed tending but mostly because he found it difficult to witness Rayan's silent suffering. A wall had gone up, their old fluidity gone. From the doctor's briefings, Mathias knew that his recovery was gradual. Rayan received daily visits from a nurse for physical therapy and weekly visits from Martin to check his progress.

Mathias parked his car around the back of the building and let himself into the lobby. He rode the elevator to Rayan's floor, not bothering to knock as he turned the silver key in the lock. The place was quiet, the blinds still drawn. He walked into the living room, which was sparse but for a couch and coffee table. At the bedroom, he pushed open the door to reveal Rayan lying on his side on top of the bed, his back to him. Mathias stood, fingers resting on the handle. Then he swung it closed and retreated into the kitchen.

It didn't him take long to find the neglected bottle of Percocet, filled almost to the brim. He shook his head in frustration. The man was so stubborn.

Mathias twisted it open and knocked two pale-yellow pills from the bottle into the lid. After depositing them on the counter, he grabbed a knife, positioned the flat side above the pills, and slammed down on it with the heel of his hand, crushing them into dust. He reached into the cabinet above his head and pulled down a glass then filled it at the sink and scraped the powdered pills into the water, where they dissolved clear.

"What are you doing here?" Rayan stood in the entrance to the hallway, his right arm wrapped tightly in a sling against his chest, preventing any movement from his shoulder to his wrist. A shirt hung from his shoulders, the empty sleeves trailing at his sides.

Mathias pushed the glass of water across the counter in Rayan's direction, pocketing the bottle of pills. "Figured I'd see how you were holding up. You're standing."

Rayan stepped forward gingerly, disguising the discomfort the movement seemed to trigger. "What a fucking accomplishment," he muttered.

The injury had been hard on him, bringing out another side than his usual stoic agreeability. He'd become curt, thorny, and uninterested in the veneer of compliance.

Mathias took down another glass and opened the cabinet above the sink to retrieve the bottle of Macallan the man kept for when he was there. Pouring his own drink, he watched as Rayan lifted the water to his lips and took a long sip.

"Is the physio helping?"

"Yes," Rayan replied guardedly, and Mathias decided not to press the issue. He was doing the recovery exercises. That was the important part. The fact that he wasn't noticeably improving—that was something else.

Rayan narrowed his eyes. "You're not going to tell me what's happened?"

Mathias knew he was struggling with the isolation, pushed to the periphery in a time of complete overhaul. "Short or long version?" He took a swig of scotch, the thick liquid lining his throat.

"Knowing your aversion to embellishment, I figure there's only a short version."

Mathias raised an eyebrow. He wasn't wrong. "Piero is dead."

He watched the news register on Rayan's face. Was it relief?

"Belkov and Truman have assisted in taking back the city," he continued as though Piero Russo was already a footnote—a mild inconvenience and not the reason for Mathias's expulsion from the city, Rayan's painful debilitation, and Tony lying six feet in the dirt.

"There's been some rebellion. The Algerians have pushed back, and rumor is the Batos are next. They got a whiff of Piero's plan and thought they'd exploit the confusion. Nothing we can't handle."

"Impressive," Rayan murmured, his features darkening. "More than I've gathered reading the paper. From the headlines, you'd think the city was imploding." His hand shot out, and he steadied himself against the counter.

"Maybe you should sit down."

Rayan gave him an icy glare. He did not like being treated as if he were anything less than capable. But he downed the rest of the water and stepped back toward the couch. Mathias followed and took a seat across from him, nursing his scotch.

"What were you going to do if I didn't drink it?" Rayan looked at him with quiet defiance. So he'd known, and he'd drunk it anyway.

"I wasn't above holding you down, if that's what you're asking," Mathias replied evenly, lifting his own drink. "Thankfully, you saved me the trouble."

Rayan stared at him. "Why haven't you come?" he asked, his voice low. "I've waited."

Mathias's gaze fell on the curve of the man's jaw. His fingers itched to reach across the table between them. Instead, he shifted his attention to the series of bandages layered across the right side of Rayan's bare chest, stopping just below his shoulder.

"Can you move it?"

They both watched as Rayan slowly bent the fingers of his right hand into a fist, his arm shuddering in protest, the pain searing across his face.

"That's enough," Mathias said.

Rayan sank back into the couch.

"You're not taking your pills."

He looked at him wordlessly.

"Martin said you're not eating—"

"What else did the doctor say?" Rayan cut in. "Seems you'd rather talk to him than ask me."

Mathias was surprised when no reprimand jumped to his lips. "Why aren't you taking them?"

"They make me cloudy, make the dreams unbearable," Rayan admitted reluctantly. "I don't recognize myself when I'm on them. My brother—" He stopped, exhaling. "I'm just one bad decision away from ending up like him."

Things began to click into place, things about him Mathias hadn't been able to put his finger on. "Choosing to get well isn't a bad decision. Shuffling around here in pain, on the other hand," he said, taking the bottle of Percocet from his pocket and placing it on the table. "Take the damn pills, Rayan. Worry about the rest when you're strong enough to fight it."

Rayan glanced away, his eyes softening as the meds kicked in.

"You should lie down." Mathias stood and was surprised when Rayan allowed himself to be guided to the bedroom. His hands brushed bare skin, stoking tendrils of electricity that pushed against his resolve.

"Must be tough," Mathias mused as he helped Rayan into bed. "Not much you can do with a busted right arm."

"I'm fine."

"Are you?"

Rayan said nothing. He'd grown too good at pretending there was nothing to want.

"How long has it been?" Mathias asked, pulling at the bedclothes, his hands moving on their own, so used to laying claim to Rayan's body that he found himself unable to hold back.

Rayan grabbed at the sheet, the muscles in his neck tensing. "Don't."

"How long?" he asked again, fingers snaking beneath the waistband of Rayan's sweats.

He jerked, his good hand gripping Mathias's wrist, attempting to hide the constriction of desire that pulled at his features. Mathias could already see the telltale flush along his neck and hear the quickening of his breath. Then, as though accepting the futility of his resistance, Rayan let go.

Mathias captured his cock in his fist, and a low moan escaped the man's mouth. Rayan's eyes flew to his face, staring up at him. Mathias was struck by the image of that same face wrenched in agony as he held him down on the kitchen table.

He froze, heart thudding. Releasing him, Mathias turned away. "You should rest," he said, catching a glimpse of himself in the closet mirror, lust filling his pupils.

Mathias stepped out of the room, closing the door behind him. He seethed with need, cursing his own weakness. Retrieving his phone and keys from the counter, he spotted the battered Saint-Exupéry paperback in a stack of books on the windowsill. Mathias picked it up, the cover falling open to reveal an inscription written neatly in black ink. He read it slowly, the words burrowing beneath his skin. Then he snapped the book shut and tucked it under his arm as he strode out of Rayan's apartment.

Mathias was once again seated in the VIP room at Le Rouge, watching the collection of family elite—albeit slightly diminished—shuffle through the door. It was the first meeting presided over by the new boss, a gathering both necessary and fraught.

Any major leadership upheaval saw members take sides, however discreetly. After weeks of bloodshed, Giovanni Bianchi had established himself as the undisputed head of the family. From here, the only way was forward. The group had come together anew, putting aside the fracture of disagreement to focus on its survival.

Mathias noted a new deference in the way the old guard treated him. While in the past they'd merely tolerated him, now his presence necessitated respect. They were afraid of him, of what he was capable of. No one in the family's history had executed a takeover with the weight of rival factions. Mathias had left the city slighted only to return unassailable—not least by the fact that his bullet had felled Giorgio Russo's son.

Truman and the Reapers had departed Montreal with a substantial increase in port access and a formal extension of their territory as far east as Gatineau—a generous reward for taking some of the heat off the family and proving a valuable resource in the campaign against Piero. Mathias's alliance with the man meant Giovanni was reluctant to relieve him entirely of his Hamilton duties. Considering how much still remained in the air, Mathias would see what he could do about that.

At the moment, his focus was on cleanup—reestablishing the status quo and ensuring that the city's various groups remain compliant. That and placating the cops. The family had stirred up enough trouble for the RCMP to get involved, and Federal attention demanded Federal-sized bribes. Fortunately for Mathias, he had several contacts embedded in the national HQ and maintained a charitable relationship with the chief of the municipal police.

The previous evening, Mathias had met with Belkov, who'd celebrated the news of Truman's departure, claiming to notice the diminished stink. They were still exploiting the Russian's muscle. His soldiers mixed in with their own as they moved through the city, stamping out sedition. In return for his support, Belkov had been awarded formerly disputed territory south of the city, padding the Russian supply route through to the States and legitimizing the group's position.

As a gesture of goodwill, Mathias had personally removed protection fees for the Bratva in Montreal and indefinitely extended the port waiver, paid for with the cut he'd negotiated on the Reapers' narcotics imports. In the end, it was a small price to pay to keep the Russians on their side. The last thing the family needed was a war on multiple fronts.

The waitress brought over his refill and placed it on the table before him. The division heads were seated to his right—with the notable exception of Collections, an absence that weighed heavy on Mathias. To his left, the remaining members of the Quintino had taken their seats: Enzo Carbone, Gabriele Giordano, and Armando Bernardi.

The boss sat at the head of the table, in no hurry to start the meeting. Giovanni had proven unflappable over the last several weeks, executing his takeover with a calculated precision. There was no question he was ready for the job, the past year merely serving as a rehearsal while Russo's health slipped deeper into decline.

Giovanni had known something different was needed to guarantee his rise to the top. Sentiment would always lean toward a bloodline succession—the family was nostalgic that way. Which was why the man had sought him out, even back then, the kernel of a plan already taking hold. Because Mathias was something different, and he'd wielded that difference, turning it into his strength. Nostalgia didn't stand a chance against brute force.

Finally, the boss raised his glass, and the room stilled. Mathias felt the tension, thick as fog. This was the first handover he'd witnessed in his lifetime, the bloody aftermath of Giorgio Russo's ascent to power having occurred long before he was born.

"In this room today, we come together as a family," Giovanni announced. "Against us is the teeming horde that exists outside these doors. Let us remember that first, especially now."

There was a murmur of agreement from the assembly of men tired of the bloodshed and infighting—men who'd much rather things returned to normal.

They wanted to go back to receiving thick envelopes of cash and enjoying the finer things in life: women, food, booze.

"I'd like to acknowledge a great absence in the room," the boss said soberly. "That of our distinguished leader, Giorgio Russo, who steered the group through fifty-two years of legacy in this town." He gave the assembly a moment to acknowledge this extraordinary feat. "And I would be remiss if I didn't honor Collections head and longtime friend, Antonio Giraldi, who was taken too soon and whose advice and expertise will be sorely missed."

Giovanni caught Mathias's eye, and he brought the scotch to his lips and drank in Tony's honor. The funeral had been modest. The disruption to the family's equilibrium meant the man wasn't extended the full rites of someone in his position. But his family had been taken care of—Giovanni had made sure of that— his wife and a daughter about Mathias's age, who had the old man's eyes. Tony had never spoken of them. All those late nights at the office, working and drinking, Mathias hadn't realized there was anyone waiting at home. Tony's wife had stood by the casket, nodding blankly while mourners filed past to shake her hand and offer condolences, like a stranger in a room full of people.

Rayan, barely walking at the time, was furious when Mathias had refused to let him attend. But Mathias's concern for his safety, a paranoia that hadn't eased since the day of the shooting, had ultimately won out. Rayan had always seemed untouchable, possessing an uncanny ability to emerge from danger unscathed. That illusion had been shattered. Mathias knew now how vulnerable he was, how easily he could die. In the end, it was good Rayan hadn't gone. He still blamed himself for Tony's death, and knowing the old man had left a family behind would only further his guilt.

"My appointment means the Quintino are a member short." Giovanni paused, allowing the implications of that fact to settle. "The council and I have discussed at length, and Mathias Beauvais has been put forward for the role. Mathias has proven his dedication, his ability, many times—and to great esteem in recent weeks. I welcome his counsel."

Mathias gripped his drink, feeling the eyes of men he'd once deferred to shift to him—men who'd known him simply as Federico Mancini's bastard son.

The boss turned to him, fixing him with a measured stare. "So, Beauvais, what do you say?"

He recalled Giovanni's words the day at the race track, cryptic at the time but now becoming clear: "There may be greater tolerance for difference, provided that difference looks the same."

"It would be an honor, boss," he replied.

Slowly, men stood, not with derision but with respect on their faces, each of them raising a glass to toast Mathias's appointment and pledge their loyalty. Mathias was no longer a shadow lurking in the background, waiting for his due. He had a seat at the table, directly below the boss, in clear line of view.

Through the haze of triumph, Mathias felt the cold hand of fear. His mind flashed to Rayan slumped against the car. To be seen meant to be subject to the full scrutiny of the family, every flaw and weakness magnified. Too many times, Mathias had caught himself looking at the man when he thought no one was watching.

How brazen he'd become.

He knew then what his acceptance meant. There was no room for error. Any defect would need to be eliminated. He had compromised himself. And if Mathias was compromised, so too was the family.

28

He'd seen more of Mathias when they lived in different cities. Weeks went by, and Rayan heard nothing. Cowed by his injury, he rarely left the apartment. He grew dizzy with the boredom of it all. When it got to be too much—when he buzzed with rage at how useless he'd become, Rayan lifted weights for hours. If his arm refused to cooperate, he would punish the rest of his body. One handed push-ups and single-arm deadlifts. Once, he passed out and woke several hours later to find the room dark. After struggling to pull himself up, he'd made it to the bed, where he'd collapsed and slept until morning.

It was late afternoon, and Rayan stood in the middle of his living room after a particularly grueling workout. He had long ago piled the furniture into one corner, giving the space a strange starkness that suited his imposed confinement. Breathing heavily, he stared at his right hand as it trembled, his arm spasming. The minute-to-minute pain had lessened, but he experienced sudden flare-ups, the wound asserting itself while he attempted simple everyday tasks—holding a knife, turning the shower handle—his body reminding him that he was a fool if he thought he could escape this penance.

The lock on the door clicked, and he was barely able to wipe the despair from his face before Mathias walked in, eyes sweeping the room, taking in Rayan and the state of the apartment.

"Interrupting something?"

Mathias's voice broke the trance. Rayan picked up the towel he'd left on the counter. He pressed it to his damp face and bare chest then threw it around his neck. "I'm done."

"With what, exactly?" Mathias asked. "Martin told you to take it easy."

Rayan frowned. "I want to be ready for when I'm needed."

"You're not," Mathias said flatly. "Not in your condition."

The fury swelled. Since the shooting, Rayan found he struggled to control simple emotions that had glanced off him before. "I'm fine. It won't be long before I'm back to where I was."

Mathias stepped over and placed a hand on his shoulder. The longing rose like an ache, immediate and physical. Mathias slipped his thumb down to the mess of scarring below Rayan's clavicle and dug it into the flesh. Rayan let out a growl and shoved Mathias backward, his hand flying to the wound. He grit his teeth as the throbbing continued, waves of pain rolling down his arm.

Mathias looked at him. "You were never much of a liar."

"You're still as much of a bastard," Rayan spat.

A flash of surprise crossed Mathias's face. The word choice, though accidental, was heavy with implications. Rayan regretted it immediately. He also regretted the way his pulse had quickened when the man touched him. In Mathias's increasing absence, Rayan had thought too much about his former capo's hands on him.

There was a thwack as his head hit the wall behind him, Mathias gripping his neck, his face dangerously close. When the man spoke, it was hard. "Wake up, Rayan. You were shot. You don't bounce back from that."

Rayan expected to feel anger but instead felt it drain from him. A piercing dread took its place. He didn't know what he was if not useful. He'd scrabbled together this pitiful life, and it was slipping through his fingers.

"Why are you avoiding me?"

Mathias dropped his hand, stepping back. Something was different. Something had changed. Rayan reached for him, but Mathias recoiled like a stranger.

The fear from before was back—the years of watching, afraid of what he might reveal. All those times he'd wanted to touch Mathias and hadn't. Rayan had become so emboldened that he'd forgotten this feeling, deluding himself by thinking he had a claim over the man—that all of it wouldn't simply disappear in an instant.

"I've been appointed to the council."

Rayan's eyes widened. "The Quintino?"

Mathias nodded.

It was an unprecedented honor, a befitting acknowledgement of Mathias's dedication, all that he'd worked for. Despite everything, Rayan felt a swell of pride. "That's... No one deserves it more."

Mathias stared at him, a coldness settling over his features. "This has to stop."

Rayan blinked. *This?*

"The family, my role—it's changing. This was a lapse in judgment. Now it stops."

Rayan heard a rush in his ears. Mathias continued to speak, but only some words made it through the noise. "I'm transferring you to Denis Larrivée, the booking head in Quebec City. He'll take you on as a favor. Starting next month."

"A favor?" Rayan echoed in disbelief.

"With your arm, you're no use in the field, and I can't justify the dead weight. The options are limited. At least you'll be working."

It came as a flurry of hits, each one harder than the next. He'd been tossed aside like he was nothing.

"Mathias..." he said, if only to stop the volley. He couldn't think. His mind was frozen.

Mathias's eyes narrowed with growing frustration.

Does he expect me to simply agree and walk away from the only thing in my life that matters?

"We're done," Mathias pronounced curtly.

A numbness crept into Rayan's chest, stealing his breath. And then one thing became clear, rising above the mess. Words he'd swallowed again and again, too afraid to give them voice.

"I've loved you for years," Rayan said, his throat constricting. "That doesn't stop because you say it does."

The admission, the first said aloud, shocked them both into silence. Mathias opened his mouth to speak but said nothing. The stillness was deafening. Something unnameable flickered in his gray eyes.

Then his face darkened, lips curling into a sneer. "You think that's what this is?" he scoffed. "What would you know about love?"

Rayan's stomach seized. Then came the surge of anger. Mathias was blind to the ways he excised his own feelings.

"More than you."

Mathias stiffened, the mask slipping to reveal a glimpse of the man beneath. But it disappeared in an instant, and Rayan found himself face-to-face with the stony glare he'd seen employed on countless jobs—menacing and dangerous, a look that whittled those who encountered it down to nothing.

"I'm done with you, Rayan," Mathias said quietly. "I don't need you anymore."

Rayan could say nothing, words abandoning him.

"Understand? This ends."

Rayan felt as though he inhabited a space outside his body. He could not make Mathias keep him.

"Do you understand?" Mathias asked again, anger lifting his voice.

Rayan spoke without hearing the words. "I understand."

Mathias drove through the streets of downtown Montreal on his way to see the boss. After months of clandestine meetings, it was strange to be invited to Giovanni's home, treated like an honored guest. Jacques had settled in well, undeterred at having to leave Hamilton behind. He seemed determined to get his stripes, hungry for the potential of life amid family ranks. While Mathias couldn't fault the man, he found himself newly cautious. Ambition, greed, power—all were accepted currencies in his world, yet they brought the potential for corruption and betrayal. It only served to highlight how completely he'd trusted his former second, someone unconcerned with such things.

Catching himself, Mathias shuffled the thoughts quickly and forced them to the back of his mind. It was a temporary exercise, leaving him exposed for when they inevitably rose again, like a dense fog, clouding his vision.

While Jacques remained unranked, Mathias preferred to keep him out of the more intimate discussions of family affairs. That day, Mathias had left him at the Collections office, figuring Franco could use the help. There was a gaping hole where Tony had once been, and almost three months after his death, they were no closer to determining his replacement.

It was still dangerous for Mathias to be out alone. A small minority continued to resist the boss's newfound clout in the city. That was to be expected. Five decades was long enough for the groove to run deep. But Mathias took his chances, less concerned these days with his own safety and more with getting the job done. It was simpler that way. Mathias operated far more efficiently when he scrubbed away the weaker parts of himself—desire, hope. No more blind spots.

In his pocket, Mathias felt the buzz of his phone. He pulled it out, not recognizing the number.

"It's Serge." The man's voice crackled in his ear.

Serge Rastelli was the regional head in Quebec City. That deep in the province, the family's presence was minimal at best, limited mostly to gambling revenue and predatory lending. It served as an outpost, primarily to keep other factions out of Atlantic Canada—the farthest one could get from the family without leaving it.

"Were you sending someone to help Larrivée?"

Mathias frowned. "I did. Weeks ago."

"He's telling me no one showed."

Mathias braked hard, pulling over. The van behind him honked, swerving across the center line to pass. He hung up, tossed his phone onto the passenger seat, and yanked the car across two lanes of traffic to speed back in the other direction. He parked outside the apartment building and scaled the stairs to the third floor, already reaching for the small silver key.

It was empty, everything gone. Only when confronted by its blankness did Mathias realize how familiar the place had become. The way the sunlight streaked across the scuffed parquet floors. The towering stacks of books, more prominent than furniture. The herbs, grown in small pots along the kitchen windowsill—parsley, mint, coriander—thrown into everything Rayan made, a lingering reverence for a homeland as strange to him as this one. Now it could have been any apartment in the city, not a hint of Rayan remaining. Nothing left to prove he'd ever been here.

That afternoon, Mathias had been sure that the man—despite the embittered fall of his face, the stricken look in his eyes—would do as he always had and follow orders. But it seemed even for Rayan—constant, loyal to a fault—there was a point of no return. After years of blind obedience, he'd taken his fate into his own hands.

Mathias closed the door and walked back down the stairs. He felt a cracking, like a layer pulling away from his skin. Back in the car, his phone began to ring. He ignored it, spinning the wheel around in the direction he had come. He was going to be late.

Giovanni raised an eyebrow when Stefano led him into the parlor of his stately Cartierville home ten minutes past their appointed meeting time. Mathias took a seat across from him and was handed a cup of black coffee from a maid who appeared and disappeared in a blur of movement.

"Don't tell me you're slipping," the boss said wryly.

"Apologies," Mathias replied, offering no explanation. He placed the coffee down on the table between them, the smell turning his stomach. He wanted a drink. Needed a drink. Something to slow the spiral.

"We need to discuss Collections," Giovanni began. "You know as well as I do Franco's out of his league."

Mathias knew the boss wanted him to take the reins, if only temporarily. The assumption rankled him. To spend his days managing the team that took care of the family's dirty work was beneath him now. Tony might have garnered a great deal of satisfaction from that, but Mathias sure as hell didn't.

All things being equal, Mathias knew who should have taken the division. Tony had said so himself—there wasn't a better man to replace him. But things weren't equal, and they certainly weren't fair. That was why he'd sent Rayan away. The man's injury was simply an excuse. There was plenty someone with his aptitude could do without setting foot outside the office. Tony had been proof of that.

The truth was he didn't want Rayan in Montreal, where he would be caught up in family politics. The farther he was from Mathias, the safer they both would be. Cutting ties had been the only way. Rayan would never have agreed to it otherwise.

Yet at the same time, Mathias had been incapable of granting his freedom. He needed to know where he was, unable to accept the prospect of Rayan vanishing entirely from his life. So he'd made arrangements. He would be gone but not gone, safe but out of reach—of both Mathias and everyone else.

An image surfaced in his mind: his mother flitting by the window of their apartment when he was growing up, like a caged bird, staring down at the street in hopes of catching a glimpse of his father. Mathias's stomach lurched again. He clenched his teeth in an effort to quell the nausea. Giovanni was still talking, but he heard nothing.

"Mathias."

He snapped back to attention.

"You don't look well," the boss remarked, cocking his head curiously. "It's been a trying few months. Perhaps you should take a couple days."

"I'm fine," he said shortly.

Giovanni studied him then smirked. "You're human after all." He rose from his chair, beckoning Stefano. "I'll be in touch."

Mathias watched as the boss left the room, smarting with humiliation yet unable to find the words to refute the man's observation. His mind reeled, stuck in a loop he couldn't break, smothering all reason. He had enough sense to gather the remainder of his composure and head home.

As Mathias drove, his phone began to ring again from the passenger seat. He glanced over at the screen then back to the road. It continued to ring, brazen, undeterred, the sound drilling into his skull. Seconds from him throwing it out of the moving car, the phone finally stopped ringing.

In the living room of his apartment, Mathias brought the bottle of scotch to his lips, barely registering how empty it had become. He was almost there. With a couple more slugs, he wouldn't even remember who Rayan was. The thought conjured the man anew, and Mathias froze midswig. He pitched the bottle against the wall, and it shattered with a crash, achieving nothing. The anger had deserted him once again.

He closed his eyes to still the throbbing in his head. Leaning back into the couch, he willed himself to think of anything but his former second. But that was the problem. That was why he was drunk on the couch in the middle of the day—because he couldn't. In his effort to exorcise Rayan from his life, Mathias had unknowingly broken something.

He picked up the book—the only evidence left of Rayan's existence—from the coffee table and absently thumbed through. Something slid from the pages and dropped to the floor. He bent to retrieve it, flipping over the small white square to reveal a photo of Rayan and his brother with their mother.

He was young but unmistakable, the same brown eyes set in a round, innocent face. His smile was wide and buoyant, revealing a missing front tooth. Mathias had never seen the man smile like that, as though at a particular point in time, the expression had been taken from him. Life got hard enough, and a person started jettisoning the things that no longer served them. He would know.

Mathias flipped open the cover to the inscription.

My precious son, today is your birthday. Forty-one weeks, I waited, but Allah's gifts cannot be rushed. Watching you grow makes my heart sore. It is hard to be small, but it will not always be so. I can already see the man you will become, noble and kind. Someone to be proud of.

The rest he couldn't read, the foreign script sloping intricately across the page. Mathias stared at the woman in the photo. How tightly she held her two boys.

From the kitchen counter, his phone started up again, unrelenting, the caller incapable of taking a hint. Mathias stood, unsteady with booze, and stalked over to the offending object. He brought it to his ear.

"I have to hear from someone else you're back in the city?" His mother's voice lilted in that self-pitying tone he remembered so well. "Spend my days sitting here alone, hoping you'll grace me with your presence?"

Mathias's mouth curled into a scathing retort, but he stopped, an icy stab in his chest. Of course she was lonely. She'd always been lonely. That was another of the traits she'd passed down to him, mother to son, starting him early, too young to protest, a sharp, cavernous seed, pushed deep within, that made her cling to people and made him push them away.

"What do you want?" he snapped.

"That's no way to speak to your mother."

"Maybe if you were more of a mother..."

"All you've ever been is critical," she accused him tearfully. "You think people are born knowing how to do this? You have no idea. Just wait until you have children."

Mathias laughed, a hard barking sound. To think he would subject someone else to an unwanted existence. Living it was more than enough. "Not in this lifetime."

He heard the sharp intake of breath through the receiver. When she spoke next, her voice was wistful. "You'll see. When you're in love, everything changes."

Mathias felt his lungs empty, a coldness enveloping him. He hung up abruptly, the phone dropping from his hand, and strode across the kitchen, making it to the sink in time to violently empty the contents of his stomach.

That doesn't stop because you say it does.

Mathias retched again, gripping the edge of the counter as his vision blurred.

29

Rayan pulled his truck into the parking lot behind the depot, careful not to clip the side mirror on the narrow entrance gate. He was three weeks into a month-long probation and didn't want to lose his security deposit.

After taking the keys from the ignition, he headed toward the open warehouse door, shielding his eyes from the glare of the afternoon sun. The sunshine here was eternal. As a small port city, Larnaca stretched along the southern coast of the island, surrounded by a crystalline ocean that lured tourists from all across Europe. It was no wonder the Cypriots were so pleasant. Life was one never-ending holiday.

Rayan greeted Nikos at the dispatch desk and handed over his completed delivery sheet before moving through to the front office to clock out for the day. He'd found a strange calm in the physicality of the job, navigating his way around an unfamiliar city, hauling goods up and down stairs, in and out of buildings. Aside from a handful of stilted pleasantries, he spoke to no one. After work, he walked home to his small apartment, ate, and went to bed. If the day had been demanding enough— his muscles sore, back aching—sometimes he fell asleep before the thoughts descended.

Rayan had always feared being alone, and now that he was, it came with a biting clarity—the realization that he was, in fact, nothing. In a world full of people, he had no one. All this time, he'd thought otherwise but had simply been deluding himself, believing he meant something to a man who meant everything to him.

Rayan had come so close to having what he most wanted only to discover he'd never had a chance. And still, the feelings lingered, more painful than before, when his greatest hope had been a nod of acknowledgment, a word of praise. Now he'd tasted him, fallen asleep in his arms, and listened to the low murmur of his voice in the dark. It was no longer a quiet yearning but a raging, blistering clamor of loss.

In the office, his boss, Andreas, was leaning against the front desk, speaking loudly to the receptionist as she finalized the following day's run sheets. He looked up when Rayan entered and fixed him with one of his high-beam grins. "Busy day, Ayari?"

He spoke in elaborately slow Greek. Rayan had been attempting to learn the language, and his boss, relieved, had taken it as a sign to stop speaking to him in English altogether.

Rayan nodded, pulling out his time card and sliding it through the black punch clock mounted to the wall. With a smile, the young receptionist handed him the next day's run from across the desk. He thanked her, folding it in half.

"You have a friend here to see you," Andreas said, thumbing toward the front door, which led out to the street. "We asked him to come in, but he wanted to wait outside."

Rayan gripped the paper in his hand, the room tilting beneath his feet. He'd been on the island barely a month. He didn't have any friends.

Throwing on an easy smile, he told his boss he would see him tomorrow. At least, that was what he thought he said. His Greek was spotty at best, and his head was churning, making it hard to concentrate. Fighting a growing panic, Rayan stepped out of the office, blinking into the sun.

There he stood, a burning cigarette in hand, leaning against the guardrail on the other side of the street—with a clear view of all who moved in and out of the building. The man was dressed in gray chinos and a light-blue shirt. He wore a pair of sleek black sunglasses, his hair combed back. To a stranger passing on the street, he would have resembled any one of the wealthy Italian tourists who made their way across the channel on vacation.

There could be only one reason Mathias had tracked him down. Leaving had been a gamble as far as family protocol was concerned. If Rayan had been a made man, there would be repercussions. But he was an outsider, and the lines were not so clear. He'd never taken an oath and was never deemed worthy enough to hold a title. He'd assumed with his track record that he would simply be allowed to disappear. Mathias was done with him. Surely it was better that he was gone.

But none of that mattered now. He had gravely miscalculated. No one crossed Mathias—not even Rayan.

Fear hit him first then a rush of relief. For years, Rayan had held a morbid fascination with how it would happen. Working as he did, seeing so many men in their last moments, he'd always imagined when he would meet his. Why not today? The sun was out, the air pleasantly warm. No one to miss him when he was gone.

Rayan walked slowly toward him, closing the distance between them until they stood facing each other on the sidewalk. Mathias straightened up, flicked his cigarette to the ground, and crushed it beneath a polished brown loafer. He pulled off his sunglasses and folded them into his breast pocket.

Their eyes met. Rayan was an open book; he was done hiding. But Mathias was closed to him, his gaze hard and impassive.

"Walk with me." It was a statement, not a question.

Rayan nodded. This was not the place. He wanted to be far from his work and the bustling streets filled with people. He would head to his apartment, a short distance from the office.

Inclining his head, Rayan gestured toward the main road. "This way."

It was almost five, and groups of high school students were gathered around shop fronts in their uniforms, men in polos and slacks slipping out from offices on their way home to their families. They walked in silence, Mathias remaining several steps behind as Rayan navigated his way through the crowd of pedestrians.

Rounding a corner, Rayan pointed up at the balcony on the second floor of an old block of apartments. "I'm up there."

Mathias said nothing as they passed through the front gate and inside to the stairs, his feet making even thumps as he followed Rayan up the two-flight climb. He could feel the hair on the back of his neck stand up. With every step, he readied himself for the cold muzzle of Mathias's gun against his head, preparing for the split second of surprise before his brains splattered along the corridor. That was how Rayan would have done it—unexpected, from behind, so he wouldn't have to see the man's face.

They reached Rayan's scuffed front door with green paint peeling around the apartment number. He pulled out his keys, let Mathias inside, and closed the door behind them. Mathias walked past him, his footsteps echoing around the sparsely furnished living room.

Besides the faded couch and a small table and chairs, Rayan hadn't felt compelled to find anything to fill the space. What was the point when eventually, inevitably, he would once again have to start over.

His former capo circled the room, studying it, as though looking for something. Then he came to a stop and stared at Rayan standing by the door. "Should have known Mulroney would roll over on you," Mathias said finally.

Rayan had gone to Deacon Mulroney, master forger, the family's go-to contact for falsified documents and IDs. It had been simple enough to get an EU passport, dropping his surname in favor of his mother's maiden name, giving Rayan access to an entire continent in which to disappear. He'd picked Cyprus on a whim, for the weather mostly, hoping to purge a lifetime of Canadian winters from his bones—drawn also to its isolation and its fractured history. The people here, like him, were not unaccustomed to hardship.

Everything he'd brought with him fit into a backpack. Despite the years that had passed, it was surprisingly easy to toss the rest, displacement a state so familiar it almost came as a reassurance. In his haste, his mind fogged with grief, he'd been unable to find his mother's book. But he'd already lost so much of himself—what was one more thing? One more tether linking him to a painful past.

Rayan stood unmoving, trying to take in what had happened in such a short time. How often had he caught himself imagining that voice, that face, and now, Mathias was standing in his living room. Yet his presence brought with it a heavy finality.

"How'd you narrow it down to here?" Rayan asked.

"Interpol. Disappointingly corruptible."

Family connections ran deep within law enforcement. Perhaps, in the back of his mind, Rayan had understood the futility of his efforts—planned it that way even, so Mathias could find him if he wanted. He had simply assumed he wouldn't. Again, a miscalculation.

"I'm impressed, Rayan," he said flatly. "Look how far you've made it from Quebec."

Rayan swallowed, caught in Mathias's unrelenting stare, unsure what to say. "I shouldn't have left like that." It slipped from his mouth, but as soon as the words were out, he knew how true they were. Rayan looked at him, searching for resonance, for understanding. "But since Junior, the shooting... everything felt wrong about that life."

"Everything," Mathias repeated with a clinical coldness.

Rayan blinked. The man stepped forward so quickly he didn't see it coming, his fist bunching the fabric of Rayan's shirt. "I am that life," he hissed, eyes flashing.

Rayan's heart thundered in his chest, a fear he thought he'd outrun staring him in the face. "When we first met, I thought you'd kill me," he murmured. "Guess we've come full circle."

A pained expression crossed Mathias's face. "What?"

"Why else would you be here?"

Rayan saw the hurt intermingle with surprise before the curtain came back down. Mathias dropped his hand and pulled away.

"I know what you're capable of," Rayan said quietly. "Others have paid for less."

"You have no idea what I'm capable of," he snarled, advancing.

Rayan drew back.

"You think—" Mathias stopped, jaw clenched. "I'm here to clip you?"

Rayan's eyebrows furrowed in confusion as a dark-red drop appeared beneath Mathias's nose. "You're bleeding."

Mathias raised a hand to his face then looked down at the blood on his fingers.

Rayan took a towel from the kitchen and pressed it against the man's nose to stem the flow. "Sit. Look up."

Mathias sat down at the kitchen table, tilting his head back.

"You should lie down."

Mathias lay on Rayan's bed. The room was as shabby as the rest of the apartment, its decor from another era, a relic of the island's heyday before the messy takeover that had led to its division.

Rayan returned with a glass of water and a pack of painkillers and set them down on the nightstand. He looked the same yet entirely different. Inaccessible, separate from Mathias. Seeing him at his work, Mathias had felt a childish sense of betrayal. How easily he'd moved on.

Mathias closed his eyes. Rayan's scent was everywhere. After so long, it came as an assault, overwhelming him. His head throbbed, and he felt woozy.

He woke suddenly without realizing he'd fallen asleep. The room was dark, the door cracked open, allowing a sliver of light to cut through the room. Rayan appeared in the frame.

"Do you need anything?"

"No."

The man sighed, pushed open the door, and sat down at the end of the bed. "You know, I'm not a stray dog. You don't get to take me in then throw me back out again."

"I'll do what I want."

"The fuck you will. I'm more to you than that."

Mathias stopped short, silent.

"I know how hard you work not to feel things," Rayan said softly. "It takes a lot to feel nothing at all."

The ache was back, cracking open his skull.

"Talk to me," Rayan murmured.

"About?"

"Anything. You, life before I met you."

"Shall we braid each other's hair while we're at it?" he scoffed.

"Mathias, it's only me."

Mathias lay back on the pillow, the fight gone out of him. He stared at the ceiling—the cracks in the molding, the exposed lightbulb hanging like a hypnotist's pendulum. "I was never meant to be here," he said finally. "I'm a mistake my mother didn't have the courage to correct."

Rayan's eyes softened. "She cares for you."

"Tell me about that." Mathias sat up, lips curling. "Since you're so clearly an expert."

Rayan stiffened, and Mathias felt a sharp spike in his chest, his mind conjuring the cruelest thing. He'd seen the file, read the coroner's report. Mathias thought of the woman's inscription, her smiling face in the photo. He remembered how Rayan had woken beside him, speaking her name.

A memory: Mathias had been a child of five or six, standing with his back pressed to the door, listening to his parents scream.

"I told you to get rid of it."

"You thought things would change because you were stupid enough to get knocked up?"

His mother had gone silent then, as though the truth could not be contested.

"For what it's worth," Rayan said, eyes on him, unflinching, "I'm glad you're here."

Mathias's gaze dropped to the man's hand resting on the bed. That night, holding him down as Martin attended to the mess of his shoulder, he'd watched Rayan dig his nails into the table, leaving marks in the wood.

I've loved you for years.

The vise tightened, black spots crowding Mathias's vision. "Get out," he growled.

Rayan stood slowly, watching him for a moment before turning and leaving the room.

Rayan awoke on the couch to discover it was morning. He'd spent the night slipping in and out of a half sleep, the events of the previous day as surreal as any dream. He stood, ignoring the tired weight of his limbs, and saw that the door to the bedroom was open, the bed empty.

Regret surged through him. There was so much he still wanted to say. He'd barely touched the man, holding himself back... for what? He would never see him again.

The previous night, he'd watched as a piece of Mathias had caught on something, beginning to fray. To speak of his past like that and see him so conflicted, his own body turning against him...

Rayan grabbed his keys and sprinted out of the apartment. The air was slowly warming, the sky a foggy blue. He strode down the street to the main road, checking in both directions for any sign of him. He knew the chances of spotting him were almost nonexistent. If Mathias had left, he would be impossible to find by now.

But Rayan could not bring himself to return home. He continued, ducking into alleyways, down side streets. Finally, with his heart in his throat, he turned back. He cursed himself. He'd been given an unprecedented chance, and he had utterly blown it.

As he rounded the corner of his apartment building, Rayan saw an unmistakable figure crossing the street ahead. The sureness of his gait, the muscular outline of his body, the way he looked straight ahead as if daring the world to challenge him—he would have recognized Mathias anywhere.

He slowed when he caught sight of Rayan approaching. He held a cigarette in one hand, his wet hair slicked back, wearing a fresh change of clothes. No doubt, he'd returned to his hotel, oblivious to Rayan's distress.

It dawned on him that this was what Mathias must have felt when Rayan had vanished without a word. But there'd been no flood of relief for him, who'd gone looking and had found nothing, the ache not abating, only intensifying. Rayan felt a barb of remorse. He'd put Mathias through that.

Rayan stopped before him. Not sure what to say, only wanting to keep him there, give himself time to think. "There's a promenade by the ocean," he offered hesitantly. "It's not far from here."

Mathias looked at him, bringing the cigarette to his lips and taking a long drag. He gave a shrug, and they fell into step, following the curve of the road as it turned toward the sea. After several blocks, they crossed onto a narrow walkway that stretched along the shorefront. It was cloudy and unseasonably cold, and the beach was practically deserted.

"Not sure why I moved to an island," Rayan said offhandedly. "I can't swim."

His mother had been afraid of the water, his father unconcerned with whether he could or not. And they'd never spent holidays at the beach or weekends at the pool. Why bother?

They walked in silence, the wind curling the smoke from Mathias's cigarette above his head. Stopping at a small lookout, he flicked the waning butt down to the sand below. From the corner of his eye, Rayan watched as Mathias stared out at the waves, his face implacable. He had trouble believing this wasn't all a daydream he was experiencing, with the real world clamoring just out of sight, trying to force its way in.

"Your father," Mathias said after a moment. "He never came back for you?"

Rayan frowned, caught off guard. Shortly after his mother died, he'd been sure his father would find them. They'd had no one else. His refusal to do so had only made their abandonment complete.

"He didn't want us. Courts can't make you take kids you don't want." A flock of seagulls circled overhead and dropped one by one to the beach. "So many ways for parents to fuck up their children," Rayan said with a shrug. "Mine left me for dead. Yours taught you about love by withholding it."

Mathias knocked him backward, and he hit the metal railing. Rayan straightened up, refusing to look away. The man's eyes were black with rage.

"Hurts, doesn't it?" he said.

Rayan had seen this look many times right before Mathias shattered a jaw, smashed a kneecap, or kicked a man until he pissed blood. The anger was a tool, a way to raze everything left in its wake.

"Doesn't mean you don't know how. Isn't that why you're here?" Rayan challenged.

Mathias turned and headed back down the walkway.

"Look at me!" Rayan knew if he let go now, he would lose the man for good.

Mathias stopped but didn't turn.

"You wanted me gone. I left. But now you're here. What does that mean?" Rayan asked.

"It means nothing."

"The hell it does!" Rayan growled. "What happens when pushing me away doesn't work anymore?"

Mathias swiveled to fix him with a deadened stare. "I can't give you what you want," he said in a low voice.

"And what's that?" Rayan countered. "There's nothing I want you haven't given me already."

"Orders?" Mathias sneered, eyes narrowing. "What happens now, with no one to tell you what to do?"

"That's what you think—I'm incapable of making my own decisions? I'm here, aren't I? And you may have given the orders, but I was the one who followed them."

Mathias stalked toward him, his mouth a hard line. "Don't act like you wanted to do the things I made you do. Once you were in deep enough, you didn't have a choice."

"There was always a choice!" Rayan cried.

"Bullshit."

"I chose you."

Mathias blinked, his shoulders slackening.

"And I'd make the same choice every fucking time." Rayan swallowed hard, his heart hammering in his throat. He stepped forward, ignoring the signs of reproach Mathias had been sending him since his arrival, moving as close to the man as he dared. "I'd choose you every time."

Their eyes locked, and he was finally granted passage past Mathias's defenses.

"When I saw you that day by the river—" Mathias's voice tightened. "I couldn't watch you die." He pulled Rayan to him, their mouths meeting, everything else falling away.

There was a ferocity to it, as though their bodies weren't privy to the shaky peace that had been hashed out along the waterfront. They confronted each other in bed like enemies, fighting for territory, for dominance. Rayan embraced the turmoil, a physical manifestation of the chaos that had plagued him for so long.

He knelt on his hands and knees, eyes veiled by a curtain of damp hair, legs trembling as Mathias thrust into him. The man wrapped a hand around his throat, tightening his grip, setting his skin on fire. The intensity of Rayan's arousal scared him, the months apart having done nothing to quell the depth of his need.

He felt a sudden spasm and dropped the weight on his right arm, pain crackling like lightning from his shoulder to the tips of his fingers. Exhaling through his teeth, he pulled away and flopped onto his back on the bed. Mathias towered over him, naked and erect, both of them breathing hard, neither of them speaking.

Mathias brushed his fingers over the scar tissue, the dimple where the bullet had entered Rayan's shoulder. His eyes were shuttered, preventing him from seeing inside.

Shame prickled across Rayan's bare skin. "I don't need your pity," he said flatly.

Mathias snorted and, in one fluid motion, scooped Rayan's legs over his shoulders. He leaned forward, capturing Rayan's tongue in his mouth as he pushed his cock inside him. Rayan let out a groan, arching into the mounting pressure. His body, so used to mitigating bouts of searing pain, had forgotten how good it could feel.

Mathias wrapped his arms around him, his lips grazing Rayan's ear. "I don't do pity."

Yet he was gentler than he would have been, his movements achingly slow, his face inches from Rayan's. Their bodies, too, began to work things out, addressing old wounds and revealing a hidden tenderness that had been quashed again and again.

Rayan tried to recall the last time they were together—whether it had been quick and frenzied, as it so often was, or languid, one of those nights where booze stripped Mathias of his cloak of stone. He couldn't remember. He also couldn't bear the man's eyes on him, missing nothing, leaving the very core of him exposed. Rayan turned his head away.

A hand cupped his chin, bringing him back. "Where are you going?"

But he no longer felt able to form words, the pleasure muddling his thoughts. Mathias here with him, inside him, scrambled everything.

"You can't hide from me," Mathias murmured.

Rayan met his gaze and saw in it the force that bound them. He twined his fingers through Mathias's hair, pulling him close, kissing him. Mathias rose to his knees, his hand finding Rayan's cock. They moved faster now, each thrust shuddering through him, making his toes curl. He felt himself slipping.

"Mathias—" he choked out.

Release slammed into him like a freight train. The edges of his vision went black. Rayan was barely aware of Mathias above him, the man's body stiffening as he came with a low growl.

They collapsed onto the bed, chests heaving, limbs intertwined. It felt like days had passed since their reunion on the street that morning. They lay side by side atop the sheets without exchanging a word. There weren't any left to say.

30

They acted as though the world didn't exist outside the four walls of his apartment. When they weren't in bed—which wasn't often—they cooked, made coffee, or leafed through books on the small balcony. Work didn't register. Rayan simply hadn't shown up. Nothing was more important than this, a lifetime of pleasure condensed into these few tenuous days.

He'd never seen Mathias sleep so much. At strange hours of the day, Rayan would find him on the couch or stretched out across the bed, dead to the world, as though his body was trying to counter a yawning deficit. He would wake groggy, surly, hair falling loose across his forehead, making him appear young and unassuming.

Rayan found himself unable to tear his eyes away, struggling to reconcile this version of the man from the one he remembered. Earlier that morning, Mathias had caught sight of himself in the bathroom mirror and scowled at his reflection.

Rayan didn't ask how long he was away from Montreal or what story he'd told to cover his absence. Sometimes Mathias took phone calls privately on the balcony, with the door shut. Rayan didn't ask about the churn of events, the responsibilities awaiting him, but with each day, he grew more anxious about the time when Mathias would have to leave.

It was almost noon one day, and Mathias sat drinking coffee at the kitchen counter while Rayan stood across from him, slicing vegetables for soup. Mathias picked up an old newspaper by his elbow, his eyes falling to the pile of papers beneath. Rayan could see the Ministère de l'Éducation logo clearly visible in the header of the letter that lay on top.

"What's this?" Without waiting for a reply, Mathias reached for it.

Rayan watched as he read, his stomach sinking.

Mathias glanced at him over the top of the letter. "You got your equivalency certificate."

It had been easier than expected. He'd shown up at a testing center before leaving the country, mobilized by a decade of self-doubt. Expecting to fail, he'd been surprised when he'd managed an almost perfect score. Rayan leaned over, yanked the letter from his hand, and returned it to the pile.

Mathias sat back, studying him. "So that's the plan—apply to university here?" he scoffed. "You'll need to work on your Greek."

Rayan picked up the knife and gripped it in his fist. He swirled with a defensive anger, the man having prodded his greatest insecurity. "You don't think I can do it?"

Mathias's face grew serious. "What would you study?"

Rayan shrugged, returning to chopping, which was easier than looking at him. "Honestly, I don't know." He waited for the derisive comments, but none came.

"Toronto has several decent programs," Mathias said, spreading the newspaper out before him. "I'm in Hamilton sometimes—more often than I'd like."

Rayan stilled, something stirring in his chest.

"If you don't want anything to do with the family, the family wants nothing to do with you," Mathias continued, idly scanning the front page. "You did your job, kept quiet. I can make it like you never existed. You don't have to learn another language, for Christ's sake."

"What are you saying?"

Mathias frowned, folding the paper tightly and tossing it aside. He stood, jaw clenched. "If you were in Canada, I wouldn't have to fly halfway across the fucking world to see you."

Rayan swallowed, his mouth dry. "Thought you were done with me."

Mathias glared at him, silent.

He felt a sharp sting and looked down to see blood blooming from a cut he'd made along his thumb. "Shit," Rayan muttered. Stupid. He'd been distracted.

"Let's see," Mathias said, rounding the counter.

"It's nothing," Rayan said, moving to the sink. "Just a cut."

But the blood was already filling his palm. Maybe it was deeper than he thought. Mathias appeared at his side, pulling his arm toward him and reaching for a dish towel. As Mathias wrapped the fabric tightly around his hand, the man's breath quickened. They stood by the sink, Mathias holding his arm aloft, waiting for the bleeding to slow.

"That night," Mathias murmured absently, staring at the blotch of red seeping into the white linen. "I had to throw out my shirt."

Rayan's stomach lurched. He finally understood. He could see the departure clearly, stemming from the moment Mathias had found him bleeding out in the parking lot—a catalyst for his extrication. Mathias, an expert at cutting off anything that endangered his well-guarded defenses, had peeled him away before he could do any more damage.

Why didn't I see it? All those days Rayan had spent wallowing in his own self-pity, resenting the distance that had opened between them, Mathias hadn't succeeded in severing himself from his humanity as Tony had believed. He'd only managed to suppress it.

The bleeding appeared to have stopped, but Rayan didn't remove his hand from the man's steady grip. "I never thanked you," he said quietly. "That's twice you've saved my life."

Mathias raised an eyebrow, his mouth curving. "It's just a cut, Rayan."

Rayan looked at him, the heaviness gone. All that remained was the pressure of Mathias's hand on his, holding tightly.

Mathias woke to Rayan's steady breath on his neck and the most aggressive morning hard-on he'd experienced in a long time. He blinked to reorientate himself, regarding the low, sagging bed, peeling blue wallpaper, and flimsy white curtains that did nothing to stop the sharp Cypriot sunshine from assaulting every inch of the room. In his waking mind, a single thought pushed itself front and center with an assailing disregard for all other things.

It had to be the alcohol that was having this effect on him, or more specifically, the lack of it—he hadn't had a drink in days. Or perhaps the fact that they'd barely left Rayan's bed, his body so easily trained. Whatever the reason, this place robbed him of his edge, his mind quietened and appetite indulged.

Mathias pulled himself up on one elbow, staring down at the sleeping man beside him. Rayan's eyelids fluttered ever so slightly, his lips parting as he took another unconscious breath. It would be a shame to wake him, but there were more pressing concerns. Mathias drew his hand under the covers, reaching for Rayan's cock. He'd barely managed to get his fist around it when Rayan shuddered awake, his body tensing, an arm raised instinctively to ward off the unexpected intrusion.

Mathias rolled over so he was above him, biting back a groan as his own erection ground against Rayan's thigh. Rayan looked up, eyes foggy with sleep. He was about to speak when Mathias lowered his head and took him into his mouth. Instead of words, Rayan only managed a hiss as he sucked air in through his teeth.

Mathias found himself compelled by the man's inability to hide the pleasure on his face. In his life working for the family, his former second had proven a master at disguising his emotions—even from Mathias. But pinned down in bed, with every sensation reflected in the tremor of his lips, the roll of his brown eyes, Rayan was intoxicating to watch.

Rayan pushed back, but Mathias would not relent, instead taking him deeper, relishing how he arched into him with a moan.

"Mathias..." he murmured, voice catching.

Releasing him, Mathias brought his face up. He let Rayan brush his neck with his lips and push his mouth open with his tongue. Mathias pressed down on Rayan's thighs, spreading him. Rayan groaned as he opened him, pushing his cock forward inch by inch. Reaching up, he wrapped his fingers around Mathias's neck, digging into the flesh. Mathias barely felt it. All his concentration was focused on holding himself back.

Jesus, that feeling—impossibly tight, the slow surrender. When he was in to the hilt, Mathias shifted so they lay face-to-face, Rayan's legs hooking instinctively around his back. Rayan's eyes were lidded, his breathing shallow, and his chin tilted toward him, making it easy for Mathias to capture his mouth with his own. And then Mathias began to move.

The pressure around his neck tightened, and he watched as Rayan bit down hard on his lip, his face twisting. Every thrust tested Mathias's self-control. He'd started too near the edge to play games and found himself brushing dangerously close to release. He tempered his movements, pulling out until just the head of his cock remained. Pushing forward, he was rewarded by the shudder of Rayan's body beneath him.

"Fuck... I'm..." Rayan muttered, a small pool of precum gathering on his belly.

Mathias reached for the man's cock and guided it through his fist in time with his strokes. Rayan's grip on him tightened, a growl tearing from his throat. And then he tensed, his face barely keeping up with the rest of his body as he shot ribbons across his chest, Mathias milking him all the way down.

Palming the wet head of Rayan's cock, he pushed deeper into him, his own release seizing him. The air stalled in his lungs as if he'd momentarily lost the ability to breathe. He lowered his head, fists gripping the sheets as the current passed through him. Why was it only like this with Rayan? This man alone possessing the ability to strip him to his very foundation?

Coming back to himself, he looked down to see Rayan staring at him, a strange wonder in his eyes. He pulled Mathias close, his kisses soft but urgent, searching and claiming, prolonging the heady high of pleasure that enveloped them both. Mathias lifted a hand and ran it through Rayan's hair, longer now that he had abandoned the clean cut he'd maintained since arriving at the Collections office. It fell about his head, tousled, unruly, begging to be wound through Mathias's fingers.

Holding Rayan's face in his palm, Mathias scanned it for everything that had changed in the time they'd been apart—skin darker, eyes brighter, dark circles gone. It pained him to realize Rayan was doing better here than he ever had in Montreal.

"Quintino," Rayan marveled, reaching for his hand and twirling the signet ring on his little finger, which was still new, still strange. He brought it to his lips and kissed it gently. "You never made me take an oath."

"You didn't have to," Mathias said.

"You didn't want me to."

Mathias was silent.

Rayan tilted his head. "So I could leave?"

Mathias withdrew, rolling onto his back with a sigh. *Is that why? All those years of feeling responsible for his involvement...*

"That time you asked if I was happy," Rayan started, propping himself up on his side. "Maybe I wasn't."

Mathias raised an eyebrow. "So you lied?"

He smiled hesitantly. "Not a lie. I just wasn't overly familiar with the concept."

"And you are now?"

Rayan looked down at him, grazing Mathias's cheek with his fingers. "Today, yes. Tomorrow? Who knows," he said, eyes sad. "Maybe you'll still be here."

They existed in a parallel plane—the apartment was a sanctuary removed from the world, with reality encroaching outside. Mathias was in Paris, attending to a family matter—that was the excuse he'd given before leaving the city, the lie that held him momentarily aloft. But as each day passed, it grew thinner under the weight of the responsibilities awaiting him back in Montreal.

Somewhere deep inside, Mathias was lured by this lazy life and the idea that he could live it with this man by his side. Being half a world away hadn't lessened the sting he felt without Rayan. But he couldn't pretend to be someone he was not. He was a stranger here—a stranger to himself.

"Come on." Mathias strode into the bedroom, already dressed, and sat on the edge of the bed to pull on his shoes.

Rayan was still tangled in the sheets, lounging in the remnants of pleasure, sufficiently laid to waste. He frowned, curious. Up until that moment, Mathias had shown no interest in leaving the apartment.

"Where are we going?"

"Out," he said, tossing Rayan his clothes from the floor.

It was midmorning, and the promenade along the beach was virtually empty. Mathias led them down the stairs to the sand, pulling off his shirt and dropping it on the ground. Rayan stood, dumbstruck, feeling as though he was missing an important piece of information.

"You figure out how to float, and the rest is easy," Mathias explained, stepping out of his shoes.

Rayan blinked. "You're going to teach me how to swim?"

"What does it look like?" Mathias scowled, turning and striding toward the water. "Hurry up."

Rayan shed his shirt, kicked off his shoes, and followed him. Mathias waded into the sea and dove under a wave as it broke. He emerged with water streaming down his shoulders, pushing his wet hair back from his face. Rayan walked into the waves until they were up to his stomach.

Mathias moved to him and eased him backward into the water, holding him up with his hands. "Find your center and trust it. Like riding a bike."

"Never learned to do that either."

Mathias snickered, glancing down at him. "Well, shit."

Rayan stared up at him, clouds parting above to let the morning sun shine through. The water lapped around his ears, moving like a giant swollen cushion, jostling him. He felt unsteady, but Mathias's hands on his back kept him from sinking. Soon, he discovered a strange calm. Rayan let his body relax and found his legs could stay afloat on their own, his arms keeping his chest up. Slowly, Mathias released him, and he floated with his arms spread, buoyed by the sea.

"At least now you won't drown." He smirked. "Try to move without sinking."

After Rayan attempted several strokes with varying degrees of success, they lay on their backs in the ocean as the sun crawled higher in the sky. Rayan glanced over at Mathias, whose eyes were closed, water slipping across his bare chest. "You're beautiful," he murmured, the reflex to hold everything inside weakening, its purpose no longer useful.

Mathias opened one eye, looking at him. "You've swallowed too much water."

Rayan grinned, staring at the cloudless canvas above. He recalled the man's admission that first night, lying stiffly on his bed, and was filled with a heavy sadness at the thought of Mathias growing up believing he was living a borrowed life, bound to a mistake that wasn't his. He wondered what kind of shadow it had cast and decisions it had tainted.

Later, they sat on the sand, drying in the sun, while Mathias smoked a cigarette. Along the beach, people began to appear—couples, families with umbrellas and chairs, children in swimsuits venturing tentatively into the water.

"Who taught you?" Rayan asked, watching as a little girl filled a bucket in the waves and ran back to her mother, who was sunbathing on a towel.

"Made us take lessons at school."

"Some school."

"The best money could buy," Mathias said dryly.

There was a collection of shrieks as a group of kids chased a soccer ball across the sand.

"You go on holidays growing up?" Rayan asked.

Mathias exhaled and made a sour expression. "Maybe. If we did, they weren't memorable."

"My mother always said we'd go to Beirut one day," Rayan said with a half smile. "Even if we had the money, my father wouldn't have let us. Probably figured she'd leave and never come back." He drew his fingers through the white sand by his toes. "It happened anyway, except we didn't make it out of the country."

"Will you go?"

He shook his head. "I have no ties there. Or anywhere, for that matter."

Mathias studied him carefully, the cigarette perched between his fingers. "Then you'll stay here?"

Rayan stared back, his heart thudding. He wanted the man to say it—to make the decision for him. "If you told me to go back, I would."

Mathias held his gaze for a moment before looking away. Stabbing the cigarette out in the sand between them, he pulled himself to his feet and shrugged on his shirt. "I don't give you orders anymore."

Mathias picked up his shoes and walked back toward the stairs. Rayan stared out at the sea—vast and sprawling, as remote as ever.

When Rayan woke the next morning, the other side of the bed was empty. He found Mathias standing in the kitchen with his bag. He was already showered and dressed, the first coffee of the day in his hand.

Rayan stood shirtless, his bare feet cooling on the brick tile. For the briefest of seconds, he contemplated pleading. But that would mean excusing his role in all of this. He'd made the choice to leave. Mathias was simply returning to where he belonged.

"You asked me once what I'd be if I never joined," Mathias said into the silence. "I'm not you. I'm not a good person with a bad past. I was built to cleave my way through life. The job is me—we're one and the same. So you understand why I can't stay."

"I know," Rayan said quietly, a stone sinking in his stomach.

Mathias raised the cup to his lips and swallowed the last mouthful of coffee then set it on the counter behind him. He bent over his bag, pulled open the zipper, and reached inside. As he removed the small paperback, Rayan felt a hot swell of relief. He'd never expected to see it again. Mathias placed Saint-Exupéry's memoir face down on the kitchen table. Rayan stared at the book as though it were a talisman from another world.

"Thought you'd want it back," Mathias said.

So he had taken it—the one thing Rayan had kept with him as he'd been tossed from place to place, hidden inside his shirt all those nights on the street. It contained the only photo Rayan had of his family, the last remaining trace of his mother. Mathias couldn't have known that. But somehow, he'd registered its significance and had taken it, a piece of Rayan he'd held onto after letting him go. The thought made his throat tighten.

They locked eyes across the kitchen, and Rayan saw frustration glittering in the man's gaze. It wasn't often Mathias didn't get what he wanted. Rayan could see that leaving things like this—unresolved, unfinished—troubled him.

He stepped forward and laid his hand on Mathias's chest. He could feel the thud of the man's heartbeat and the warmth of his skin beneath the fabric of his shirt. He was here, standing in his apartment, in the flesh. In a moment, he would be gone, and Rayan would have to unearth the memories once again and recreate him anew.

He wished he knew how to give voice to the feelings that surfaced when he was this close to him. But words didn't apply where Mathias was concerned. Words meant nothing. He reached up, threaded his fingers through Mathias's hair, and pulled him close, tasting him. Coffee and saliva—bittersweet.

Rayan broke away, taking in the slate-gray eyes, the curve of his brow, the tug of his lips—features he'd long ago committed to memory after seeing them every morning at the Collections office. "This is how we should've left it."

Mathias shook his head, the corners of his mouth curving into a frown. "No," he said, gripping Rayan's neck and leaning in so their heads touched. "If this was how we'd left it, I wouldn't have let you go."

Then he pulled away, picked up his bag, and strode out of the room without looking back. Rayan stood, unmoving, as he listened to the front door shut with a thud. The man was gone.

Rayan exhaled slowly, his gaze falling to the book on the table. He reached for it, marveling at how familiar it felt in his hand, as though he'd been reunited with an old friend. He flipped through the pages until he found the photo—his mother's face staring up at him. Lifting it from the book, he found a slip of creamy-white paper beneath. On it, written in Mathias's meticulous hand, was a series of numbers followed by a twelve-digit code. And there, watermarked into the thick paper stock, was the logo of the Capital Bank of Cyprus.

Rayan let the paper slide soundlessly through his fingers. He'd worked in Collections long enough to recognize a foreign bank account when he saw one.

It took him a week to pluck up the courage to walk into the nearest Capital Bank. Rayan pushed the piece of paper over the counter to the teller without a word.

Breezily, she tapped her long pink nails against the keyboard, transferring the numbers onto the computer in front of her. "All right, Mr. Ayari, I'll just need one form of ID before we continue."

Rayan blanched. "I'm sorry?"

"Rayan Ayari. You are the account holder, correct?"

He gripped the edge of the counter. *What doesn't Mathias know?* Rayan's efforts to disappear seemed laughable in the face of how completely the man had uncovered him.

"Sir?"

Rayan blinked, reaching for his wallet and pulling out his Cypriot driver's license. "That's right."

"Thank you, sir," she said, smiling with bright-red lips as she took the license from him. The teller made another series of taps on her computer before turning back to him. "How can I help you today?"

"The balance," he asked hesitantly. "What's the balance on the account?" The woman turned to the screen and was just about to speak when Rayan cut in. "Actually, could you write it down?"

The teller gave him a quizzical look but took a small yellow pad from beside the computer and jotted down a figure. She passed it back across the counter toward Rayan. He glanced down, his mind reeling.

It was suddenly all too much. Rayan took a step back, regretting having come, not because of the money but because of how the man had given it to him— unconditionally, with no interest in what he used it for. Mathias had handed him a blank slate, challenging him to rebuild his life anew. He remembered his question, back in Montreal—"When you're done surviving, what then?"

Rayan had never before been confronted with that possibility.

"Was there anything else today, sir?" the teller asked.

"No," Rayan said, shaking his head as if to clear it. "That's all."

31

Mathias lowered his club, reaching for the cigarette between his teeth. He watched the white speck of the ball tumble down the green and stop several feet from the twelfth hole.

"Decent backswing you've got there, Beauvais," Enzo Carbone declared, slapping him on the shoulder. "Not bad for a rookie."

Mathias shrugged. "I didn't get into the game to play golf."

It was a clear August afternoon, the blue sky stretching above the Cedarbrook Golf Course in West Montreal. From behind the wheel of the cart, Armando Bernardi chuckled, knocking back his third beer. "But here's betting you're no stranger to a club."

The remaining members of the Quintino laughed. The man wasn't wrong. A nine iron made a particularly satisfying sound when it hit bone.

"Wait till you get to be our age, Beauvais," Gabriele Giordano warned conspiratorially, sitting beside Armando and nursing a can of Labatt Blue. "You'll come around."

Mathias doubted it. He surveyed the clusters of men dotting the course—a sea of gray hair and designer polos. He was no more partial to golf than he was to most mindless leisure activities. Aside from it being a way to mine information, he didn't see the point.

Enzo lined up his shot and swung. The ball arched through the air to land close to his own. "What do you make of the construction-bid changes?" he asked as Gabriele and Armando came down to join them on the grass.

"We need to tread lightly," Mathias said, squinting against the sun. "The new government campaigned on the back of harsher legislation. I'd hold off on any bids until they find the next tree to bark up."

Armando snorted, selecting a club from his bag and weighing it in his palm. "The Feds are getting bolder, that's for sure. Heard one of De Luca's drivers was caught with a wire the other day."

"Are we in need of a scapegoat?" Enzo asked, the lines on his forehead deepening. "Toss some meat their way to throw them off the scent?"

Gabriele lit a cigarette, crossing his arms. "I have some names if you want them."

"I'll let you know," Mathias said tactfully, watching Armando ready his ball.

"And what does boss make of it?" Enzo cut in.

Gabriele pulled on his smoke and sent a cloud downwind. "Boss doesn't want to upset the apple cart. Not yet, anyway."

They all watched Armando take his swing. The ball jetted sideways and bounced into the sand. "Fucking piece of shit!" he hollered.

Enzo chuckled. "Maybe Beauvais should give you some pointers."

"Beginner's luck." Mathias smirked.

Gabriele eyed him with amusement. "If I've learned one thing, that don't apply to you."

The four councilmen walked back to the cart, and Armando took his seat behind the wheel and steered them across the course to the next hole. Mathias stared out at the brilliant green of the fairway and the line of maple trees along the perimeter, lush with summer leaves, his mind pulling him back as it always did. It had been almost four months since his return from Cyprus, and the only thing that kept the thoughts at bay was the sheer amount of work. Mathias had taken Collections in the end, unable to let the division fall into Franco's slippery fingers. Tony would have been rolling in his grave. The least he could do was ensure that the man's legacy didn't go to waste.

His responsibilities to the Quintino ate into the limited time remaining, and then there was Hamilton. The family had installed a new regional head there, but for high-level negotiations, Truman refused to deal with anyone besides Mathias. Using their shared clout, Mathias and the Reapers' head had been able to stamp out Nostra dealings all the way to Ottawa, so every month or two, he made the trip out there and entertained Truman's whims—less indulgently now that he'd risen so high in the family's ranks.

Still, in those elusive moments of downtime—driving between the two cities, stuck in traffic, or lying in bed before falling asleep—he thought of Rayan.

Mathias had been able to unite warring criminal factions and forge alliances with irrational lunatics. He had a knack for manipulating people, convincing them they were getting exactly what they wanted, when he was really bending them to his will.

Yet here he was, powerless, unable to influence the outcome when it mattered most. Because Rayan was an enigma. Mathias had no idea what the man wanted or how to give it to him.

The envelope was small, the size of a postcard. It sat on top of the pile of mail inside his collection box in the building foyer. Mathias retrieved the stack of letters, stepped into the elevator, and punched in the access code for his floor. Once inside the apartment, he turned the envelope in his hand, noting no return address, then tore it open with his thumb. Inside was a single cream-colored card. On it in neatly printed script, was an address: *18 Lower Jarvis, Box 4001*. The city and country had been left out, as had the postal code.

Mathias flipped the card to reveal a tiny brass key taped to the back. He removed it, placing it down on the counter, and turned to study the handwritten text on the front. When he was sure he'd committed it to memory, Mathias picked up the envelope and walked over to the sink. He slipped the lighter out of his pocket and held the flame to the corner of the card, watching as the paper caught and seared through the ink. After flicking the burning card into the sink, he lifted the envelope, and it met the same fate.

Two weeks later, Mathias rounded the corner of Lower Jarvis and King, just west of Toronto's distillery district. He pushed open the glass doors of the Canada Post office at 18 Lower Jarvis, grateful for the relief of the air-conditioned interior. The country was in the midst of a heat wave, suffering through record high temperatures despite the summer having officially come to an end. Water levels along the Saint Lawrence River were low, so the ships were restricting cargo, reducing import volume between the provincial ports and fucking with his margins.

Inside the store, across the far wall, were rows of small gray mailboxes. Mathias walked slowly, scanning the numbers, and stopped in front of 4001. Not for the first time since the envelope had arrived, he felt a flare of annoyance at being jerked around on some cryptic scavenger hunt.

The box opened easily. It was empty except for a plain silver key tied to a slip of blue paper. *#317, 55 Erskine Avenue,* the note said.

Mathias held the key in his palm, stilling the sudden race of his pulse. Then he pocketed it, locked the mailbox, and stepped back out onto the street.

The door to the apartment opened to reveal a small sun-soaked living room. Ceiling-high windows faced the street, cracked open slightly to let in the air. It was stripped back, the interior designed with the blocky quality that dominated the brutalist buildings this side of town. Books littered every available surface, piled by the door and on the coffee table. But the man had made an effort with the furnishings, keeping the feel of the place simple and clean.

Mathias couldn't help but smirk. He'd given Rayan a fortune. He could have picked anywhere, and this was what he'd chosen.

He shut the door behind him and walked idly through the room. Rayan had assembled a jungle of plants of varying sizes along the windowsill, some faring better than others. Mathias didn't own a single living thing. He saw no point in having anything else rely on him for its survival.

Mathias shrugged off his jacket and threw it over the back of one of the kitchen chairs. He picked up a dog-eared textbook lying open on the table, its pages marked with colored tags. *Evolutionary Epistemology*. Mathias placed it back down, careful not to lose Rayan's place.

He stepped over to the counter, opening cabinets at random, not entirely sure what he was looking for. Pulling open the cupboard above the sink, his hand froze midair when he saw the unopened bottle of Macallan. Mathias stood, struck by the yearning that had lingered since he'd last seen Rayan's face. Despite being here, so close to relief, he found the feeling even more difficult to fight. He stared at the bottle, proof he wasn't the only one who thought of the time they would see each other again.

Mathias took the scotch down from the cabinet and cracked the seal to pour two fingers into a glass tumbler. He raised the drink to his lips and took a measured sip. After placing it back on the counter, he continued his unfettered exploration of Rayan's apartment. He stalked down the hallway, opening doors as he went. Finding himself in the bedroom, Mathias attempted to quell his growing sense of frustration. He was trapped in a world of Rayan without access to the real thing— the man of flesh and blood.

Then he heard the sound of a key in the lock. He turned, his feet moving on their own, and walked back through the hallway, stopping abruptly before he reached the living room. From where he stood, Mathias could see the front door swing open.

Rayan stepped in, a sheen of sweat on his face and dark hair falling across his forehead. His jaw was brushed with stubble. Over his shoulder hung a scuffed leather satchel that, coupled with the casual cut of his clothes, made him look like an innocent college kid—like a different person, someone whose path Mathias would never have crossed.

But Rayan still had his old instincts. His eyes snapped to Mathias in the hallway, his body tensing long before his hand left the doorknob. He hung there for the briefest of moments before dropping his shoulders, letting the bag slip to the floor as he closed the door quietly behind him.

"Nice place," Mathias said. Neither of them moved. "Could have done without the trail of breadcrumbs." But he knew that Rayan had understood how careful he needed to be.

Rayan's lips moved from a smile to a grimace, finally settling in a hard line. "You're here," he said, his voice strained.

"I'm here," Mathias echoed woodenly, the distance between them yawning.

Rayan was the one to approach. He stopped when they were close enough to touch and exhaled slowly, looking up at Mathias, his forehead creasing, eyes hiding nothing. "Christ, I've missed you."

Mathias felt the warmth of Rayan's mouth against his own—the deep jolt it sent through his insides. And then his hands were on the man's shoulders, pushing him against the wall, desperate for all of him, any of him, as much as he could get.

A Life Betrayed

Here it was again: the impossible situation. Their lives were fundamentally incompatible but inherently intertwined. He did not know how to unravel what they had without first unraveling himself.

The Feds have taken a renewed interest in the spate of criminal activity in Quebec, and Mathias Beauvais, a consigliere in the Montreal mafia, discovers it's not just him they're after. Can he deal to this challenge like the ones before, or is it possible he's no longer the man he once thought he was?

Despite his desire for a new life, Rayan Nadeau's past has caught up to him, and he's thrown back into the very world he tried to escape. With Mathias willing to put Rayan's freedom before his own, he may have to abandon all hope of them remaining together.

About the Author

Sydney Rutherford is fond of travel, a morally ambiguous protagonist, and the fragility of the human condition. She writes contemporary m/m romance with a penchant for noir, and currently resides in Aotearoa New Zealand.

Find out more about her books at sydneyrutherford.com or sign up to the mailing list for bonus content and upcoming releases.

Thank you for reading. If you enjoyed this book, please leave a review.

www.ingramcontent.com/pod-product-compliance
Lightning Source LLC
Chambersburg PA
CBHW051247250626
47155CB00009B/3204